"Don't think you can do

"You know very well that is not the issue."

"Uh-huh. Sure," she said, a real honest-to-goodness smile forming.

He worked up the nerve to shove her shoulder with his, and for a moment, it almost felt like old times. A fact they both seemed to notice at the same time and the moment devolved back into uncomfortable silence.

"I have an idea," Shane said. "What if we just...didn't make this weird? What if we're just two old friends who know they're reuniting for a short time and won't see each other again after that? It will be great to catch up, do a little work together, and then it will be just as great to go our separate ways with nothing but fond memories."

"Just two old friends, huh?" she said, interest showing behind her dark lashes.

He nodded once. "Exactly." Even though he couldn't help but think their relationship had never been remotely anything anyone would have ever called just "friendly."

"So, what are we proposing here? Pretending this whole thing isn't weird and uncomfortable and utterly ridiculous?" she asked.

"Yes, that sounds like an excellent plan."

Dear Reader,

If you love a good heist—the twists, the turns, the adventure, the action—you've landed in the right place.

I came to love the characters in *Undercover Heist* so much while writing, and I hope you come to love them just as much while reading. Ruby Alexander is a brilliant and capable ex-thief who wants nothing more than to put that world behind her. That is until ex-partner Shane Meyers sneaks back into her life and turns that notion—and a few other things—upside down.

It doesn't take long to get the gang together to save their old friend and mentor—once again stealing for all the right reasons, even while everything around them is going terribly wrong...especially those old emotions that Ruby is absolutely, positively *not* supposed to be feeling.

Fun fact: During the writing of *Undercover Heist*, while Ruby and Shane were searching for their happy ending atop a mountain, I got to experience a happy ending (beginning?), too—getting engaged at the top of Sulphur Mountain in Banff National Park.

Thank you so much for reading!

Rachel

UNDERCOVER HEIST

RACHEL ASTOR

Recycling programs for this product may not exist in your area.

ISBN-13: 978-1-335-59413-6

Undercover Heist

This is a work of fiction. Names, characters, places and incidents are either the product of the author's imagination or are used fictitiously. Any resemblance to actual persons, living or dead, businesses, companies, events or locales is entirely coincidental.

For questions and comments about the quality of this book, please contact us at CustomerService@Harlequin.com.

TM and ® are trademarks of Harlequin Enterprises ULC.

Harlequin Enterprises ULC
22 Adelaide St. West, 41st Floor
Toronto, Ontario M5H 4E3, Canada
www.Harlequin.com

Printed in Lithuania

Rachel Astor is equal parts country girl and city dweller who spends an alarming amount of time correcting the word *the*. Rachel has had a lot of jobs (bookseller, real estate agent, 834 assorted admin roles), but none as, *ahem*, interesting as when she waitressed at a bar named after a dog. She is now a *USA TODAY* bestselling author who splits her time between the city, the lake and as many made-up worlds as possible.

Books by Rachel Astor

Harlequin Romantic Suspense

The Suspect Next Door
Undercover Heist

Visit the Author Profile
page at Harlequin.com.

Prologue

Max Redfield's eyes became a bit misty as the two most talented students in his current class stood for their bow. The audience roared with appreciation after the story had swept them completely away for one hour and forty-eight minutes. He never tired of watching his actors succeed in stealing the full attention of a rapt audience…the way you could hear a pin drop inside a theater of a thousand, everyone holding their breath to catch each word.

That was *real* power. Sharing time with someone, taking their troubles away, if only for a moment. Getting them off their screens and out of their heads. These days that was almost a miracle.

He sighed a happy sigh, which turned wistful as it drifted off.

If only it was enough. If only the other life didn't call him. The life of excitement, and drama, and all the things that created a great story. Except in the other life, he got to live great stories instead of portraying them. He could never give up the con. He'd tried, of course, and even quit for a few months after Scotland, but the thrill drew him in again and again. He couldn't live without it—it was the one vice he couldn't quite give up.

His two protégés were far too promising. He couldn't let their talents go to waste.

One of two things usually happened after someone with

real talent went through Max's acting school—they headed for Broadway or Hollywood—great contacts to have, especially when they felt indebted to you—or they graduated to a con.

Acting was a highly underrated talent in that world. The art of making people believe could get a person into most places far more effectively than methods other people swore by. At least he thought so. But Max supposed he was old-fashioned.

After the excitement of the evening faded, and the last of the guests and actors departed, Max found himself daydreaming, trying to think of the perfect story for his star students to tell. This was how he thought of his cons. They were stories—and he relished in finding the perfect role for each actor to play. The ultimate director's high.

Sadly, his stories—his cons—were never quite as elegant as Ash's. Such a waste she left the biz, but Max would have to do his best with the skill he did have.

And so, as he walked home, he thought of stories. Of new ways to deliver a con—but only to those who deserved it, of course. Never innocents. Only real criminals, the kind who used drug money or blood money or the souls of the young and innocent, and with the world in its current state, there was never a shortage of targets. The challenging part, though, was that these were also the kinds of people who tended to be naturally suspicious and more dangerous than the average person.

It was much harder to swindle a swindler.

But sometimes that was the fun part too.

So lost in his thoughts, Max had missed the signs. A noise, easily written off as a feral cat, then a faraway click, escaping on the wind as quickly as it came. A glint of something in the reflection of a window, which might have been anything.

But it had all been something. The noise, a careless footstep, the click, a gun cocked several yards away and the reflection? The flash of a watch, left on because it wouldn't matter anyway.

Max thought nothing of any of these things.

Until, that was, a heavy hood was pulled over his head, his arms yanked painfully behind his body and cuffed as a vehicle pulled up alongside—a van, judging by the sound of the sliding doors—and whisked him away.

And in that moment, in the black and the speed and the terror, one thought entered his mind—perhaps it wasn't so hard to swindle a swindler, after all.

Chapter 1

Most people didn't always know why they weren't successful, but Shane Meyers knew exactly why he was failing so miserably.

Because he had to.

"Buddy—" his agent said. Shane hated when he called him that—made him think the guy had forgotten his name. Although, Shane thought with a tilt of his head, maybe that wasn't such a bad thing. "—this could have been your big break. *Again*," the agent finished after a dramatic pause. "What happened in there this time?"

Shane let out a long, rehearsed breath. "I don't know, man. I guess I just wasn't feeling the part."

It had been an incredible opportunity. Shane honestly didn't know how Christoph had managed to land him the audition. It would have been a huge role. The lead in a small but potentially significant film. There was no way he'd paid the kind of dues it took to land an audition like that, but something in his film reel had caught the producers' attention.

And then he blew it.

He blew that sucker like a five-year-old blows dandelion wishes, the knowledge that he had no intention of taking the part—even if he had miraculously landed it—solidly planted in the forefront of his mind.

"Not feeling the part?" Christoph was saying, his voice rising to little-girl-squeal-like proportions, though Shane wasn't really paying attention. "Do you know how hard I work to get you the kind of attention you need to become a breakout star? Do you know how many other people would die to have this kind of opportunity?"

"I know, man, and I appreciate it," Shane said, though he was becoming increasingly more interested in the party going on around him than in the conversation. "But I've told you before, I'm not interested in the leading-man roles."

"Shane," Christoph said, exasperated. "That is the whole point of being an actor—to become a star. Get famous and be adored."

Shane rolled his eyes. He wanted to tell Christoph where he could neatly tuck his spiel, but the guy would never understand, no matter how clearly and precisely Shane spoke. Famous and adored was the last thing Shane wanted. Sure, there was a time when he thought those things were important, but none of that held any interest anymore.

To be in the spotlight would ruin everything. Famous would mean he'd be as incognito as a grizzly bear in a fuchsia crop top wandering undetected through a food court. He'd never go unrecognized, which had been essential in his previous line of work.

He would never be able to have the thing he really wanted again. And sure, the thing he really wanted was about as likely to happen as Santa beating the Easter Bunny in a foot race on Boxing Day, but he couldn't take the risk.

He could only take small parts on TV and in movies—the kinds of roles that paid but would never throw him into the spotlight. It was a nice way to live. Gave him the connections that put him in the places he wanted to be. Places like the party he'd been trying to enjoy before his phone had so rudely interrupted him.

His life had become a steady stream of parties, flowing

alcohol, attractive women and flying under the radar. It was what he wanted. Well…as close to what he wanted as he could reasonably expect under the circumstances.

Christoph would never understand Shane's reasons for not aspiring higher. But his acting training had so far helped him keep Christoph's ambitions at bay. "It's not about the fame for me. It's about the craft. The art."

Admittedly, the delivery of that line had not been his best performance.

But Christoph bought it, or at least pretended to. "Whatever you say, buddy. But mark my words—someday, I'm gonna make you a star."

"Great. Looking forward to it," Shane said, trying his best not to hurt himself rolling his eyes too hard.

If there had ever been a cheesier line in the history of the movies, Shane had yet to hear it. But he supposed it was the job of agents to sell dreams, so he could hardly blame the guy. And so far, Shane had been impressed by the things Christoph had done to move his happily mediocre career along, especially considering the utter lack of cooperation from his client.

Shane tucked his phone into his pocket and turned back to the party. He watched a gorgeous brunette in a bathing suit, which left little to be desired, dive gracefully into the pool. *Now this is more like it.* It never ceased to amaze him that in LA it was perfectly normal for swimwear to be right at home in the company of expensive suits…along with everything in between. There was a familiar-looking guy—had Shane worked with him once? Or seen him in something recently?—in board shorts, a hooded sweater and wavy long hair that looked like it hadn't been washed in a while. An attractive woman in a sequined evening gown was sitting on his lap. Only in LA would she be the one fawning all over the guy instead of the other way around.

Shane couldn't help but smile. The inconsistency and oddness of the town were what had drawn him there in the first place. Easier to blend in where anything and everything goes.

He wandered over to the bar, enjoying his life now. Maybe he wasn't 100 percent content, but parties on random Sunday nights—complete with bartenders, waitstaff, caterers and everyone else who made these kinds of events run without a hitch—weren't too shabby. It would be a dream to pull a job at an event like this. So many options for characters to perform.

He pushed the thought from his head. That wasn't his life anymore. No matter how hard it was to stop himself from planning how, exactly, he might get to the painting above the TV. It wasn't the artwork he cared about, it was the thrill of the job, the adrenaline gained from taking the risk.

A voice came from beside him. "It's beautiful, isn't it?"

Shane hadn't heard the woman come up to him. He'd been so lost in his daydream, or rather day-*scheme*, he'd let his guard down. It was nice he was able to do that now. For years he'd been so "on" all the time he'd begun to worry the stress might be affecting his health. Not that he was ever as interested in his health as he was getting to the next thrill.

"Incredible," Shane said, guiding his showstopper smile toward the woman. He knew from experience what this seemed to do to those who'd shown interest in him.

The woman was attractive—auburn hair, great body, a twinkle in her eye suggesting she might like a little mischief almost as much as Shane did.

"Are you an art connoisseur?" she asked.

Shane chuckled. "Not really," he said, turning away from the painting to face her. "I suppose I just like to look at beautiful things."

The woman raised her eyebrows with a little smirk, as if to say "nice play." "Does that line work on all the girls?" she asked.

Shane tilted his head in thought. "Surprisingly, yes," he said, "though I'm not sure if it's the line itself, or the professional delivery."

"Is that your way of subtly letting me know you're some kind of famous actor?" the woman asked.

"Oh, I am very far from famous, but the actor part is accurate." Shane motioned to the bartender to get them two more drinks. "And yes, I suppose I hoped it would impress you in some small, silly way."

She smiled. "Fair enough."

"But let me guess something about you," he said.

The woman looked intrigued and nodded for him to continue.

Shane's heart sped, knowing he was about to enter his area of expertise. He didn't know if it was because he'd studied acting and spent so much time thinking about motivations, or if he was just a natural at it, but he was always able to read people. Well, almost always.

"Well," he began. "I think you have an expectation about what you think I will say, which is that you are an actress."

The woman smiled, her eyes impressed and amused.

"It makes sense. You're at a Hollywood party filled to the brim with actors and actresses, and you certainly have the looks for it. Of course—" he squinted his eyes "—it's clear you have a lot going on behind those intelligent eyes, so you could just as easily be a producer or a director, but I don't think that's quite right either." Shane picked up the drinks from the bar and handed her a fresh glass of the wine she held, taking her almost empty glass and setting it down.

Her eyes sparkled. She was clearly enjoying herself more than she'd expected, which, for someone like Shane, was simply another clue.

"You're here because someone important to you asked you to come, but it's not your usual scene. Perhaps a roommate."

She smiled wider.

"The roommate is an actress, and you love her enough to come to these kinds of parties even though you find them superficial and tedious. You both moved here from the same small town after high school. Her for Hollywood and you for…school, I think," he said.

"Impressive," the woman said, and Shane could tell she wasn't just saying it. He knew he'd gotten it dead right.

But he still had a bit more in his arsenal that he hoped to blow her mind with.

"And I suspect you are a psychology major."

Her eyes widened, her lips parting in surprise. "How did you—"

"Just a lucky guess," Shane said, flashing her his—thankfully less than—famous smile once more.

It wasn't just a lucky guess, of course. It was what Shane did. He read people better than most people read books. She squinted, not quite believing him, but he was nothing if not good at feigning innocence. His boyish charm had gotten him far in life.

"Can you excuse me for a minute?" she asked, starting to walk away. "I'm Isabelle, by the way," she said, "and I'll be right back."

"Shane," he said, shaking her hand. "It's very nice to meet you."

Shane wandered over to the edge of the patio. He'd been in this position more times than he could count. Isabelle would go off to her roommate and let her know she was leaving, then come back and Shane would take her to his place, where they'd finish off the evening enjoying each other's company in various fun and energetic ways.

But he wasn't sure, as he looked out over the gorgeous view of the hills and the ocean beyond, why it didn't feel as exciting as it used to. Maybe it was because he knew he'd never own a view like this one. Then again, with his charm and skills, why would he ever need to? He'd always have plenty of friends in high places who'd let him borrow their views. His thoughts hung a little longer on Isabelle, and how there'd been so many women like her, but nothing that ever stuck.

Not since Ruby.

Maybe he was just bored of everything, since nothing could ever live up to the life he used to have. In fact, when Shane really thought about it—something he tried hard not to do—his life was starting to feel a lot like a psychology major might feel at a Hollywood party.

That it was all a little superficial and tedious.

Ruby Alexander sighed and slammed the enormous book shut, shoving it across the desk. "Flipping comatose sloths!" she said, under her breath.

"Ruby?" Barb said, raising an eyebrow as she poked her head into Ruby's office. "Is everything okay?"

Ruby rubbed her temples. "Yeah. No. I don't know." She shook her head. "It's just…all this red tape. These laws. Some days it feels like everything is working against us."

Barb sat across from Ruby, sighing. "I wish I had words of wisdom to make it better, but unfortunately, this is the work. The art world has a complicated relationship with these governments. The negotiations are always delicate and a lot of the time it's going to be one step forward, two steps back."

Ruby let out a low growl. "But half these people are war criminals."

Barb nodded. "And many of them are all we've got to negotiate with."

Ruby leaned back and gazed out the window. "It all feels so futile. Like nothing we're doing here matters."

"It matters, Ruby," Barb said emphatically. "We're the only support these poor families have to lean on. The only place they can turn."

Ruby nodded even though she knew something Barb didn't. The families whose art was pillaged in various war raids throughout history did have another option. And knowing *that* left her with even more guilt than not being able to do more for these families. She'd left that world behind years ago. It was just…once in a while she wondered if getting out of the heist game had been the right choice.

"Thanks, Barb," Ruby said. "You're right. Sometimes the snail's pace of the whole thing just gets to me."

Barb nodded and stood. "It gets to all of us, hon. It gets to all of us," she said, walking out with a little wave.

Deep down, Ruby knew she'd made the right choice getting out when she did. Things were getting too hot after everything imploded in Scotland. The authorities were starting to close in on the team, and so were some of the dealers trying to sell the black-market pieces. And while a typical art dealer might not be the most terrifying kind of person on earth, the people who protected the shady ones certainly could be.

Still, as she sat in her office day after day pushing paper, she sometimes missed the intrigue, the danger, the pure fun of it.

But she could never go back to that life, to breaking all the rules. She had way too much to lose now. She was a rising star in the legitimate art world, landing her first apprentice curator position at the age of twenty-seven. Over the past three years she'd been working her way up the ladder. After a few incredible recoveries of stolen art, she'd been asked to specialize in helping governments around the world make pacts and agreements to carry out the arduous process of returning stolen art to their rightful owners—ancestors of victims of art raids around the world and throughout history.

And Ruby was becoming a leading expert, able to spot and identify stolen art faster than a high-speed getaway driver.

Of course, her expertise wasn't quite as uncanny as everyone thought. Truth be told, she'd had years of research and hands-on experience, though she couldn't tell anyone about that.

Doing everything through "proper channels" was an exercise in frustration compared to the way she and the team used to work. Still, she was doing good in the world, no matter how slow the process. She helped without having to risk her life or break the law. Without having to always look over her shoulder. It was almost worth the day-to-day slog in the trenches of already found stolen art.

Ruby packed up her things and got ready to head out for the day. She smiled as she strolled down the hall past her colleagues who were also getting ready to leave. Imagine what they would think if they knew about her past, she thought as she waved at Gordon, who would pop his toupee if he had any inkling.

She bet none of them had ever played the part of a damsel in distress inside the mansion of a criminal—a decoy as her team pilfered the man's jewels from right under his nose. Or raided a secret warehouse filled with original artwork stolen in war crimes. And likely none of them had scaled the outside of a thirty-six-story building to retrieve a priceless Ming dynasty vase.

Of course, it wasn't like she could do that anymore either. It wasn't an option, even if she were willing to leave her new world, which she loved, no matter how frustrating. She wasn't equipped anymore. She tried to keep in shape but sitting in front of a computer doing office work for the past three years had made her soft. She worried she'd lost her edge mentally too. She used to be able to peg a criminal's thoughts with shocking accuracy, but she hadn't let her mind go there for a long time.

Ruby stepped out of the museum into a chilly day, the wind sweeping her hair sideways. She pulled her coat tight and walked toward her apartment—another perk of this new life. The museum owned residences nearby for the employees to rent at a discounted rate, and Ruby loved her place—modern and sleek, but with plenty of soft surfaces and artwork to warm the space up.

As Ruby made her way down the street, a strange feeling crawled through her. In her old life, she'd always been on high alert, glancing over her shoulder to make sure no one followed her, but she'd given up the habit a long time ago. Still, sometimes old habits died hard, and she risked a peek back.

Nothing.

But she couldn't shake the sense she was being watched.

She looked again.

If she were being followed, her training was still sharp enough to notice. She shook her head and kept walking, a little faster now, wanting to get home, have a long hot shower and relax with a glass of wine.

Hurrying into her building, Ruby took a final glance back then shrugged, deciding she was being paranoid because she'd been thinking so much about her old life. But that was ages ago, and all that business was a long way behind her. She was grateful for that, though perhaps there was a small pang of nostalgia on the side.

Ruby opened a bottle of cabernet and poured a glass to breathe, then began to undress as she made her way to the bathroom, dropping clothes as she went. It was an old habit, and she felt decadent as she disrobed—a simple luxury, yet it gave her so much pleasure to take those last few steps into the bathroom completely naked. A little jolt of naughty as a throwback to her old life, she supposed.

The shower felt glorious. Another little gift to herself, a ritual to wash the stress of the day down the drain before she indulged in her art, needing to cleanse herself of the traitorous people she helped hunt down before her creative juices could flow.

She wrapped a towel around herself before making her way

back down the hall to retrieve her wine. Halfway to the kitchen she realized something was off and stopped, heart racing. There didn't appear to be an immediate threat, but impossibly, her clothes were no longer scattered on the floor. A sound of a glass clinking came from the kitchen where the clothes she'd discarded sat neatly folded on the counter.

A voice floated from the shadows. "Still doing the same old rituals, I see."

Chapter 2

Shane thought he was prepared to see Ruby after all this time. From the moment their former contact got hold of him, Shane had been warring with himself—one moment filled with dread, and the next, trying to keep his excitement at bay. One glance at Ruby's face—a face he'd believed he'd never see again—was almost more than his wounded heart could take. The fact that she wore nothing but a towel and still looked as good as the day she left—better even—did not help either the dread or the excitement.

Thankfully he had always been the best actor in the room. He reminded himself he was there to play his part and nothing more. Slowing his breath, he tried to calm his heart—the one part of him doing a terrible job at staying in character.

"Jesus, Shane, what the hell are you doing here? How did you find me? And how did you get in?" Ruby's voice rose as the questions poured out of her.

"I think you know the answer to the last question, at least," he said, smirking. "You know I can pretty much break in anywhere I want, anytime I want."

Shane knew the look on her face well. Fuming, with a side of livid.

"Just because you *can* go somewhere, Shane..."

The way she said his name twigged something in him,

made his stomach tighten. He never did handle it well when she was mad at him.

"…doesn't mean you should."

Her eyes still flashed the way they used to, as if her anger lit a flame somewhere deep in her core.

Shane's plan had been to pour himself a glass of wine to match hers and be sitting in the dark recesses of the living room before she got out of the shower. But she'd come out before the plan was fully executed and, as she usually did, caught him a bit off guard.

Good thing he was a master at keeping his cool under pressure.

Of course, there was no greater pressure than the kind only Ruby Alexander could apply.

He continued to pour his glass of wine, slowly, deliberately, then picked up both glasses and sauntered over to Ruby, handing her one. He caught her eye and held it a moment longer than necessary, then turned. "We may as well make ourselves comfortable. You, my friend," he said, catching her eye again as he sat, "are expecting company."

He made himself comfortable, one hand on the back of the couch as he sat, playing the part, acting as if he owned the place.

Ruby, to her credit, played it cool, taking a step toward him. She lowered her hand from the towel, knowing that even a hint that the towel might drop at any moment was enough to throw him off his game.

"I certainly wasn't expecting anything besides a quiet night at home, but since you never bring anything but trouble with you, I guess I should get dressed and prepare for the worst." She took a long sip of her wine and moved to set her glass down on the coffee table. She leaned farther forward than she needed to, affording him a view he tried to resist, but failed.

She caught his eye knowingly and stood up, heading back down the hallway.

He watched her go, his jaw working as if grinding his emotions into submission. As she took the last step into her room, her towel slipped—just a little—and Shane couldn't help but think she did it on purpose to torture him. He leaned back and took a drink, trying not to think about Ruby in there that very moment, letting the towel fall to the floor.

He closed his eyes and breathed, remembering the exquisite torture being around her had always been. Never knowing where he stood, but never being able to walk away either.

Remembering how easy it had seemed for her when she'd finally left.

A knock sounded at the door.

Shane moved to stand, but Ruby was already headed back down the hall, looking as though the couple of minutes in the bedroom had done nothing to ease her anger.

Of course, the anger was completely justified. Especially considering behind that door was the one person Ruby was absolutely not going to want to see.

Having Shane Meyers sitting on her couch as if there was nothing out of the ordinary was making Ruby feel like she had been hit by a toddler on a runaway scooter—dazed, confused and like she'd fielded a solid thwack right to the crotch.

She hadn't seen him in three years, but he was acting as if not a day had gone by. Something about him looked different, though. A little more tense around the jaw. A little shaggier around the edges. A little sexier than she remembered.

Shit.

She got a sense that somehow life had not been kind to Shane in the years since she'd seen him. Perhaps he hadn't landed on his feet in quite the same way she had. The degrees she'd worked for on the side of their…other business…

had been the safety net all those teachers and parental types back in school had warned her she'd better have. She'd never quite bought into those ideas, but school had come easily for her—things tended to be like that when you picked something to study that you were already passionate about. She had to grudgingly admit they'd been right. In her case, at least. She doubted it would have been quite as valuable for people who hadn't ended up with their lives in the kind of massive destruction hers had catapulted into.

Something similar might have helped Shane, though, she mused, noticing a scar above his right eyebrow that hadn't been there before. It was small, but she knew it hadn't been there before, given all the nights she'd stayed up watching him breathe as they lay tangled in bed. But school hadn't come so easily to Shane. Hell, it had been a miracle he'd made it through Max's program… Then again, there was the whole thing about passion. Something Shane never lacked when it came to a job, since playing the part of someone else was his favorite thing in the world to do. Ruby tried very hard never to think about that. Going down the rabbit hole of what had been real and what hadn't could turn into a spiral of doubt, fear and a whole lot of paranoia.

She hated this. Hated feeling shaken in her own damn place, her only sanctuary, and she was pissed he had the nerve—and the ability—to break in even though her security was one of the top systems available. Of course, that had never stopped any of them before, herself included. Still, there was a code people in her former line of work were supposed to stick to.

But frankly, none of that mattered. If she was being honest, her anger was really pointed at herself. She was angry for the way she felt. And the way those feelings snuck up on her in less time than it had taken to say "Be careful with the bloody Rembrandt!" that time in southern Italy. Time should have made it all go away but seeing him again after all these years stirred up…feelings, and that was what *really* pissed her off.

Screw the slightly longer hair, which somehow made him look both more boyish and more mature at the same time. Screw the new, slimmer style of jeans that showed off just how much better he'd been at keeping in performance shape than she had. Screw those hands that looked just as dexterous as ever…and Holy Mother of Pearl, could she remember the way those dexterous hands felt sliding slowly from her hip to her breast as if it were yesterday.

Double shit.

She needed to stop. She moved toward the door, shooting Shane a glare she hoped said, *This is my house and I will open my own damn door, thank you very much.*

Ruby knew the person on the other side of the damn door was likely to be one of three people.

Please be Bug or Max, she silently prayed. *Please be Bug or Max.*

She eased the door open and let out a long, weighty sigh. She wanted so badly to slam the door shut again, especially since she couldn't think of a single reason for this woman to waltz back into her life. But—although she hated herself for it—Ruby was curious. She hated when she couldn't immediately figure out the end game.

Ruby pulled her shoulders back. "Ashlyn," she said, nodding to the woman before her.

"Ruby!" the woman said, as if meeting up with a long-lost friend.

Which of course she was. Long-lost at least, though Ruby would not consider her and Ash friends anymore.

Ruby rolled her eyes and opened the door wider to let Ash in.

The woman looked like she hadn't aged a day, which Ruby found unreasonably annoying. In fact, Ashlyn Greaves looked as though she had grown younger. Ruby wondered if she'd had some work done, though she supposed the relaxed lifestyle of no longer being a criminal was bound to give a person a little pep to their step.

Ash was as put-together as always—pencil skirt, tailored blouse, fabulous coat and perfect accessories, looking as if she'd been professionally styled. Ruby made an attempt to smooth her wrinkled sweatshirt, trying not to think about how she must look—straight out of the shower with the first clothes she grabbed from the heaping pile in her hamper thrown on. Ash had that effect on people. No matter how far you'd come, no matter how respected you were in your field, she had a way of transforming you into your most awkward, uncomfortable, seventh-grade-in-the-change-room self. It was what made her so good at her job. Or used to. Ruby had no idea what Ash had been up to since that night in Scotland.

She tried to push it out of her mind, but seeing Ash brought it back like it was yesterday.

Ruby had felt the job going south and wanted to abort—knew they needed to abort—but it was Ashlyn's call. The plan had worried Ruby from the start. For every other job, the team, without fail, made sure to have three exit strategies. Surprises always came up when pulling off a heist, and contingency plans were the most important piece. Always.

But Ash—the group leader and the strategist—insisted that even though she didn't have a plan C, the score would be worth it and there wouldn't be any surprises.

But surprises were the one thing you could count on.

The team got into the castle, no problem. It was supposed to be vacant. Max and Shane had cased the place for a week straight, and not a single person had come or gone. The family was on vacation off the coast of Morocco and the only security consisted of the nonliving variety. Plenty of cameras, alarms and even a pressure-sensitive floor around the most valuable items, but the team had dealt with all that before. Human interference was always the most volatile kind, and they were confident it wouldn't be a problem.

It was Ash's job to confirm the whereabouts of the family.

But she hadn't been thorough enough.

The teenage daughter had come home from college a few days early for her holiday break, and Kaden had surprised her as he walked into the foyer with a duffel bag full of antiquities.

The family was a paranoid one—most families who collected illegal artifacts were—and they'd had guns stashed everywhere.

The team knew this ahead of time—Bug was always thorough with his recon work—but no one had thought the guns would be a problem. They assured themselves it would be the easiest job they'd ever pulled. Thought they had all the time in the world. When Ruby woke up that morning, she hadn't even been nervous.

What a dazzling fool she'd been.

They'd retrieved everything they went there to steal back, but the cost had been far too high.

The others panicked, but they'd gotten themselves together and succeeded in taking the daughter down. Not to kill her—they tried never to kill people, and certainly not an innocent teenage girl. As innocent as a teenage daughter of an exporter of…let's just say contraband, could be, at least. She'd simply stumbled upon an intruder in her own house. But they had been able to restrain her in a cell in the basement. Even Ruby had to admit that was extraordinarily convenient in the end. They stocked her with plenty of food and water, and only once they were safely out of the country did they alert her family to her whereabouts.

But Ruby hadn't been panicked. Instead, she had been left holding Kaden in her arms as he bled out. It was the exact moment Ruby had decided she was out. Out of the team and out of the lifestyle. She vowed she would never work a con again.

And now, trying to keep her cool as her two ex-partners stood in her living room, she was determined not to let anyone convince her otherwise.

Chapter 3

Shane hadn't realized he'd been holding his breath until he started to feel light-headed. Thankfully the acting classes he'd taken all his life had included breathing exercises, which helped calm him and get back on track.

He wasn't in any sort of character, but he was still playing a part. When he thought about it, he was always playing a part. Then again, wasn't everybody?

Ash sauntered in, removing a pair of expensive-looking gloves and surveying the place.

Ruby did have some nice digs, Shane realized. That museum job of hers must pay pretty well. A whole lot better than the odd acting jobs he'd picked up here and there in the years since the team had disbanded.

Ash looked like she was doing pretty well, too, for that matter.

Shane knew what this little unplanned visit concerned, but Ruby was about to hear it for the first time. Ash knew she could never go to Ruby on her own, not after everything that had happened, but they thought together they might have a chance at convincing her.

"So," Ruby said, grabbing her wine again, probably realizing that with the two of them in her apartment, she was going to need it. "Is anyone going to tell me what the hell is going on?"

Shane had never been so nervous in his life. He didn't get

nervous—that was the whole point. It was what made him better than anyone else at acting, and better than anyone else at the lifestyle. But sitting there, working as hard as he could to appear calm, he realized he didn't like the feeling one bit. But if he and Ash couldn't convince Ruby to make a brief foray back into the world of the wrong side of the law…well, he couldn't think about that.

They needed her. Desperately.

This, he realized, was another feeling he wasn't terribly familiar with, and was even less fond of—desperation. But here they were. A full-on "desperate times calls for desperate measures" situation, sitting in the apartment of a person they'd all sworn never to see again. Ruby had made them promise on their lives.

Given the circumstances, she was being rather…*cordial* was the word coming to Shane's mind. She poured Ash a glass of the cabernet before they all sat down on various minimalist-style furniture pieces around the room, which would have been called stark if not for the decorative items from Ruby's travels around the world. There was even the odd thing he recognized from…well, from before.

They sipped their wine, faster than Shane would have liked. But frankly the tension was thick and the only thing cutting through it was the alcohol. Or the alcohol was making it worse. He couldn't really tell.

"You're looking well," Ash said to Ruby.

Shane couldn't help but notice Ruby stiffen, though to the untrained eye, Ruby was hiding it well. Of course, there wasn't a single untrained eye in the room, so it hardly mattered.

Ash continued as if there was nothing out of the ordinary—just three old friends catching up after a long time apart. Shane would bet his life that Ruby wished it had been much, much longer.

"I'm not surprised you've been doing so well since going

legit. You always did have the best eye of all of us for the pieces," Ash continued, running her finger along an African statue on the bookcase.

Ruby cleared her throat, eyeing Ash like she was afraid she might break something. Not that she didn't have good reason—the last time they were all together, Ash had made the decisions that had broken pretty much everything. The rules, the job… Kaden. In essence, the whole team.

"My team doesn't seem to be complaining," Ruby finally said, a note of "unlike yours" underscoring her words.

Ash let a smirk slide across her lips, almost as if she was finding all this exceedingly amusing. "All the bureaucracy must be frustrating, though, I'd imagine."

Ruby took another sip of her wine, which was already half-gone, anger burning in her expression.

After a moment of seething silence, Ash turned her attention to Shane, making him wish he were anywhere else but in that room. If he didn't already know the reason for the impromptu reunion, he would have been out at the first glance from Ash. But this was too important.

"You, on the other hand, seem to be having a bit of a go with life," Ash continued.

"How nice of you to notice," Shane said, as if it were a compliment.

Truth be told, he'd had nothing but fun in the past few years, living off the spoils of their labors. Sure, they returned artifacts to their rightful owners, but it wasn't like they weren't still paid handsomely. Deals had always been worked out ahead of time for the team's commissions—usually a percentage of what was recovered—and the families were often so happy to get their items back they would throw in a hefty bonus.

Shane had enjoyed suddenly having enough time on his hands to enjoy the money he'd accumulated over the years particularly well. He found days of soaking in the sun on private yachts and drowning in the island club nightlife suited him quite well. Lately, though, it had all been feeling a little empty.

And seeing what Ruby had done with her life in the time since the last job made his lifestyle feel a little shallow. Which was fair enough, he supposed, though he was surprised at the spark of shame he felt. Why the hell shouldn't he use his money whatever damn way he pleased? But the moment *that* thought crept into his mind was the same moment he realized it wasn't the judgment from the others bothering him, it was the judgment he was clearly blanketing on himself. And it was only in that moment he realized he'd been blanketing it on himself all along. Loathing himself for the decadence combined with a healthy dose of idleness. Truly, a case could be made for each of the seven deadly sins having infiltrated his life. Not that he could blame the sins. No, the blame was squarely on him.

"Look, can we just stop with all the niceties and get to the point here?" Ruby said, suddenly out of patience with the song and dance they were all performing.

Ash didn't bother trying to hide her smile this time. "I was wondering when you were going to get jumpy. You always were the first to get impatient with everyone."

"Ash, come on," Shane jumped in. "Getting after each other isn't going to help the situation."

"Which brings me to my point," Ruby said, another sip going down the hatch.

Shane was hard-pressed to believe Ruby was nervous, but the wine swigging was about something. Maybe it was impatience, or maybe it was because she knew exactly why the two of them were sitting in her living room.

"What," she continued, "is the actual situation?"

Ash sighed and set down her glass. "There's a job."

"No," Ruby said, so fast Shane wasn't sure Ash had even finished her sentence.

"If you would just let me finish what I was going to say, I'd like to—"

"I said no," Ruby said, standing and putting her hand up as if to say that was the end of it. "There's no way it's ever going to happen."

"Ruby, just hear her out, please," Shane said.

Ruby shot him a glare. "Hear her out?" she said, her voice rising. "The woman who nearly got us all killed the last time she planned a job for us, and now you just want me to hear her out?"

"I think saying I nearly got everyone killed is a little unfair," Ash said.

"Tell that to Kaden," Ruby fired back.

"Look, I get it. You are angry with me and probably always will be. I've come to terms with that, but just listen to me, please. It's not what you think," Ash said.

Ruby shook her head. "This conversation is over. I don't know why I was even stupid enough to open the door for you." As she spoke, she moved over to the very door she spoke of and put her hand on the knob.

"Ruby." Ash sighed. "It's Max. They have Max."

Ruby's eyes darted from Shane to Ash, then back to Shane again. Then she closed them, a pained expression coming over her face.

Her hand dropped from the doorknob.

"What in the shit do you mean they have Max?" Ruby said, knowing exactly what in the shit they meant, but couldn't stop herself from asking anyway.

"No one has seen him since he left the theater production of his latest graduating class," Shane said.

"How long ago was that?"

"He left late two nights ago. They had all been celebrating after the final show and as far as anyone knows, Max was the last to leave."

Ruby nodded. She remembered Max was usually the last to leave after every show. He always said there was something about the dichotomy between a packed house and an empty theater in a single evening that gave him a sense of balance.

"But he never made it home," Shane finished.

Ruby began to pace. She'd tried to push Max—and all the others—from her mind every time they strayed in there, but she never forgot what an important figure he'd once been in her life. She supposed because her actual father had been largely absent while she was growing up and she'd never had an older, male influence in her life. Or maybe it was just that he'd become a friend. Of course, there was also the fact that he'd given her the first big opportunity she'd ever had in her life.

Without Max, nothing would have been the same.

"We have to get him back," she said, her pacing picking up speed. "This is Max."

"We know," Shane said.

"That's why we're here," Ash added.

"Shit," Ruby spit out, her mind suddenly racing faster than she could keep up. "What do we know?"

"Quite a bit," Ash said, going into her mastermind mode, as the team used to like to call it. Ruby was less than enthusiastic about being reminded that Ash's mastermind mode consisted of pacing as well, which made Ruby sit, though she couldn't keep her leg from jiggling.

"The kidnappers haven't kept it a secret. The moment they had him safely stowed away, I received a text instructing me to check my email."

"I'm assuming you've attempted a trace on the origin?"

"Of course," Ash said, and to her credit, she wasn't even snarky about it.

Had it been Ash questioning Ruby about it, Ruby would have been snarky times a thousand.

"Through the email, we discovered several things. First, we know Max is alive. They've provided proof of life via a video feed on a secured and encoded website."

Ruby stood. "Let me see."

"You can if you want," Shane jumped in, "but we can only assume they're able to track the IP of anyone who logs in, so unless you want these guys to know where you live, we might want to wait until we get somewhere else, or until we can get Bug on board."

Ruby sighed. "Fine. What else do we know?"

Ash tilted her head as if to say, *Could you possibly let me finish before you ask your requisite immeasurable sum of questions?* It took all Ruby had in her not to roll her eyes, since her very reasonable number of questions was usually what saved the team from certain disaster.

She did risk a glance at Shane, who just shrugged and gave her a knowing little smirk that was damned delectable, letting her know they were on the same wavelength. The "yes, Ash is an ogre's buttcrack but we have to humor her for Max's sake" wavelength.

This had to be about Max.

Max, who had taken her under his wing and showed her she had acting chops, at a time she didn't think she had any kind of chops. Hell, she couldn't even afford pork chops back then.

Max, who had been the only father figure she'd ever known, who'd brought her into the fold of his inner circle and made her the star of his show—well, one of the stars—the year she and Shane were set to graduate.

Max, whose inner circle was so much more than just an acting gig at some mostly unknown theater program—it was a real job, out there in the world doing good work. To this day Ruby still believed it had been good work, no matter how illegal most people would have considered it.

Max, who had warned her that love was never a good idea on the job.

And Max, who was the first to console her when that love had gone south and never, ever said, "I told you so."

He'd given her everything back then—her livelihood, his friendship, his acceptance. She'd had to fight for those things with everyone else, but Max just gave them easily and freely.

And he had done the same for Ash and Shane, and countless others along the way. They couldn't just leave him hanging.

Unfortunately, the people pulling Ash's strings must have known all that as well as Ruby did.

"The message was from the same people we used to work for. Max used to be the go-between for the jobs, but now that they have him, they somehow found me," she said, shrugging. "Who knows, maybe Max gave them something on me."

"Did Max even know where you were?" Shane jumped in with a question. And it was a good thing he did, since if he hadn't, Ruby would have called her out about throwing their friend under the bus, and that would have sent Ash over the edge. Ruby paused for a moment to imagine Ash sailing, quite literally, over the edge of a cliff, then spent the next twenty seconds trying to hide the smile attempting to force its way across her face.

"Of course not. When you guys insisted on no contact, I swore to you I would honor that, but Max always did have a way of finding things out," Ash said.

Ruby waved away her comment. "Whatever. Tell us what you know."

Ash looked like she wanted to continue to argue the point, but they all knew their most important resource now was time. "So, these people. They're not necessarily bad people—they do good things in the world—but they're not necessarily good people either. The one thing I do know for sure is that they are reasonable."

"Right," Shane jumped in. "Kidnapping an old man is a super-reasonable thing to do."

Exasperation coated Ash's face, but she did her best to ignore the interruption. "They are reasonable in the sense that they are fair—as I'm sure you well remember, the pay will be generous."

"I don't want their money," Ruby said, "I just want Max back."

"We can figure all that out later," Ash said. "The problem these people are having is they can't find a team they deem good enough to do a particular job. They still have people around the world doing the same kind of work we used to do, but something…special has come up and they don't trust anyone else."

Ruby closed her eyes and shook her head a little. "You know, for the way I can usually see every imaginable outcome to any given situation, I gotta say…being forced back into a life of crime because I was so damn trustworthy was not number one on my list of things I wanted to have happen today."

Chapter 4

If the whole thing hadn't been so disastrous, Shane would have laughed. As it stood, with Max at stake—one of his favorite people in the world, his mentor, for Christ's sake—he was having a hard time not letting the emotions of the situation get to him. Clearly, he'd been out of the practice of compartmentalizing for too long. He used to be so good at it. Then again, when everything in life was going your way, there wasn't a whole hell of a lot to have to shove into a tiny box and lock away on some high dusty shelf somewhere in the back of your brain. He'd filled that shelf right up to the top after Scotland, then kept the door on the memory storage unit locked down—with a little help from a ton of traveling, partying and booze ever since.

When Ash found him and pried the door open again, all the emotions had come oozing out, sitting right on the surface ever since.

Maybe that was why seeing Ruby again made it seem like his whole world was shifting off its axis.

She looked different. Her hair was cut shorter than the bob she used to wear, like she'd started getting the expensive haircuts that looked amazing even straight out of the shower. It suited her, made her edgier, like she was ready to take on anyone and anything. Not that she wasn't always like that, but now she was just…more herself somehow. It wasn't going to be good for the job, though—made her stand out too much.

Of course, she always stood out more than the rest of them, constantly having to use makeup to play down her features, make them more like everyone else's. Especially her lips—which he was trying very hard not to stare at as he watched her talk—shaped almost like a heart. And then there were those piercing gray eyes she hid under brown contacts when they were on the job. Eyes that kept flashing toward him as if looking for some kind of reassurance, of which, of course, he had none to give. He took another swig of wine, wishing it was something a whole lot stronger.

"Even if we agree to do this," Ruby said, "how do we know they're not just going to keep doing it over and over? Snatching one of us in the middle of the most inconvenient time ever and forcing us back into the game?"

"Look," Ash said, sounding impatient, "they've given me their word. They don't know who either of you are, or the rest of the team. They know Max and they know me, that's it. Once we're done with this and have Max back, I'll make sure they can never find either of us again."

"Um," Shane said, "how do you plan to do that?"

Ruby turned to Ash and raised a perfect eyebrow, as if to say, *Yeah, exactly.*

Ash sighed. "When I'm not on the job, I'm unfindable. As for Max…well, he's going to be difficult. Maybe this little kidnapping stint will help convince him. He's going to have to close the school and go into hiding."

"He's never going to do that," Ruby said.

"For you guys, he might," Ash said, knowing Max might not do anything for her anymore, not after Kaden.

Max had felt an unreasonable amount of guilt over the Kaden disaster, since he'd been the one who'd brought him in. Max had brought everyone into the crew—his acting school was an incredible source, but with Kaden, it had been different. Scotland had been his first job. Max had plucked him from his class earlier that month and essentially sent him to his death, and while the rest of the crew hadn't known him very well yet, they'd all known he would have been a star in the business. He had the power to make people around him feel good. Hell, even Shane missed the damn kid and he'd barely known him. Kaden had been one of those guys who just…left a mark on people wherever he went.

Shane put his elbows on his knees and ran his hands through his hair as Ruby let out a long sigh.

"If it wasn't for Max, you wouldn't still be standing in my living room," Ruby said to Ash, spitting the words out like they tasted foul.

"Well, it is for Max," was all Ash said, taking a long drink from her wineglass. "So, are you in or not?"

Ruby glanced from Ash to Shane. "Are you in?" she asked him.

He shrugged one shoulder. "I wouldn't be here if I wasn't. I mean, it's Max, right?"

Ruby's shoulders slumped ever so slightly, then she straightened and turned to Ash. "Yeah, I'm in."

Shane felt a weight lift. He hadn't known if Ruby would agree to do it, even if it were to save Max. As he leaned back in relief, his eyes landed on the master's degree from Columbia she had sitting in a nondescript frame on her bookshelf. He didn't know how she did it. During all those years they were pulling jobs, Ruby had kept at her studies—more than kept at them, excelled at them—and had come out of it all barely breaking a sweat. She'd gone so far in life, a fact that was obvious in everything—the way she looked, the way she acted, hell, even the way they were sitting in this very expensive apartment drinking wine Shane knew was worth more than anything he'd had to drink in the past three years. And she hadn't even known she was expecting company.

There were no two ways about it—Ruby Alexander was so

far out of his league he was pretty sure they weren't even playing the same damn game anymore.

"So, what are we in for?" Ruby asked, what small bit of the patience she had left waning.

Ash raised her eyebrows. "As you would expect, it's not going to be easy."

The urge to strike at Ash with some kind of comment about the word *easy* even leaving her lips flooded through Ruby. Scotland was supposed to have been easy, then turned out to be the end of everything. But she couldn't delay this any longer. She had to know what they were up against.

"We've been tasked to steal back an emerald scepter rumored to have once belonged to a Swiss family of high nobility. It's made of pure gold and is encrusted with three hundred sixty-eight diamonds, which comprise an ornate cage-like enclosure for the centerpiece—a massive round emerald."

"Value?" Shane asked as he leaned over Ruby's shoulder.

He smelled sweet and fresh—a scent that brought back way too many memories and made something twinge low in her stomach.

"There are whispers of a hundred million," Ash said.

"Who did it belong to?" Ruby asked.

"We haven't been told specifically. We can only assume, based on our previous work with these people, that they hope to return it to the rightful owners, which more likely than not is some aristocrat in Switzerland."

The answer was vague. Different from their other jobs with these people. Normally they laid out specifically what the job was and who it was for. Ruby had always had the understanding that the people they worked for were a sort of broker—a go-between—liaising with the team and those families who'd had their valuables stolen at one time or another throughout history. It was a tricky business given the way history tended to get skewed and rewritten according to the people in power at any given time. It had always been Ruby's job to confirm all the recovered goods would be going to the legitimate, rightful owners, and being given such imprecise information didn't sit well.

Ash swiped to the next photo on her phone. "The destination we'll be headed to is…remote."

Ruby didn't like the way she said the word *remote*.

"How remote?" Shane asked, clearly thinking the same thing as Ruby.

"About as remote as it gets. Nestled into the top of a mountain. The Swiss Alps, to be precise, on an unnamed peak—the nearest town is Grindelwald."

Ruby let out a long sigh. The top of a damned mountain. That was a new one.

"And security?" Shane asked.

Ash tilted her head. "Pretty much what you'd expect from people paranoid enough to build their complex on the top of a mountain. There are two ways in…helicopter or the large private gondola, which is operated by guards at the top and bottom of the mountain. Once you get to the top, there are additional guards in four perimeter towers."

"These guys are paranoid," Ruby couldn't help but point out.

Of course, she also couldn't help but think that since her team was planning a heist, the intense caution was more than warranted.

Ash nodded. "The main structure itself is massive—almost more like a castle than a modern house. As far as technology, we don't know much, other than to assume it's top-of-the-line."

"Up there, any network would have to be run through satellite," Shane said.

"We're going to need Bug," Ruby added.

"We are," Ash said, an expression crossing her face like she was not particularly happy with that situation.

Not that Ruby could blame her. Ash and Bug had a complicated relationship, considering Bug was completely in love with her. The infatuation may have faded a little after Scotland, but Bug had defended Ash to the end, saying it had all been an accident and couldn't have been avoided. Of course, all of it could have been avoided if they'd all had a little more time to go through all the proper checks and procedures, but there wasn't much sense arguing with Bug. He would defend Ash with his dying breath. The fact that Ash barely gave him the time of day didn't seem to matter.

Ruby's insides coiled up like a not-so-fun little whirlwind. Why were they following this woman again?

Max.

She had to think of Max. And do whatever she could to mitigate the situation. Ruby glanced at Shane, who looked like he was thinking the exact same thing.

If Ash was going to give her vague information, then they'd just have to work harder.

This was not going to be another Scotland.

"Do we need anyone else?" Ruby asked.

"I want to keep the team small. The fewer people who know about this the better," Ash said.

Besides, Ruby thought, there wasn't anyone else, was there?

"These pictures are pretty far away," Shane said. "Couldn't we get in there with a drone or something for some better intel?"

"These were from a drone," Ash said, "which fed these few images to us before it was shot down."

Shane raised an eyebrow. "So, these guys aren't messing around."

"They are not," Ash said, her voice clipped, like she might have been a little annoyed by her precious drone being destroyed. No doubt it had cost an arm and a lung and obtained through some mysterious techno-wizard network, since it would have to be untraceable.

"Doesn't sound like there's a whole lot of good news," Ruby said. "I don't see an 'in' here."

Ash took a deep breath. "These people don't build a place like this for tourists. It's elite. It's remote. And it's damn near impenetrable."

"So, what's the good news?" Ruby asked, sensing Ash was leading to something important.

"The good news is that in three days, they're having a party. And we're going to make sure we're all invited."

Chapter 5

Ash assigned the task of finding Bug to Shane and Ruby, then left before they could argue.

"I guess the longer she can put off that inevitable uncomfortable situation, the better," Shane said.

"Ugh, poor Bug is an awkward mess around the woman," Ruby said.

"I do not get what the draw is," Shane replied, but then again, when Ruby was anywhere in the vicinity, he had a hard time seeing other women, period.

"I don't know," Ruby said. "I think he likes the way she wields power. In his regular life he always needs to be the one calling the shots." She shrugged. "Maybe he likes being bossed around."

Shane made a face. "I do not love the visual that conjures up," he said, a flash of a bedroom scene flitting through his head.

"Ew, stop," Ruby said, apparently reading his mind.

"So, are we doing this now?" he asked.

Ruby let out a long sigh and tipped back the rest of her wine. "I guess we have to," she said, knowing as well as Shane did that Bug was a creature of the night and if they didn't find him before sunup, he'd be in hibernation until this time tomorrow. She glanced down at the clothes she'd thrown on. "But just to be clear, I do not give one rat's ass about how Ash is starting to make this look like a heist. I just want to get in, get Max and get out. That's it."

Shane nodded once. "Sounds good to me."

"Okay, good," Ruby said. "I'm glad we're on the same page. Just let me get changed."

"I think you look great," Shane said, tossing her his most dazzling smile, but Ruby just kept walking, throwing one of her famous eye rolls right back at him.

It was a reaction he was more than used to, and he loved it. Honestly, he loved any reaction he could get out of her. He'd meant it about looking great too. Even standing beside Ash, who was in her heels and fancy little skirt, Ruby outshone her in bare feet and rumpled clothes she'd clearly picked up off the floor or something and thrown on. Tenfold.

Ruby emerged from her room in jeans and a white T-shirt, throwing on an oversize leather jacket and combat boots. Shane marveled at how the woman could pull off pretty much any look. She was damn sexy in anything from her sweatpants to the red evening gown she'd worn on the job in Kosovo that no matter how long he lived, he would never forget.

"Any thoughts on where to start?" she asked, opening the door and motioning for him to go through so she could lock up behind them.

"I was thinking our best bet would be—"

"His sister," Ruby said, saying it with him as he said the last words.

He nodded and they were off, not needing to say more. They both knew where to find her, and Shane briefly wondered if they should be concerned. If they knew where to find Penny Elliot, then so might anyone else. Of course, the man they referred to as Bug—Jacob Elliot—would likely be pegged as an elite hacker about as readily as a still-frozen ice-cream cone might burst forth from Lucifer's butt.

But that was only because the man was a master at hiding in plain sight.

An hour later they were easing into the parking lot of a bar called Twisted Trance, conveniently and purposefully located just outside the outskirts of town. They could have made it in twenty minutes, but Shane had used every evasion trick he knew in case they were being followed.

"What's the play here?" Ruby asked, already appearing to know the answer. She wasn't even trying to hide that she was going to enjoy watching it all go down.

"Obviously I'll do the talking," Shane said, throwing her a side-eye.

Penny had never kept the fact that she was 100.7 percent enamored of Shane a secret. In fact, the next ten minutes were very likely going to prove to be the most uncomfortable ten minutes Shane had experienced in a while. And it wasn't just the fact that the woman liked to flirt—hell, Shane liked to flirt too—but it was the way she flirted. Crawling up all over a guy, which was a tad uncomfortable given her love of weightlifting and tossing drunken bikers out of her bar.

Without even breaking a sweat.

Shane assumed she could do some real physical damage in the bedroom, and *that* was not something he wanted to ever find out for sure.

"It'll be fine, she's a sweetheart," Ruby said, trying to coax him out of the car.

It was a fair point—Penny was a sweetheart—but it wasn't her sweet heart Shane was worried about. It was her biceps that could likely pop the head right off a guy if she ever caught him in a choke hold.

He tilted his head from side to side, cracking his neck. "Okay, let's do this."

Ruby followed, trying—and failing—to hide what could only be categorized as a snicker.

Inside, the bar was…atmospheric. If, by atmospheric, one meant smoky, smelly and dark. Exactly the way a biker bar wanted to be. Just sketchy enough to make anyone too much on the up-and-up turn straight around and peel out of there as fast as the speed limit would allow. It used to be raided by cops on the regular, but they never found anything, likely because they were searching for signs of drugs, prostitution, maybe a little human trafficking.

But none of that was the kind of shady that happened here.

It was genius, really—the absolute last place a law enforcement agency—or anyone else—would ever look for one of the world's most elite hackers.

Even as they headed toward the bar, Shane couldn't see a single sign of tech at all. It had to be there. Bug was the foremost expert in the latest security measures and wasn't about to leave himself exposed, but he did a damn fine job hiding it. There were, however, about thirty uneasy eyes following their every move.

"Well, look what the smitten kitten dragged in," the booming voice said from somewhere in the smoky depths behind the bar.

"Hey, Penny," Shane said, hoping his acting was a lot steadier than his stomach was. "How've you been doing?"

Penny raised one heavy eyebrow. "Doing a lot better now that your fine ass has graced my presence," she said, tilting her head liberally in an attempt to get a better view of said ass.

"Hey, Pen," Ruby said, hoisting herself onto one of the bar stools, looking as comfortable as if she was lounging in her own house. "How about a beer?" She glanced at Shane. "You better get one for him too. And maybe a shot of something. Looks like he could use it."

"He sure does," Penny said, her eyes grazing all the way up him nice and slowly.

Once Penny's gaze turned away to get their drinks, Shane finally found the fortitude to prop himself on the stool beside Ruby.

"You can saunter into the Palace of the High King of Zendovia like you own the place, but this one woman reduces you to a nineteen eighties potluck jelly salad," Ruby teased, just loud enough for him to hear. "You know, all jiggly inside," she finished with a goofy grin.

Shane gave her a glare. "Hilarious."

Penny returned with the drinks. She actually did have a shot of whiskey, which she set in front of Shane with a beer. He might have even been offended if he hadn't needed it so bad, downing it in a flash and enjoying the distracting burn.

"What brings you to our neck of the woods, handsome?" Penny asked, laser focused on Shane, barely paying attention to Ruby, who sipped her beer, quietly enjoying every second of the Squirming Shane Show.

"Oh, you know," Shane said, clearing his throat. Honestly, Penny brought out the worst performances of his life. "Just feeling restless and looking for something to do."

Of course, Penny knew there was precisely one reason Shane and Ruby would ever set foot in Twisted Trance—they were looking for Bug. She also knew it would never happen unless something big was going down. But she was well aware of the drill.

"Well, if you're feeling restless," Penny said, shooting him an actual wink, "I've been known to rid a man of his jitters real quick." She licked her lips, which then spread into a scandalous smile.

Oh, dear god, was about all Shane could think, but he recovered, saying, "I bet you have," and sending his own, somewhat less scandalous, smile her way.

"I get off at two," Penny said, grabbing his coaster and writing on the back. "Call me." She laid down the coaster, with one more wink for good measure.

Blessedly, she headed off to take care of some of her other customers.

Shane got down to the business of drinking his beer, sipping rather more quickly than he needed to, but they'd gotten what they came for and he wanted to get the hell out. They also didn't want to look suspicious, so they needed to make an attempt at finishing their beers. This was a place to drink, not the kind of place people sauntered into, took two sips of a cocktail and went on their merry way.

Mercifully, Ruby was on the same page, and did a damn good job at finishing her beer faster than even he did. He laid thirty bucks on the counter and pocketed the coaster as they headed out the door.

Once they were safely outside, Shane made sure they were alone, then checked what Penny had written, showing the single word to Ruby.

"Barn?" she whispered, but they kept heading for the car.

When they drove in, they'd both noticed the huge, decrepit barn out behind the roadside bar, but hadn't thought much of it—places like this were often remodeled old farmhouses.

They drove back out of the parking lot anyway, not wanting to leave a strange car a regular would recognize as out of place faster than you could say "dive bar."

About a mile up the road, Shane eased the car onto a trail that led toward a cluster of trees, which he pulled behind. It wasn't the best disguise job in the world, but unless someone came down this particular trail, no one would see it until the sun rose.

They ran back off the road, sneaking onto the property from the back, making their way to the barn.

This time it was Shane's turn to ask, "What's the play here?"

But Ruby just shook her head. "There is no play."

Before Shane could stop her, Ruby sauntered right up to the barn and pushed one of the giant doors open with a lot of effort and an alarming amount of noise. He hurried in behind her, heaving the door shut behind him, but before he could even turn all the way around, a light flicked on, and ominous clicks sounded around them.

"Well, I guess we can safely say we've found Bug," Shane said, his eyes darting from one gun barrel to the next to the next.

He followed Ruby's lead and put up his hands.

"I gotta say—" A voice came from somewhere in the back of the barn where Ruby didn't dare glance, since the throng of men and guns pointed at her face were a tad distracting. The voice was punctuated by slow, heavy footsteps. "—this was not the way I saw my night turning out."

The men with guns parted, and Ruby had never been so happy to see a six-foot-two, heavily muscled man with arms covered in tattoos in her life.

"Hey, Bug," she said, rushing forward to clutch him into a big hug.

There was nothing on earth that felt quite like one of Bug's bear hugs, swallowing her like she was the bug and he was the cocoon keeping her safe.

"At ease, my friends," Bug said as he released Ruby and noticed the men still had their aim squarely on Shane.

Ruby wasn't sure if she should be happy or offended that they'd all determined Shane was the one to keep their eyes on.

"I'm going to have to train them better," Bug whispered to Ruby. "You and I both know you're the real danger around here."

Ruby smiled. At least someone appreciated her. "And that's why you're my favorite," Ruby said, leaning up on her tiptoes to give the massive lug a kiss on the cheek.

The men lowered their guns and Shane joined them before Bug started walking toward the back of the barn.

"Let's go to my lair," he said, without a hint of irony.

"Lair?" Ruby couldn't help but ask.

Bug shrugged a heavily muscled shoulder. "Always wanted a lair and now I have one. I feel like it would be a shame to call it something boring like a hangout or, worse, man cave." He gave a little shudder.

"Touché," Shane said as Bug lifted a small, unassuming panel up from the floor and began his descent into it.

Ruby raised an eyebrow at Shane as they followed into the dark space. The idea they could be headed into a trap flitted through her mind briefly, but there were few people she trusted as much as she did Bug. She didn't doubt for a second that Bug had some sort of top-tier security measures in place if someone outside his chosen circle got in, though. And she'd bet her life it was some kind of *Mission Impossible* spy level shit too.

As they landed on the floor below, Ruby had to admit she was a bit disappointed. She wasn't sure what she'd expected, but it hadn't been another barren level of wood walls, wood floor and a single wooden desk slapped right in the middle.

Bug started toward the desk.

"Not quite what I expected," Shane said, sounding both tentative and amused, like one might sound wandering through a carnival funhouse just waiting for something to jump out at them.

"Have a seat," Bug said, motioning to the two seats across from him as he sat in his own chair and fired up the monitor on the desk.

"As far as lairs go, I thought there'd be a little more to—" Ruby started to say, but was cut off by a sudden movement of the floor.

The entire desk, all three chairs and the floor it all sat on started to slowly drop below the rest of the floor, like some sort of giant elevator.

As they continued down, Ruby got her first glimpses of an honest-to-goodness, for-real lair—dozens of screens, banks of computers and a plethora of additional gadgets and machines.

"Right. This is more like it," she finished as the floor came to a gentle halt and a panel slid across the opening above their heads to hide the real lair once again.

With utter satisfaction on his face, Bug spoke. "So, what brings you to my humble abode?"

Shane tilted his head. "How long have you been waiting to be able to see someone's reaction to that little trick?"

Bug's expression slid into a grin. "Since shortly after our last job. It's not like I can invite just anyone down here."

"No, I would think not," Ruby said, her grin almost as wide as Bug's. "This place is amazing."

He nodded his thanks. "But seriously, what's up? I figure it's got to be big if it brought the two of you together on my doorstep."

Ruby's and Shane's expressions turned serious.

"It's Max," Ruby said. "He's been taken."

"When? Where?" Bug asked, getting up from the boring desk and sauntering up to a very different one, the workstation all glass, metal and with stunningly copious amounts of technology.

"We don't know where. We only sort of know a who," Shane said. "The people we all used to work for."

Ruby didn't know what Bug was already typing so furiously away at, but he stopped and spun around on his chair. "Bastards," he said, shaking his head as he turned back around. "Let's start with where he was when he was taken, then."

"Two nights ago, somewhere between the theater and his house," Ruby said.

It never did cease to amaze her the way Bug—this giant, hulking mass of a man—could work a keyboard, his massive fingers whipping over the keys, the tattoos on his forearms a frenzy of movement.

"There he is," Bug said after an astonishingly short amount of time.

Ruby and Shane turned their attention to the large screen on the wall several feet beyond Bug's workstation, where Bug was already pulling up the footage. As the image of Max sauntering down the empty street flickered on, a swell of something—nostalgia, a sense of missing him, fear—washed over her.

Shane made a musing sound. "He looks happy."

Ruby nodded. "Opening night must have gone well," she said, knowing how much Max lived for those nights, where all his hard work paid off through his newest students up on stage. The buzz of the always sold-out crowd, the rush of nerves, the pride so apparent on his face after every performance. Ruby could tell it was all there, dancing behind a glint in Max's eye as he walked along, seemingly without a care in the world.

"Still the last one to leave, I see," Bug said.

"I don't know how many times one man needs to hear that he should change up his routine," Ruby said, frustrated that Max never did heed the warning they'd all given him time and time again.

"Pick a cliché, any cliché," Shane said, with a smirk. "Can't teach an old dog new tricks, perhaps?"

Ruby rolled her eyes, but she knew it was true. It wasn't for any lack of knowledge that Max had been careless—he just didn't seem to think he'd ever be important enough to get in trouble. Strange idea for a man who'd made the better part of his living in crime, but here they were. Maybe Max was just so used to being deep in the shadows of the theater, allowing everyone else to take the spotlight, that he thought the same went for his other life too.

As they watched, Max seemed to tense, so slightly they might not have noticed had they not been waiting for it. Then out of nowhere, a van pulled up and, in a flash, they were beside him, throwing the door open and hauling Max inside before he had a chance to react.

The screen switched from camera to camera as Bug transferred from feed to feed, following the van, while a lump formed in Ruby's throat. A few minutes later, the van found a more remote area of the city, which also meant the street cam feeds ended.

"Shit," Bug said. "They knew where to go."

Ruby nodded. "We gave them the intel back when we used to pull jobs for them."

Shane let out a heavy sigh. "What next?"

Ruby swallowed, willing her throat to return to normal. But they were a hell of a long way from normal.

"Next we go see what Max has been up to for the past three years."

Chapter 6

Shane had forgotten what it was like to be this close to Ruby. Or, more accurately, he'd pushed those memories from existence with a force of will rivaling that of a professional marathon runner.

But now that he was back in her company, he found his fortitude starting to wane. Quickly. Ruby was so much the same as she used to be, but she was different somehow too. She was both softer and stronger, and worse, she smelled like a damned strawberry sundae dipped in moonlight.

Jesus, was he a freakin' poet now? What the hell did "dipped in moonlight" even mean?

The only way he could think of to describe the bloody intoxicating smell, was what it meant.

He let out a long sigh, trying to focus on the road instead of the intense awareness that she was sitting right there. So close all he could think of was dipping strawberries into moonlight, for god's sake.

"What?" she asked, shooting him a quizzical look.

"It's just…surreal being in this place. I never thought any of us would see each other again," he said.

I never thought I'd see you *again.*

Ruby stared at him, making him shift in his seat, like she could read his mind. She'd always had a way of doing that. Looking at him like she was sure she knew what he was thinking but couldn't decide whether she thought he was a genius or an absolutely atrocious human being.

Her stare always felt like this intense, significant thing, but for all he knew, she might just be trying to figure out what she was going to have for dinner.

Bug pulled the car to a stop a few blocks from their destination. The world felt a little haunted as Shane and Ruby stepped out of the car.

"This is close to where it happened," Bug said, noting the cameras with a tilt of his head.

If they'd been able to hack into the feeds, it was likely whoever had Max could do the same.

"We have to assume we're being watched," Shane said.

They were used to the idea. They'd all trained under Max, after all. The only reason any of them were there was because they'd felt at home in the spotlight—or were at least willing to tolerate it. Shane got the feeling Bug wasn't into being adored but was able to become someone else the way intense acting situations allowed him to do, like it was simply part of the game. Shane, on the other hand, had to admit he loved the adoration. What wasn't to like? Honestly, he couldn't understand what introversion was even about. People had to be kidding themselves, right? For him, life was all about feeling seen. Because, what the hell else was there?

Bug peeled off down an alley while Shane and Ruby kept walking toward Max's place.

"You got us?" Shane said quietly into the comms equipment they'd gotten together at Bug's.

"Loud and clear," Bug replied.

"Let us know when we're good," Ruby said as she slowly eased the gate open in front of Max's house.

The neighborhood was shockingly quiet. Sure, it was the middle of the night, but Shane would have thought someone would be up. Maybe he'd just gotten used to a different kind of nightlife—the kind where a lot of alcohol and loud music were involved. Maybe this was how normal people lived.

"The area has a lot of seniors," Ruby said, which Shane supposed made sense, though he would have felt better if there'd been a TV on in one of the windows.

It was hard to believe every single resident on the block slept so well. It felt like he hadn't had a full night's sleep in decades.

"Shit!" Ruby whisper-yelled as a bright spark lit up the night momentarily.

"What the hell was that?" Shane asked.

But Ruby was already scrambling, whipping something out of her pocket and crouching to the ground, frantically chopping/stabbing/sawing at something down there.

Shane crouched in front of her to get a better look but was shooed away.

"Out of the light, I need to see," Ruby said, as she continued, more frantic by the second.

In his hurry—brought on by the scolding and vehemence in her voice—Shane sort of flung himself backward, landing on his butt. Which might not have been so bad, except Max had his sprinklers on a timer, as evidenced by the giant wet patch thoroughly soaking the ass of his jeans.

Ruby finally stopped hacking and let her shoulders relax.

"What the hell was that?" Bug said, the comms cluing him in to something clearly going down.

"Detonator fuse," Ruby said, her eyes following the wiry line almost directly to where Shane's hand sat.

"Jesus," Shane said, gingerly lifting his hand and leaning away from the explosive. "What if a kid had come in here or something? Or, like, doesn't he have a mailman?"

Ruby leaned in close to the device now that the danger had been neutralized. "It's just firecrackers," she said with a shrug. "Just a warning system."

"Would have been one hell of a warning if my hand had been sitting right on top of it," Shane said, easing himself up to his feet, wiping the back of his jeans even though it was futile.

"Stay alert, guys," Ruby said. "Something's definitely going on here."

"Well. Ho. Lee. Shit," Bug said.

"What?" Shane asked.

"That little welcome warning got me checking a little closer than I normally would—since this is a simple security system—and sure enough, Max has this thing enhanced."

"Enhanced how?" Shane asked.

"Like an innocuous little wire I might not have normally noticed, and just so happens to lead to something a little more intense than a firecracker, how," Bug replied.

"What does Max have himself mixed up in?" Ruby said.

Shane and Ruby made it to the front door, going slow, making sure there weren't any additional fun surprises that would signal the entire neighborhood to their presence.

"In position," Ruby said, scanning the area, the little knife she'd used to cut the fuse still in her hand.

"Give me a second," Bug said.

Hacking a security system never took Bug this long, Shane thought, as he caught Ruby's eye. The look in it didn't make him feel much better.

"Okay, cameras and alarm are disarmed but keep your guard up. This is some old-school stuff he's using here. Manual. A lot of it is unhackable."

"Copy," Shane said, his hand on the doorknob, turning slowly.

He pushed on the door so it would swing open, allowing him to assess the situation before he moved to step inside. Across the house, he could see the back door slowly opening as Bug did the same at the rear of the building.

Almost in unison, two arrows released, whizzing past each

door into the line of fire where a less cautious person would likely be standing had they opened the door and stepped straight in.

Bug let out a low whistle. “That is some real Indiana Jones type shit right there.”

The team spent the next hour clearing the house. Gingerly searching for actual, honest-to-god booby traps—disarming them where they could and setting them off while safely out of the way where they couldn’t.

“How the hell did he even live in this place?” Shane said, as he searched a desk for hidden dangers.

“I suppose once you know where they all are, it only takes a few minutes to disarm them,” Ruby said.

“It’s a lot of work every time you come and go from a place,” he continued. “I’d hate to have to run back in if I forgot my phone or something.”

Ruby smiled, nodding a little. “One thing’s for sure. Something was definitely going on with Max. This is not your normal theater director kind of place.”

They had all sworn they were getting out of the game, but maybe Max had a harder time letting go than the rest of them. If so, Shane could relate.

Bug was at the back of the house, doing a final sweep for out-of-place electronic equipment such as listening devices, cameras or anything that could potentially blow up in their faces. Literally.

Ruby stuck close to Shane. Or maybe it was Shane sticking close to Ruby. He never could tell. They were always drawn to each other no matter who else was around or what else might be going on.

He watched as she began her search at the desk.

“What do you think we’ll find?” Shane asked as he started pulling books off the bookshelf, opening them to see if they had any hidden compartments or loose papers hidden inside.

"Well, I guess we can assume Max was still up to something... less than legitimate," Ruby said, "maybe something similar to what we used to do. Hell, maybe it was *exactly* what we used to do. Max was the one who started us all in the business, after all."

"But he was never the mastermind. Ash was always the one calling the shots."

"Speaking of," Ruby said. "Why the hell are we out here risking our asses and she's off doing who knows what?"

It was the way things usually were. The team out doing the dirty work while Ash was holed up in some undisclosed location being the brains of the operation. Shane was pretty sure she wasn't any smarter than the rest of them, she was just incredibly organized. And truth be told, she wasn't great in the field since her acting left something to be desired. But she'd been one of Max's first students and Max had a soft spot for her. To be fair, Shane hadn't had any misgivings about her role on the team until...well, until he did.

"Oh, you know," Shane said. "She's just off planning a diabolical heist. The usual."

Ruby smiled. The unexpected flip his stomach made caught him off guard. She must have seen something change on his face. She quickly looked away, sorting through some papers on the desk.

They fell into a comfortable silence as they got to work. There was nothing on the bookshelf even hinting at anything out of the ordinary going on in Max's life.

"You got anything over there?" he asked.

"Nothing besides some questionable deductions on his annual tax return and a few cryptic entries in his calendar, although *meet F.P. for lunch* isn't all that damning."

Shane moved from the bookshelf to a small table beside the couch, but it only took about three seconds to determine it held nothing but a couple remotes. He spent some time searching for potential hidden compartments but came up empty.

When the living room was exhausted, Shane moved to the kitchen. He hated searching kitchens. It was rare they ever found anything valuable in a kitchen, and there were just so many damned places to look. But he dove in and started with the freezer. It was honestly weird how often people literally "froze their assets" even though it was one of the oldest tricks on every detective show there was. He supposed people thought they were being clever.

But Max was not one of those people. There was nothing in there but a few microwave meals and a large bottle of vodka.

The fridge was equally uninteresting.

It sounded like Bug was in the room just above, walking slowly and steadily. Everyone had their jobs, and Bug's was tech. Tech in the form of surveillance, tech in the form of communication devices and tech in the form of digital intel. He sighed. What he wouldn't give for an expertly hidden thumb drive right about then.

Ruby had already started on the lower cabinets, so Shane moved to the uppers. It was a tedious routine, but one they'd done a thousand times. It was funny how the movies always made it seem like the day of a heist was the only day that mattered. Of course, Shane supposed, depicting the days upon days of recon would be exceedingly dull.

After a thorough sweep above the cupboards, behind the appliances, and on the floor for any loose linoleum or marks indicating a trap door, they finished in the kitchen and moved on to the main bedroom, which looked like the most used room in the house. It made sense, considering Max spent the majority of his time at the theater.

"Shit," Shane said.

As was their way, Ruby was just coming into the room behind him. "What?"

"I think we're in the wrong damn place."

It's odd how some cities have neighborhoods with such a robust night life you'd never find yourself alone on the streets at night, and then there are other neighborhoods that are more like ghost towns after a certain time of day. The Guardian Theater was in one of the ghost town places.

It was a testament to the quality of Max's productions that he never had a hard time filling the place. The Guardian wasn't in a bad neighborhood. In fact, it was in a nice part of town. But it was on the edge of a suburban area, so there weren't a whole lot of people out and about at four in the morning.

The sun would be coming up soon, though, and that would change everything.

"We should hurry," Ruby said.

The last thing they needed was some overcurious early riser who just happened to glance out their window at the beginning of a new day to see three strangers wandering down the street.

Ruby was suddenly very aware of her new hair. She's spent so many years wearing it just past her shoulders in soft waves—like half the female population tended to lean toward, which was exactly the point. Once she was out of the business, she could do with it what she wanted, and she may have gone a little over the top. Her current short, edgy cut was rather more…standout-ish than was optimal, given the current circumstance.

Shane didn't have any particularly stand-out features, other than the fact that he was infuriatingly attractive, which made him the person most people looked at in any room. Add in Bug, a massively muscled, heavily tattooed bald guy, and the trio was not especially incognito.

They'd decided to walk, trying to get a sense of what the

area would have been like for Max on the night he was taken, but Ruby was questioning their choice.

"Yeah, sun'll be up soon," Shane said.

Always the best one with locks, Shane coaxed the back door of the theater open moments later without a sound.

The theater was even more eerily quiet than the street. The smell of the place instantly brought Ruby back to a time when it had felt like home. *Was* a second home, really, considering she'd spent way more time there than she did the shabby two-bedroom she'd shared with Maurine, another theater student, whom she'd lost touch with pretty much immediately after the season's class ended. Max hadn't asked Maurine to stay on for the other type of work once the theater season was over.

Once inside, the three of them lit up the flashlights on their phones, confident no one would see from the street. There were large windows at the front of the theater, but the performance area was closed off from the lobby and they'd come in the backstage entrance.

"I won't be able to do a full sweep," Bug said, "but I'll check for any obvious signs that they were watching Max…or listening in."

Ruby nodded and moved toward the stage, her breath catching when Shane's hand landed on the small of her back. It was a maneuver they'd done a thousand times in dark places. A protective thing, a reassurance that the other was still there with them.

Shane had done it instinctually—an old habit coming back to haunt him. Maybe it was because Ruby stiffened a little, but he jerked his hand away and quietly cleared his throat.

"Sorry," he whispered.

"It's fine," Ruby replied.

But the jolt of energy that shot through her at the heat of his touch made her realize things were very far from fine.

"I'm going to check out the dressing rooms for old times'

sake," Shane said, though Ruby suspected he was giving her some space. Which she desperately needed, but she also hated that he knew it was what she needed.

As Ruby entered Max's office, the door squeaking the way it always had, more of those familiar feelings started to come back.

As far as offices went, Max's was enormous. He loved being surrounded by people—the actors, the crew, even some of his favorites from the audience sometimes. Ruby couldn't count how many times there'd been a full-fledged party going on in that very space.

But there had been quiet times too. The day Max had explained to her and Shane about the other jobs he did, inviting them to join one of his crews. The man could convince anyone of anything. He'd let them know in no uncertain terms it was dangerous work, and it was definitely not on the right side of the law, but he'd convinced them it was the right thing to do. They'd be helping people. Making a difference in the world.

And it had felt right for a long time.

Ruby flicked on the light, realizing she could because there were no windows in the room. She'd never thought it was strange before, but she wondered if it had been on purpose—a precaution Max had planned out. After the booby trap situation at his house, nothing would have surprised her.

Her eyes landed on the lamp standing in the back corner of the room with the crack in its stained-glass shade. The crack that had been her fault. Well, hers and Shane's. Ruby still didn't know who'd stumbled first that night at the tail end of one of Max's famous end-of-the-week parties. She remembered the day itself like it had been five days ago instead of five years, even though she'd had her fair share of the wine Max had provided.

Ruby had wondered how he could afford to buy so much booze and food for everyone, but that was before she knew about his side gig. She thought it would be a onetime thing and should enjoy the opportunity to its fullest.

Just as she was starting to feel the warm buzz, the kind that felt like relaxing into a hot tub on a cool summer night, Shane had sauntered over. They'd met earlier in the week but hadn't talked much, though every time he'd glance in her direction, Ruby could feel something. It might have been one of those "all in her head" kind of somethings, but she didn't think so, and was anxious to find out for sure.

"Hey," he'd said, looking adorably shy, though Ruby couldn't help think he had to be putting his acting on display.

"Um, hey," she'd said back, her brain frantically searching for something interesting to say.

"So, is The Guardian Academy of Dramatic Arts all you'd hoped it would be?" He said it in the cheesiest voice he could muster, which made his question pretty endearing.

She'd smiled, wondering for a moment if his sweet woodsy scent was meant to lull women away from their senses and out of their clothes, because that was the exact effect it was having on her. Her first instinct was to volley some sort of melodramatic answer back, but something about Shane made her want to be more honest. More herself.

"It's exceeding my expectations so far," she'd finally said, the wine confidence she was feeling making the words more suggestive than she'd intended.

But one can't argue with wine confidence so she went with it, letting her eyes take a little stroll down his torso and back up, being way bolder than she should be, especially considering she had to finish out the class with this guy. But when her gaze met his again, he did not seem to mind.

"So, why acting?" she'd asked.

Shane shrugged. "I never could figure out what I wanted to be when I grew up, so I figured, why not everything?"

She nodded. "Choices *are* hard." She grinned.

"Some of them are," he'd said, leaning a bit closer.

"I'm Shane, by the way," he'd said, holding out his hand, though as close as they were standing, the handshake was a bit crowded, to say the least.

Still, she'd taken his hand, enjoying the warmth radiating through her at his touch. "Ruby."

"Like the gem," he'd said, tilting his head. "Makes sense."

She'd given him a grin and rolled her eyes as if he were being very unoriginal even though the truth was, she'd always wished a hot guy would say something like that about her name, though none ever had. Until then.

"I'm afraid I can't come up with something witty to say about your name," she'd said.

"It's what I get for having a boring old name."

"Definitely not boring," she'd said. "It's a good acting name. And it suits you."

"Thanks," he'd said, like it was a question.

She'd smiled. "The real question is, what is the last name to go with it? With that information, I'd be able to tell if you're going to make it as a famous actor."

He'd grinned back, sort of scrunching his face. "I'm not sure I want to know," he said. "What if it's bad news?"

"I don't think it will be bad news," she'd said, her voice becoming flirtier of its own accord, apparently along with her body, which also seemed to be moving of its own accord, leaning in even farther.

He let out a big breath. "Okay, then, it's Meyers. Shane Meyers."

Her eyes lit up. "Ah, very good. Yes, I think that's a fine stage name."

"It's my real name."

She nodded. "Sure, but all that matters is whether people will remember it."

Shane tilted his head in agreement. "Okay, maybe that's true," he'd said. "But I can promise you one thing, Ruby…"

Her eyebrows rose in question.

"It doesn't matter what your last name is," he'd said, the gap between them shrinking even more, "there is no way in hell I'd ever forget you."

His gaze moved from her eyes to her lips, the air between them heavy with that fresh woodsy smell. Ruby was acutely aware of the delicate gap between them—so tenuous, so easy to close. Ruby let herself give in fully to the wine confidence, traveling the final small distance, brushing her lips on his, then drawing away, as if asking a question.

Shane had answered, kissing her back, his hand tracing the curve of her waist, curling around to pull her in. But it was Ruby who'd kept the moment going, her hand climbing up his arm, finding the back of his neck and drawing him closer.

She knew there was a side table somewhere close by. She was sure if she could just think straight for one second, she'd be able to find it, her drink-holding hand searching, only finding thin air as she begged it to please just find the bloody thing already. But feeling more like a passenger in her body rather than in control, she'd stumbled back, taking poor Shane with her, straight into the lamp, a meaningful crack sounding from behind.

They'd frozen midkiss, the lamp snugly lodged between Ruby's head and the wall.

Ruby's eyes had opened wide, like she'd been caught doing something she wasn't supposed to be doing, a giggle escaping her. Shane smiled against her lips, then maneuvered to steady her with one hand, reaching out for the lamp with the other. Ruby had glanced around sheepishly, waiting for the crowd to start heckling them, but it turned out the room had emptied out sometime during their conversation without her noticing. It startled her—made her come back to her senses for a second.

"Just so we're clear," Ruby had said, "I'm not looking for anything serious."

Shane had smiled. "Perfect, I'm not either."

And so it was settled. This…whatever this was…was only going to be for fun. No messy relationship nonsense to worry about.

And that was how it had always stayed…at least in practice.

"Find anything?" Shane's voice jolted Ruby back to the present, making her jump.

She cleared her throat. "Not yet," she said, hurrying over to the desk, hoping he couldn't see the flush heating her cheeks.

Chapter 7

Shane couldn't help but notice what Ruby had been staring at. Their lamp. The lamp that had become their little secret. The reminder of the moment that changed everything. The moment they became inseparable. Until they weren't.

Until everything got so monumentally screwed up it could never be repaired.

No, scratch that. Until *he* monumentally screwed things up so they could never be repaired.

"Hey," Ruby said, rifling through some papers on the desk. "Look at this."

Shane went over to her, acutely aware of how close he was standing. He was careful not to get too much into her space, even though it was all he wanted to do.

"I think we were right that Max might not have been quite as retired as the rest of us," Ruby said, sliding some papers toward him.

It only took a quick glance for Shane to know what he was looking at. Schematics for a large house—a mansion really—with various routes in and out.

"He was doing jobs without us," Shane said, only realizing after he'd said it how sulky his voice sounded. He cleared his throat.

But Ruby just nodded, seemingly not bothered in the slightest. Then again, Shane supposed it was because after Scotland, Ruby appeared to have landed on her feet…and then some. She'd gone completely legit, still able to do the same kind of work, though it had to be challenging with how slow it must all be.

Ruby had moved on to the bottom drawer of Max's desk. "There are dozens of jobs here," she said as she flipped through the papers.

Shane tried not to let the pang of emotion get the better of him.

"What the hell was he up to?" he said, even though it was more than clear by the massive pile of documents.

"The drawer wasn't even locked," Ruby said. "Anyone could have come in here and gone through them."

"I guess the average person might not have known what it all was?" Shane said. "And we never used names on documentation, so the team would be safe."

"Yeah, but what about Max? All this in his possession would be pretty damning if authorities ever came knocking. These jobs go back at least a couple of years. It doesn't make sense."

She had a point. Back when they were still a team and Ash was taking care of this part of the operation, she never hung on to any documents once the jobs were done. She talked about it all the time. "Lose the evidence" was one of her favorite sayings.

"I guess Max doesn't work the same way Ash does," Shane said. "Are you sure the drawer hasn't been jimmied?"

Ruby shook her head. "Not unless they had the key or were good at picking locks. But even if someone had come in here, why would they leave everything? It's not safe for the clients either. Not that their names are in the files, obviously, but it wouldn't take a genius to figure out where all these places are."

Shane nodded, then opened the top drawer on the left side of the desk. "There's one more file," he said, pulling it out and flipping it open.

But Ruby was distracted. Too busy going through the pile on the desk, trying to figure out why on earth Max would be so careless. Back in the day he was never the mastermind, but he wasn't stupid either.

"Shit," Shane said, the contents of the file he was holding starting to sink in. "You're right. He was being surprisingly careless."

"What is it?" Ruby asked, moving in close.

She was so close Shane could smell her shampoo—the same one she'd always used, the damn strawberries. It was also the same one that brought back way too many memories.

"It's our job," Shane said. "The scepter."

"You're kidding," Ruby said, taking the file from his hands.

"And by the looks of things, Max already had a whole lot more figured out than we do."

Ruby flipped through the pages, nodding absently. "He even has the night of the party all laid out. The only thing missing are the names of the operatives."

A low rumble of uneasiness began to swirl deep in Shane's guts. Something was starting to feel a bit off about this job. About Max having all this information. It was a little too handy. "Here's the real question," he said. "If Max had all this planned out and had it pretty much just sitting out in the open for anyone to come along and see it, why the hell didn't the kidnappers take all this with them?"

Ruby stopped flipping, staring at Shane like she was searching for something.

"Because," she said, finding the answer, "they didn't need the specifics of the plans." She shook her head. "These guys don't do the dirty work. They don't need the plans…they need us, the team."

"And Max was the only way to get our attention."

Shane decided he was not a fan of being a pawn in someone else's game. Then another thought struck him. "Bug," he yelled.

A few seconds later, Bug poked his gloriously shiny head

through the door, laptop in hand and a very weird set of goggles with blinking lights over his eyes.

"What in the hell are those?" Shane asked.

Bug shrugged as if he wasn't sure why Shane was questioning him. He shot him a "nothing to see here—so what if I'm sporting a little steampunk tech" look, but just said, "I like to call them Bug's Bug Busters. They find and detect surveillance devices so I can, you know, bust them." Bug appeared exceedingly thrilled to have unveiled his fun little tool, although he seemed prouder of the name than anything.

"Sure," Shane said, "just as I thought."

It was not, in fact, just as he thought—he'd been expecting some long scientific explanation about what the contraptions could do. But, as was his way, Bug defied expectations.

"Anyway, could we bring up the proof-of-life feed?"

Bug started typing away—faster with one hand than Shane could have been even if he'd had three—and moments later, the screen lit up with Max's face. Which, much to Shane's disappointment, was covered with duct tape.

He wasn't entirely surprised. Max did have a talent for being able to speak without pausing in a way that suggested he was simply narrating his stream of consciousness—a bit like those gaming guys who talk nonstop as they play games online for hours. He was probably driving his kidnappers up the wall—a thought that he might have even smiled at, had something else not been glaringly apparent.

"Shit," he said.

Ruby came over and took a spot behind Bug's other shoulder. "Damn."

"What?" Bug asked, though in his defense, Shane thought, maybe he couldn't see the screen well with those ridiculous glasses on.

"They've moved him," he said.

"The background is completely different. It's like he's in a desert or something," Ruby added.

"I'll see if I can pinpoint his new location," Bug said, moving toward the desk so he could set the laptop down and get to some serious work.

But Shane held up his hand. "Don't bother," he said. "By the time you get anything figured out, they will have moved him again."

"How do you know?" Bug asked.

Shane pulled in a deep breath. "Because it's what I would do."

Ruby's hopes plummeted. This whole time she'd been hoping to avoid the con, skip the heist, escape any and all ventures that could potentially jeopardize her new life. She'd spent years cultivating a legitimate career, forging her way into a notoriously challenging field and doing a pretty successful job of it, too, if she did say so herself.

Helping an old friend out of a spot of trouble—okay, more like a giant splotch—was one thing, but pulling a heist was something else completely.

But seeing those plans—where Max had everything laid out so meticulously—and knowing the kidnappers were on the move and likely to remain on the move, made her realize these people would have thought of all that. They would have known Ruby and the team would just want Max back. They'd gotten out of the game a long time ago and didn't seem to have any interest in playing it again. And that was why she knew, beyond any doubt, there would be no getting to Max unless they completed the heist. He was their number one priority and the people who took him would know all the tricks and secrets the team might use to get to him.

Hell, through the years the team had shown the kidnappers their entire playbook.

She let out a long sigh, which Shane picked up on right away.

"You were thinking we would just go rescue Max, easy peasy, right?" he said.

She nodded. "I just... I hate that I have to go back. I promised myself I never would."

"I know," Shane said, and he sounded sincere.

Shane never had a problem with the life of a con, but he'd never made fun of her for wanting to be such a rule-follower either. She closed her eyes and went back to the desk, hoping she could find something, anything that could point them in another direction. Bug headed back out of the room without another word and Shane gave Ruby some space, knowing her moods as well as anyone.

After Scotland, she'd vowed her life of doing things the wrong way was behind her. That breaking any rule of any kind was behind her. It just wasn't worth it. In the end—no matter how good her intentions—everything always went to shit when she broke the rules.

Funny how life always seems to punch you in the face with the same lessons over and over. She should have learned once and for all back in her freshman year of high school. She'd been headed in for her first big final.

"Hey, Jenn," Ruby had said. "All ready for the test?"

Ruby had been nervous but prepared. She was always prepared. Jenn looked a little fidgety, hands squeezing and unsqueezing the binder she held close to her chest. Her gaze was planted squarely on the floor.

"Is everything okay?" Ruby had asked.

She knew Jenn always had trouble with exams. It struck Ruby as unfair that some people were able to take tests no problem, but others struggled, even if they knew the material inside and out. Jenn was one of those people.

And the poor girl looked on the verge of tears.

Jenn shook her head. "I just... I studied so hard, and I know this stuff, but these tests… It's like my mind goes completely blank the second I step foot through the door."

"It'll be okay," Ruby had said, though she wasn't really sure it would be.

She'd seen Jenn struggle with test after test, and that was just middle school. This time the stakes were even higher—permanent record and everything.

The first tear escaped Jenn's eye as she shook her head. "I don't see how."

Ruby was desperate to help her. Jenn had done so much for her over the years—talked to her when she was too shy to speak to anyone the first day of school all those years ago, taken her camping that one summer in grade three, shown her how to be cooler than she could have ever hoped to be if she'd been left to her own devices.

Ruby had never broken a rule in her life, but suddenly it seemed like the whole system was discriminating against people like Jenn. The way she saw it, she owed Jenn, so she swallowed her fear and decided for once, she was going to be brave. She pulled Jenn aside and spoke to her quietly.

"Look, I know you know the answers, and I also know tests aren't your thing. Maybe you just need a little reassurance. Do you think you could try to forget about the stress of taking the test if you like, had a backup?"

"What do you mean a backup?" Jenn asked.

"Like if you could double-check your answers after you've written them."

Jenn looked dubious. "No way—I'm way too scared to bring in cheat notes. If I get caught my parents would send me to Pittsburgh to live with my grandma. And believe me, Grandma Janice is no joke. My life would be like living with a drill sergeant."

Ruby giggled, picturing Grandma Janice supervising while poor Jenn marched for days on end. "That's not what I meant.

I just meant maybe we could sit beside each other," she whispered. "That way you could glance over—you know…just to make sure you're on the right track."

Jenn tilted her head, thinking. "Maybe that could work," she'd said with a little shrug, still doubtful.

But Ruby was excited. She had a chance to help her friend and she was going to take it. And it wasn't like she was cheating—she knew every answer in the book. But she could still do something to help her friend, right?

As they entered the classroom, everything seemed to go perfectly. There were tons of desks open beside each other and Ruby and Jenn slid into two of them. As the exam began, Ruby tried to answer quickly, to be more efficient for Jenn. Making sure to still look natural, Ruby angled her paper toward Jenn to give her the best chance at being able to see as much as she could.

Everything went smoothly for the first hour or so. Ruby had been so lost in writing the exam she barely noticed anything around her. Every now and again she glanced over at Jenn, who was writing away, not even nervous.

See, she thought to herself, *Jenn knows this stuff.* She just needed a little extra boost of confidence.

Ruby finished soon after and spent some time pretending like she was going over her answers, not ready to give up her role as moral support. In fact, she was feeling pretty proud of the way she'd found a solution to her friend's problem and stuck with her through it.

Just before the bell was supposed to ring, she heard a shuffling from Jenn's general area and glanced over.

Jenn didn't say a peep, but mouthed the words, *Is this right?*

Later, Ruby would wonder what she'd had been thinking. Maybe she'd been finished with the test for so long she'd forgotten what she was even still sitting there for, but whatever the case, she instinctively leaned over to take a peek at her friend's work.

"Ruby Alexander and Jennifer Dales!" a voice came booming from behind them.

Mr. Porter came by and whisked both their test papers off their desks. "To the principal's office…now!"

Jenn looked at Ruby and Ruby looked at Jenn—both with eyes as wide as the gaping chasm of doom opening in Ruby's chest.

"I said now!" Mr. Porter reiterated.

The girls scrambled out of their desks and straight to the principal's office, which was just down the hall. Neither knew what they were supposed to do once inside, so they sat, both too scared to speak.

Soon Principal Chen came out of her office and called Jenn in first.

Ruby had never felt so sick over anything in her entire life, but she reminded herself she was just trying to help a friend. The system was broken, and it wasn't their fault if some people didn't do so well with tests. Surely, she could explain that, and an educator like Principal Chen would have to agree with her.

What felt like hours later, but was probably only twenty minutes, Jenn emerged from the office. She walked straight past Ruby without meeting her eyes and hurried out the door.

The worry train slowly chugging through Ruby's stomach suddenly turned into a runaway locomotive.

"Ruby, come in please," Principal Chen said, motioning her into the office.

She got up and walked slowly, a thousand scenarios playing through her mind. If only she knew what Jenn had said.

Too soon, Ruby was seated across from the principal.

"So, Jenn tells me it was your idea to cheat off her paper," Principal Chen started.

Ruby's mouth slid open in shock. "No… I—"

But the woman held her hand up to stop her. *What was even happening?* There was no way Jenn would have thrown her under the bus like that. They were friends. Friends didn't do that to each other.

"Frankly, it makes no difference whose idea it was," she'd said. "Cheating is cheating, and it cannot happen in this school. You're lucky you have a spotless record thus far."

Ruby nodded vigorously. "Exactly. I always do well on tests. But I think if you look back, you'll find Jenn, like many other students, has trouble with exams no matter how well she knows the material and—"

The hand rose to cut her off again. "The punishment is two weeks' detention, and you should be happy this wasn't a suspension. You will both, of course, receive zeroes on this exam, which will affect your final mark significantly. You can't break the rules and not expect consequences."

The train in Ruby's guts had finally derailed and she'd thought she might be sick. "I didn't even cheat. I was just trying to help..." But her words trailed off. Principal Chen was angrier by the second. "I was just trying to help," Ruby had said again, though she wasn't sure if the words even made it past her lips.

"You're dismissed," Principal Chen said with an air of finality.

Ruby wanted so badly to keep talking, to try to make Principal Chen understand, but as she opened her mouth, a realization washed over her. It didn't matter. Rules were rules and she'd broken them. She might not agree with them completely, but she knew she was supposed to follow them. She was supposed to do the right thing. So she'd done the only thing she could do. She'd closed her mouth back up and walked out of the office, swearing she'd never break another rule as long as she lived.

Of course, that vow didn't last. She'd made the choice to

break the rules for a damn living, for Pete's sake. And then she'd paid the price again with Scotland.

A sick feeling welled in her guts all over again, just like that derailed train all those years ago, and Ruby couldn't help but wonder how high the price was going to be this time.

Chapter 8

"This is kind of the perfect place to headquarter for a job," Shane said, noticing more tech everywhere his eyes fell.

After the theater, the team had gone back to Bug's hideaway to regroup.

The first time he'd entered the underground bunker/war room—or lair, as Bug kept insisting they call it—the sheer expanse and appearance had been almost overwhelming to Shane. His eyes ran along the vast network of wires, which he assumed allowed Bug to enjoy computing power that could give a government organization a run for its money.

Now that Shane was taking a closer look, though, that hadn't been the full story. The place had everything they were going to need, and then some. The tech alone was mind-blowing—Shane couldn't begin to understand what it all did. But on top of all the computer stuff, there was a weapons room, what appeared to be a fully functional crime lab and shelf upon shelf full of gadgets that would have been right at home in a spy museum.

The place legitimately rivaled the Batcave, and Shane conceded that perhaps the place was best referred to as a lair.

"We need to show these to Ash," Shane said, spreading out the plans from Max's place out on a large table in the center of the room.

Bug's face turned gray at the mention of Ash's name.

Shane smiled and slapped his friend on the back. "Don't worry, man, she'd going to love it."

"It's pretty much the coolest place I've ever seen. Really," Ruby added.

Shane would never know why the woman intimidated Bug so much, or why he was so infatuated with her, but to each their own, he supposed. It wasn't like he was immune to feeling sick around a certain team member, who was currently leaning over the table in an incredibly distracting way.

Shane aggressively averted his gaze before something catastrophically embarrassing happened.

Suddenly the room jumped to life. Flashing lights, a death wail of a siren and a computerized voice flooding the air. "Warning! Warning!"

"What the hell is that?" Shane asked, his heart pounding as his mind raced through possible scenarios and checked for exits.

"Don't worry about it," Bug said, "it's just the elevator."

Sure enough, the ceiling above began to descend slowly.

"You don't think that's a little overkill?" Shane asked.

But Bug just shrugged. "I didn't want anyone to get crushed."

Shane's eyes widened. "Is that possible?"

"Only if the pressure-sensitive floor, the movement sensors and the heat signature reader all give out at the same time."

Shane slow-blinked at his friend. "Somehow I don't think that's likely to happen all at once. But hey, I haven't been in an adrenaline-induced coma in a while, so yeah, keep all the flashing lights and ear-fracturing alarms."

Bug smirked as if to say, *Thanks, I think I will.*

Shane was surprised he hadn't witnessed the extreme warning system when he'd been on the elevator, but as the elevator walls moved past the ceiling above, the noises and lights immediately stopped.

The room must be noiseproof, he thought. Which meant

they could be testing explosions down here and the world above would never know. Not that he thought testing explosions in an underground lair was a good idea, but hey, they could if they wanted to.

As Ash and another one of Bug's guys came into view, Bug looked as though he was about to be sick. He was staring at the woman like a lost puppy, though Shane realized he was probably monitoring Ash for her first reaction to the place. No matter how much brilliant work Bug did, none of it seemed to mean anything to him unless it was approved by Ash.

Of course, Ash barely reacted at all—her poker face had always been one of her strengths.

Bug rushed over to the elevator floor to take Ash's hand, assisting her off the single-step platform. Shane caught Ruby rolling her eyes in his periphery, but he thought it was cute, and Ash didn't seem to mind a bit, even flashing a smile Bug's way.

"Thank you, Bug, great place you've got here," Ash said, as she stepped down and took her first scan around. "Very acceptable."

Bug looked like he might faint. "Er, thanks, Ash," he squeaked out.

"Okay," Ash said loudly. "Ruby, you've got the artwork. Find out everything you can. Shane, I need you to verify everything we know about this compound. I need layouts, surrounding area, any obstacles that could get in our way. Bug, you're on security obviously." She clapped her hands twice. "Come on, people, we have a heist to plan."

Bug smiled and jumped into action. "You got it, boss."

This time Ruby rolled her eyes so hard Shane thought she was going to pass out from the strain. Not that she didn't have a point. Ash came storming in and barking orders as if they weren't all already doing exactly what she'd ordered them to, but that was Ash. The woman loved to be in charge. It drove

Ruby nuts, but it didn't bother Shane. The woman was good at what she did and if her ego needed a little stroking along the way, it was an easy trade-off.

So Shane did what he always did. He got back to work.

Ruby had already been researching the scepter and all the other treasures that could potentially show up at the "party," which they all knew was just a code word for black-market auction. The job specified they were only supposed to take the scepter. It seemed like a strange ask, since, according to some sources Ruby reconnected with, there were dozens of other treasures up for auction. But sometimes that was the job. A family only wanted what belonged to them, and they weren't about to claim someone else's stuff.

But Ruby was nothing if not thorough. If they were going to do this thing, she wanted to be as informed as possible. The rumored treasures for this particular "party" included gold, silver, rings, tapestries, jewels, fine china and religious artifacts.

The scepter itself was the star of the show. The gold was of the highest quality and the diamonds were rumored to have come from an uncharted mine somewhere in the Australian outback—an intriguing history in and of itself that Ruby vowed to research more fully when this job was complete. The origin of the magnificent 117-carat emerald crowning the whole thing was unknown.

The last time the scepter was accounted for was hundreds of years ago—it was logged at a Swiss castle. Castello di Siegenthaler had been perched high in the hills, one of three fortresses that once protected the ancient town of Santenal Obli in the Alpine region of Europe. The town no longer existed, but the treasure was well documented if a person knew where to look.

It was Ruby's job to know where to look.

From what Ruby could gather, the three fortresses were

attacked sometime in the fifteenth century, overtaken and raided. The town was completely destroyed, and hundreds of people were killed, including the noble families who lived in the castles. It was a well-planned and well-executed attack. If a few of the people hadn't made a daring escape, eventually making it to the border of Austria, history may never have known about it.

The scepter showed up again briefly just before World War I, where an unnamed Swiss family sent a photograph of it to a museum that was potentially interested in purchasing it. The purchase did not go through, and at last mention the scepter was rumored to have been among the treasure looted by the Nazis during World War II.

No family had ever come forward to claim the scepter when it was found, most likely because those first founding noble families of Santenal Obli were obliterated during the original attack. It was a fascinating piece, and Ruby couldn't help but wonder who the kidnappers' client was. In each of the jobs they'd done back in her con days, Ruby had been assured the clients were fully vetted and authenticated as the rightful owners of each recovered treasure.

Ruby zoomed in on the grainy picture of the scepter to get a better view of the coat of arms. It appeared to show a picturesque valley with a waterfall feeding into a body of water. Something prickled in Ruby, as if she'd seen something similar before, though she couldn't place when or where.

"Ruby?" Ash was saying. And then again, louder, with a snap of her fingers. "Ruby!"

Ruby had been so engrossed in her research she'd barely noticed the team making plans around her. "What?"

"Do you still have your info to get into The Vault?"

"Oh, uh, yeah, I think so. I'll have to double-check, I guess."

Ash let out a long, exasperated sigh.

"What?" Ruby asked. "I was out of the game. I was never

supposed to have to need any of this again. You're lucky I didn't destroy everything the minute I left Scotland."

The room fell silent at the mention of their final, failed job.

But the team recovered, as Ash faced them. "I'll work on compiling everything we've found out. In the meantime, you all need to go get your stuff in order. Pack what you need."

"I need to take time off work," Ruby added.

Ash shook her head. "Fine, take time off work if you must," she said, making it sound like work was some kind of ridiculous frivolity Ruby was just killing a bit of time with. "As always, we'll be taking different flights out to avoid any connections between us, and we'll meet in Switzerland. Everyone got it?"

"Sounds good, boss," Bug said.

Ruby really hated when Bug called Ash that. No one was supposed to be the boss of the team, they were all equal partners. But somehow, Ash had become their unofficial leader, something Ruby was not too fond of.

"See you on the other side," Shane said, packing up the papers from the theater, along with printouts of additional research.

Ruby began to save all the information she'd gathered, sending it to a special folder on the computer even though she'd already tucked most of it away in her head. Bug would encrypt everything and keep it ready in case they needed the info during the job. He'd digitize what they'd found at the theater so they'd have it at their fingertips no matter where they were in the world in what they called The Vault.

"Ruby," Ash said in her most stern schoolmarm manner. "You got that?"

Ruby pulled in a slow, fortifying breath. "Yes, Ash, I've got it."

Ash nodded once and turned on her heel, making her way back to the elevator. Bug scrambled behind to accompany her back up to ground level. God forbid the woman had to push a button all by herself.

"I guess she hasn't changed much," Shane said, sidling up beside Ruby as she turned the computer screen off.

His scent drifted past then, and Ruby tried not to think about being even closer to it, nuzzling into his neck…kissing along his jawline.

"Guess not," she said, trying to hide the way her pulse sped up so much she could hardly catch her breath.

After a moment of strange silence—not quite awkward, but certainly not comfortable—Shane straightened. "Well, safe travels," he said.

She nodded, trying to push down the feeling of regret creeping in, telling herself it was because they had to do this job, and definitely not because she had to part ways with Shane so soon after seeing him again. "Yeah, you too."

Three hours later, Ruby was packed and logging in to The Vault. It was essentially a digital safety-deposit box—a highly encrypted space where the team kept and managed their most essential documents. Logging in gave her the same sense of anticipation mixed with dread it always had. She clicked on the icon of the red gem—for Ruby, of course. Inside was her itinerary and digital flight information.

Great. She had to take three flights before she reached her final destination—no doubt the worst travel plans of them all. Ruby guessed Ash had her own private jet and was flying direct. Bug and Shane probably had a couple flights, maybe one domestic and one international, but of course Ruby got stuck flying through Canada and France before finally making it to Switzerland.

At least it would give her time to do more research, she supposed.

It was interesting the job was taking them to Switzerland, right back to the origin of the scepter itself. If Ruby was lucky, maybe she'd have some time to go through local records and see if she could trace the family.

From the outside, people thought her job was boring, but Ruby loved nothing more than digging into lost treasures, to uncover the stories they told.

The only thing left was to pick up her passport and other documentation, and hopefully, enough cash in various currencies to get her to Switzerland comfortably. The process of document retrieval was different every time, and The Vault told her this time she was off to a local waterpark. She wasn't in the mood for a bunch of hyper kids, but she was a professional and she would simply get to work like she always did.

Twenty minutes and thirty dollars to get into the park later, she was standing in front of locker 213 in the change room. She consulted her phone for the five-digit code and punched it in, pretending like she was about to put her bag inside. Once the area was clear of other people, she tucked the small envelope into the bag and made her way back out without encountering too many screaming children.

She arrived at the airport with a renewed sense that this was what was going to help get Max back. She almost felt a jolt of excitement.

Until an aggravatingly familiar and even more aggravatingly handsome face greeted her at her gate.

Chapter 9

She hadn't noticed him yet, and Shane was making the most of his opportunity to watch her unnoticed. A twinge of something squeezed his heart. The way she walked, only half paying attention to where she was going, and half paying attention to whatever bit of research she had on her phone. An untrained observer might have thought she was a little careless…distracted. But Shane knew better. It was part of her cover—what better way to blend in these days than have your attention focused on your phone?

In the hours since he'd last seen her, she'd already changed her hair. Shane didn't know if it was extensions, or a convincing wig, but she was back to her old bob style, a little past her shoulders—the kind of style no one would pay any particular attention to. Sure, she was going to get looks no matter what she did—she was too beautiful to completely fly under the radar—but this was about as incognito as she could get.

As she neared the waiting area at the gate, she glanced up from her phone and Shane gave her a little wave.

He did not particularly love the way the color drained from her face.

"Hey, honey," Shane said, pulling a shocked Ruby into a hug. "Don't worry," he continued quietly into her ear. "I'm not stalking you."

Which obviously made it sound like he was, in fact, stalking her.

He pulled her to a quiet corner with only the slightest bit of resistance. Ruby was probably in a full-on mental war with herself, both desperately wanting to get away from him, but equally curious as to why he was there. At her airport. Taking her flight.

“Ash didn’t think you would show up if you knew the plan was you and I posing as a couple traveling together to Switzerland.”

Ruby’s face stayed neutral. She was always one to stay in character when a job called for it, even in an unexpected conundrum like the one she found herself in. But Shane knew from experience Ruby was far from okay.

She pulled the boarding pass out of Shane’s hand, confirming they did, indeed, share a last name. “Why do they even need us to be in disguise for this?” she asked, her eyes darting around. “Presumably the people who took Max already know who all of us are at this point.”

Shane tilted his head in agreement. “Maybe, but the people who have the item we are going to retrieve do not.”

“I feel like this is a bit overkill,” she said.

“It is, but I don’t think we’re in any position to push back on an abundance of caution…especially after Scotland.”

She let out a long sigh. “I guess.”

She walked away from Shane without another word and sat on a nearby chair to wait for their boarding call. Shane followed. It was no doubt completely obvious to anyone who might be paying them the least bit of attention that they were not particularly getting along, but Shane figured it wasn’t necessarily uncommon for a married couple to do just that—especially when traveling.

“I’m sorry,” he said. “This wasn’t my idea.”

She glanced at him out of the corner of her eye. Shane

wasn't sure if the look she gave him was because she didn't believe him, or if it was because she knew it would never be his call either way.

She let out a low growl. "What the hell is Ash even thinking?"

"Well," Shane said, a small grin forming, "I honestly prefer not to think about that. I imagine it's kind of a flurry of mathematics whipped up into a whirlwind of blueprints and security briefings. Maybe with a hint of commanding power fashion lurking around the edges."

Shane couldn't be sure, but he thought the corner of Ruby's mouth twitched. "She does tend to dress to make an impression," she finally said, her shoulders relaxing.

Shane's relaxed along with hers.

After a beat, he spoke again. "None of this is ideal, obviously, but it's good to see you."

She nodded absently. "All things considered, it's good to see you too. A little discombobulating, but good, I guess."

Shane chuckled. "I suppose I can see how I have that effect on people."

Ruby finally looked at him then. "That's not what I meant. I don't mean *you're* discombobulating, it's just… I don't know, I never thought I'd see you guys again and it's kind of thrown me off, I guess. And the whole thing with Max…" She drifted off, pulling her knee up onto the seat. She turned to face him. "What if we can't get Max back?" she asked, her eyes shimmering.

It was the first note of vulnerability Shane had seen since the moment they reunited back in her apartment, and he had to fight the urge to reach for her.

"We'll get him back," Shane said. "We have to."

"He's done so much for us," Ruby said. "If anything happens—"

Shane shook his head. "We'll get him back. They can't

afford to do anything to him. Max is the only thing keeping us going on this job. If they really want that damned scepter, they can't risk touching a hair on his head. They know we'd be gone in a heartbeat."

She nodded, though she looked far from convinced. "I wish I could check the proof-of-life feed again," she said.

Shane had been wishing the same thing. But for all intents and purposes, they were a couple on vacation—it wouldn't make sense to be traveling around with a bunch of state-of-the-art tech.

Ruby straightened in her seat and pulled back her shoulders. "Okay, we're going to do this. Positive attitude and all that, right?"

"Right."

"But I will tell you one thing. I am going to kick Ash's pencil-skirted ass for giving us all this bloody itinerary."

Shane grinned.

"How about you go up to that young staff member up there and see if we can get an upgrade?" Ruby asked.

He lifted an eyebrow. "I thought we were supposed to be flying under the radar."

She narrowed her eyes, though a glimmer shone through them. "Don't think you can do it, huh?"

"You know very well that is not the issue."

"Uh-huh. Sure," she said, a real honest-to-goodness smile forming.

He worked up the nerve to shove her shoulder with his and for a moment, it almost felt like old times. A fact they both seemed to notice at the same time and the moment devolved back into uncomfortable silence.

"I have an idea," Shane said. "What if we just...didn't make this weird? What if we're just two old friends who know they're reuniting for a short time and won't see each other again after that? It will be great to catch up, do a little work together and then it will be just as great to go our separate ways with nothing but fond memories."

"Just two old friends, hey?" she said, interest showing behind her dark lashes.

He nodded once. "Exactly," even though he couldn't help but think their relationship had never been remotely anything anyone would have ever called just "friendly."

"So, what are we proposing here? Pretending this whole thing isn't weird and uncomfortable and utterly ridiculous?" she asked.

"Yes, that sounds like an excellent plan."

The weird, uncomfortable and utterly ridiculous fact they were even having this conversation was not lost on Ruby. Still, Shane's proposal did seem better than the alternative.

"I suppose it does beat spending the next twenty hours traveling in a smelly cloud of awkwardness," she said.

"It does," Shane said, getting comfortable in his seat, his legs relaxing, one knee falling open to touch hers, causing a little zing to shoot through her.

This was not going to be an easy twenty hours.

She wanted to throttle Ash. Ruby just knew she had some sort of ulterior motive too. Hell, she was probably trying to get Ruby and Shane comfortable again by forcing them to spend a bunch of hours together.

Ruby hated that it was already working. Not that she wanted to be on edge with Shane, but she did not want Ash to have the satisfaction of knowing her plan had worked. Yes, there had been good reasons for her and Shane to be apart, but for now, they were stuck together. There was no reason to make this mission more difficult than it had to be. Working together was going to be key to getting Max back, which was all that mattered. Even if Ash being right was one of Ruby's least favorite things in the world.

Their first flight was announced, and Ruby and Shane played their parts the way they needed to. Ruby tried not to notice how familiar and comfortable Shane's hand felt on the small of her back as he led her toward the check-in desk, then tried not to miss it when it was gone. She tried not to notice the way he fiddled with his passport and sent a smile to the woman who was checking him in, which was sexier than Ruby would have liked. And she tried very hard not to notice the sparkle in the eyes of the woman as she smiled back.

"You want to maybe cool that a little?" Ruby asked as they made their way down the walkway.

"Cool what?"

"The obvious flirting with the airline staff," Ruby said. "We're supposed to be acting like we're in love, or whatever."

His eyebrows knitted together in a way that said he didn't have a clue what she was talking about. Ruby knew Shane well enough to know it was sincere—he truly didn't know what he'd done.

Cripes, Ruby thought. That smile—that charming, disarming smile—wasn't even rehearsed. It was just his smile. She remembered hating it back then, and she hated it now. That smile for any lucky soul who happened to cross his path in a day—a cashier, waitstaff, a stranger coming his way down the street. Of course, if she was being honest with herself, she didn't hate it. She loved it, as a matter of fact. What she hated was that he never used that smile on her. The smiles she got weren't any less beautiful, but still, it was hard not to want all the smiles to be just for her.

Lord, she was being ridiculous.

"Never mind," she said, giving herself a solid headshake inside her mind.

Ruby crossed her fingers they would at least have a row to themselves on the plane, ideally with the middle seat empty, but as she approached their row, her hopes began to fall. Of course, she was assigned the middle seat, and of course Shane was going to be snugged up right beside her for the five-hour flight, almost touching her the entire time. Which was about the worst thing that could happen, since Ruby could feel her defenses starting to crumble with each moment she spent with Shane.

She had forgotten how easy things were with him.

Ruby gave the woman sitting in the window seat a smile as she sat down, hoping she wouldn't be much of a talker. Ruby preferred to catch up on sleep or do some quiet contemplating rather than chat nonstop with strangers on a flight. She liked people just fine, but she never did seem to find enough time to just sit and think, which was one of her favorite pastimes. She couldn't understand when people said they hated being alone with their thoughts. How else was anyone supposed to solve problems or come up with new ideas? Those people were almost as strange to Ruby as the ones who said they hated silence.

"Oh, don't you two make a lovely couple," the older woman said as Shane sat—much too close for comfort—in his seat beside Ruby.

Ruby was about to correct the woman, let her know they were not a couple, when Shane reminded her they were supposed to be playing a part by gifting the woman with his flirtatious smile and replying with a gracious thank-you. Ruby shot a quick smile toward her new seatmate, noticing how the woman was flushed. Shane had that effect on women. Ugh.

What Ruby wished they could do, even more than sleeping or getting some good thinking in, was to discuss their next moves. She wanted to know what else had been in Shane's

Vault package. Or compare notes on the other tidbits of info Ash might have conveniently left out of Ruby's Vault. But that would be impossible with the woman so close by.

Unfortunately, sleeping and/or thinking proved to be wildly unsuccessful for two reasons. One, Shane was watching some kind of uproariously hilarious movie. Or at least he thought it was funny. Every time she would get settled enough to close her eyes and begin, Shane would let out another massive laugh, effectively jolting her out of her thoughts. The second problem was, when the movie was finally done, Shane decided to strike up a conversation with their seatmate. He asked her all about her grandkids and hobbies, making it impossible for Ruby to relax.

Ruby couldn't help but think Shane was doing it just to spite her. Sure, he may have just been passing the time on a long and uneventful flight, but how he could be so interested in little Jesse's piano lessons was beyond Ruby.

By the time they were making their final descent, the woman—Rose—was more smitten than a schoolgirl at her favorite boyband concert. And as they deplaned, Shane walked Rose all the way to the exit, stopping only because if he went any farther, he'd have to go through security all over again.

"Quite the charmer," Ruby said, once Shane had returned to find their next gate.

"Got to keep up appearances," he said, his eyes practically sparkling.

"Which appearance is that? The one where you're much more like a trusty shadow than the doting partner you're supposed to be?"

Shane pulled off a flawless performance of mock offense. "What kind of a partner would I be if I didn't take an interest in my fellow travelers?"

"Your fellow female travelers?" Ruby couldn't help but point out.

"Ruby Walters!" Shane spouted, and Ruby had to admit she was impressed he'd even memorized her false name, no pause or anything. "That woman was old enough to be my grandmother, what are you implying?" He grinned wide.

Ruby couldn't help but grin right back. She'd forgotten how fun being with Shane could be, even when they weren't doing anything. "Oh, nothing, dear," she said, knowing he hated being called *dear*, always saying it made him feel like he was ninety-three. But she knew he couldn't do anything about it since they were supposed to be playing the happy couple.

"You know you love it. Who would I even be if I didn't flirt with cute little elderly ladies?"

"I honestly have no idea," Ruby said, smiling, and she meant it.

Shane had more "people person" personality in his pinky finger than Ruby had in her whole body. She hated that she loved the way the twinkle in his eye brightened with their exchange. He was enjoying this.

Then again, so was Ruby.

Oh, no. What was she thinking, trying to flirt with Shane of all people? Although, one might be hard-pressed *not* to flirt with Shane. He was the master at it, bringing out the flirt in most everyone he talked to. Rose had been a prime example.

Their second, and longest, flight was slightly better, since much of it was spent flying over the ocean in the dark. The flight was full again, so no such luck on talking strategy, but at least Ruby thought she could get some peace and quiet and even a little sleep. Quality thinking time was still eluding her, since she was finding it a bit difficult to concentrate on anything besides the way Shane still smelled like a damn forest-scented candle—sweet with just a hint of pine in the morning.

Apparently, she was the only one who was having trouble focusing. By the time they reached elevation, Shane was already peacefully asleep.

Chapter 10

Shane knew how to get people on his side. Sure, their seatmate Rose had been an easy target, but still, he knew how to work situations to his advantage. But no matter how good he was with people, he was still surprised every time Ruby played along.

There were just certain people whom he'd always feel nervous around, no matter how confident he appeared on the outside, and Ruby was one of them. So he closed his eyes when they boarded their last flight, not wanting to jinx the moment.

The Meyerses had always been winners, no doubt about that. It was in their DNA, threaded deep into every cell. Shane had grown up knowing this to the core of his soul, and he never questioned it.

Until, of course, he did.

He would always remember the feeling of inadequacy at the most inopportune moments. Admit to himself there might be certain situations where he didn't quite measure up. He tried to push the thoughts away, to keep his confidence. He'd never have admitted it out loud, but back when he still lived in his hometown and his name commanded respect, he secretly felt like he was just a little better than everybody else.

But that was before Renaye came to town in his senior year. Shane wasn't sure if it was because she was new, or if it was her incredible looks that caught his attention first. He'd had his fair share of girls pay attention to him, and frankly, the girls from his small town were starting to get boring.

Yeah, Shane knew how bad that made him sound, which was why he'd never say it out loud—his mother taught him better than that. But a small town with the same twenty girls in your age range got a little stale after fifteen years of knowing them inside and out. Besides, he'd already kissed all the ones he wanted to, and there was the additional problem of having all their parents know you too.

Small towns. Everyone always all up in your face.

It was a strange place to be—both itching to get out of Dodge the moment you graduated, yet knowing you'd be taken care of—and well—for the rest of your life if you stayed. There was no lack of admiration or people fawning all over you where he grew up.

The Meyers men had always been the ones people in town called troublemakers—but with a wink to go with the word. They were a little too handsome, had a little too much charm and were maybe a little short in the smarts department. But that didn't matter. School was a joke anyway—his family owned half the town and most of the "smart" people relied on them for their jobs.

"Hey," he'd said, waltzing up to this new, gorgeous being, flashing the winning smile that worked every time.

Renaye glanced up from her book, slight annoyance crossing her face, which Shane was surprised didn't go away after she got a good look at him. His smile faltered, just a little.

"I'm Shane. Shane Meyers." He hated that he threw in the last name, just to make sure she really knew who he was. Something about this girl made him feel like he needed all the arsenal he had available to him.

"Renaye," she said, turning her gaze back to her book.

But Shane had been taught well. He knew how to talk to girls. And this one had already given him some insight into her interests. "So, uh, what are you reading?" he asked, expecting her to get excited, to start droning on about ever minuscule plot detail.

His dad had taught him a long time ago that girls wanted to be seen, wanted someone to pay a bit of attention to them. "And that, son, is the fastest way to get what you want," he'd said with a double pump of his beefy eyebrows. Shane had felt a bit of an uneasy twinge when his dad first said it, but over the years, he'd discovered his dad had not been wrong. So he'd mentally prepared himself for the plot onslaught, readying to go into fake listening mode.

"It's the new Suzanne Collins," she'd said.

Shane nodded, waiting for her to continue into her diatribe.

But that diatribe never came.

"Oh, yeah? Is it any good?"

The girl actually sighed. "Yeah, I guess."

Okay, this girl was a hard nut to crack. But Shane wasn't one to give up easily. "So, what's it about?"

She'd looked up at him again, kind of squinting since the sun was behind Shane. Maybe that was the problem—maybe she couldn't see him very well.

"Shane?" she'd asked, seeming like she had to dig a little harder than Shane would have liked to remember his name.

"Yeah?" he'd said, flashing the smile again.

"What was the last book you read?"

Shane had made a face. "I don't know. Something in school, I guess."

"And did you finish it? Like read the whole book?"

Shane shrugged. "Doubt it."

Why read a whole book when you could get a girl to give you the lowdown? They loved to do that kind of shit for guys they liked.

She'd nodded. "That's what I thought."

"I guess I'm not that into reading," Shane had said, not thinking much about it.

Reading had never been important. Like yeah, he *could* read, of course, but beyond the bare minimum that helped a person comfortably get by in the world, he didn't see the appeal.

"Well, Shane," Renaye said, "I guess I'm not that into guys who don't read."

She'd said it in a way that made it clear it was the end of the conversation and she had no desire to ever have another.

"Oh, um, okay," Shane said, walking away, wondering what in the hell was wrong with her.

He never tried to talk to her again.

It was his first lesson in reputation. As in, it wasn't going to get you everything you wanted in life, contrary to what his family would have him believe.

It was a lesson Shane was thankful for now. The satisfaction in winning someone over with his own skills—using his own charm, his own intelligence, which he'd finally started to hone after the Renaye incident—was so much greater than just being somebody in some small town in the middle of nowhere.

Shane had gotten a little melancholy, thinking about the past during the final plane ride. He had been thinking of it as they got off the plane and headed to the luggage carousel. He was even still thinking about it the moment he realized something wasn't quite right.

"Hey," he said, moving in close to Ruby's ear. He felt her stiffen, and hoped their audience didn't catch it. "We have company."

The sensation of Shane's breath on her ear raised goose bumps on Ruby's skin. How the man still had that effect on her even with all they'd been through, she'd never understand.

But she didn't have the luxury to think about any of that at the moment. Not if they were being tailed. She turned her full attention to Shane, pivoting to meet his eyes, though she was hoping to get a glimpse of whoever the "company" was in her peripheral, but nothing obvious jumped out at her. Although, she supposed, the tail wouldn't be much of a tail if they'd been obvious. Still, she was trained to know what to look for and was frustrated she couldn't spot them. Or maybe she was just frustrated Shane had spotted them first.

"So, what's the plan?" Ruby said, keeping her voice light so she wouldn't attract suspicion in case the person following could hear.

Shane pulled her into an unexpected hug, one which might have sent her into shock if she wasn't so focused on staying in character. It was a smart move—they'd be able to talk for a minute quietly enough so no one could hear—but Ruby wished it didn't make her feel so…discombobulated.

"We need to figure out if this is one of the guys who have Max, or if it's someone else," Shane said.

"Who else could it possibly be?"

"I don't know. Maybe someone's keeping track of anyone researching the scepter. Maybe our passports got flagged somehow. Maybe I just have a very eager secret admirer," he said, pulling away from the hug with a grin.

Ruby smiled back. "Are you saying it's a woman?" she asked, her eyes darting to the left.

Shane adopted an expression of mock hurt. "Are you saying I couldn't attract the attentions of a male admirer?"

Ruby raised her eyebrows. "Solid point."

The alarms had started for the luggage carousel, and they turned their attention toward it. Shane took the opportunity to speak while the noise was assaulting the air. "We'll just grab our luggage and head for the taxis. I didn't get a good look. Maybe I'm being paranoid."

Ruby squinted her eyes at him, feeling like he was up to something. "Are you going to ditch me?"

Shane looked a little wounded for real this time. "Of course I'm not going to ditch you. I just think our best bet is to lose them as soon as possible. Ideally before we make it out of the airport."

"Fine," Ruby said, realizing Shane was using it as an opportunity to challenge himself.

They'd both been out of the game for a long time. Ruby assumed she was a little rusty—which was confirmed by the fact that she hadn't even spotted the tail—and she could only assume Shane felt the same.

"Like we did in Cairo?" Shane said.

"Should work," Ruby agreed.

They stepped toward the carousel, Shane moving left and Ruby moving more to the right, both jostling their way to the front the way the most obnoxious passengers tended to do. For the plan to work, there had to be a bit of confusion. They had to get separated.

Ruby spotted Shane grabbing his bag first, taking off toward the exit. Ruby hung back a bit, but only for a few moments, snagging her bag off the turnstile at the last possible second, heading in the opposite direction.

Because Shane had taken off first, they assumed the person watching would go after him, but if there was more than a single person, this maneuver was designed to get them apart. It meant Ruby and Shane would be separated, too, but this way they'd regain the upper hand. Take back the element of surprise.

Ruby strolled relatively slowly—the trick was to walk at a different pace than the people around so you could try to pick up on anyone who might be matching your pace. She glanced as surreptitiously as possible into every reflective surface—windows, signs, even the bars of luggage trolleys. But she heard nothing…saw nothing.

Still, she couldn't shake the feeling someone was back there. Maybe it was paranoia from being away from the con game for so long, but back in the day she'd had a sixth sense for these things…and her "Spidey-senses" were tingling. As Ruby neared an almost deserted area of the airport, she snuck into a washroom.

Back at Bug's, they'd all been given special suitcases with handles that came all the way out. The ends of the metal posts were angled, creating a concealed, but highly effective weapon. She hid around the corner of the entrance, heart beating, every sense on high alert.

As the woman on Ruby's tail walked in, she was met with quite a surprise in the form of a headlock and—much to Ruby's astonishment and Bug's credit—a rather effective-looking, bladelike object nestled along her neck.

Chapter 11

Airports are interesting spaces. Some areas are packed with people, and others are ghost towns. Thankfully, Shane knew how to navigate both. The question was, which area to choose? The answer depended on who his pursuer was, of course.

But Shane had no clue who that might be.

By now the person tailing him would know something was up. A couple traveling together doesn't usually just split up. Shane had to assume his follower had at least some idea who he and Ruby were, and their suspicions would be on high alert.

At first, Shane chose to keep to the places with people, following the throng filing out of the baggage area, out toward the area where hotel shuttles, taxis and families waiting in long drive-through lanes congregated in a flurry of activity. But he wasn't about to leave the airport without Ruby. They had plans in place if they got separated—they both knew where to meet and several routes to get there, but Shane didn't think they'd gotten to that point yet. Plan A—a little evasion work, then meet back up near the domestic security gate—was still in place.

Shane weaved through the people, glancing around as if he was a lost tourist, speaking briefly to an airport employee helping people find the right combination of taxis, shuttles and buses for their needs. Shane felt bad for taking up so much of the man's time when there were clearly people needing help more than he did, but he wanted to get another look at his tail and the man had presented the perfect opportunity.

But a good look was not to be had—the guy was competent, intuitive, trained. Shane only got a shadow of a glimpse that told him nothing besides what he already knew. His tail appeared to be a man, and a rather commanding one at that, well-muscled and on the tall side.

Shane thanked the airport employee for all his help and continued his winding route. There were plenty of places he could sneak into if he wanted to confront his pursuer—empty spaces, walkways, between large trucks—but he didn't want to risk it with so many people around.

Shane spotted an entrance propped open with a small brick, an employee smoking a few feet away with his back turned.

Perfect.

Pulling his luggage close to squeeze through, he ducked into the door, hoping the guy smoking would finish quickly, too quickly for his tail to follow, but no such luck—the guy apparently hell-bent on using every last second of his break time.

Inside, Shane found what he was looking for. He was in some kind of secure, employees-only space—dark and extremely quiet. He considered confronting his tail right there, but he knew the employee was bound to stumble upon them if he stayed, so he jogged down the dark corridor. He didn't bother testing door handles for anything that might be unlocked—an enclosed space like a small room would be his last resort. What he needed was a space where he could hide, take his shadow by surprise, but still have at least a few options for exits. He was a good fighter, but by the size and skill of his shadow, he couldn't assume he'd come out on top in a hand-to-hand battle.

The annoying thing was, Shane couldn't figure out why this person would follow him. Even if someone had guessed what they were up to—and that was a big if—the people watching them wanted the team to succeed in their mission. This whole bloody thing was about securing the scepter and trading it for Max. Nothing was making any sense.

Thankfully, his pursuer was moving slowly, knowing Shane could jump out at him from any of the nooks or doorways along the hall, which bought Shane a little time to find the kind of spot he needed. The end of the hall opened into a large room filled with chairs and tables, like some sort of staffroom or cafeteria for employees. It was deserted. A quick survey told Shane there were three exits. He wouldn't get a better opportunity than this to find out what his new friend was up to.

It felt like forever. Shane slid Bug's special handle from his suitcase, readying for anything, though after three long flights, he knew his energy would be less than optimal and hoped whoever this was just wanted to talk. Unfortunately, Shane knew from experience that wasn't often the case.

He ducked behind a serving counter to wait.

And wait.

Seriously, was this guy even following him anymore? Shane was about to come out of his hiding spot and head to the meetup point to find Ruby when he heard the tiniest scrape of a footstep entering into the cafeteria. The man moved with caution, which Shane hoped was a good sign. His pursuer was a thinker, not making sudden moves or charging in like a drunk rhino. Which also meant he was calculating every possible situation, just like Shane was. This was the exact reason Shane had chosen the hiding spot he did—because it was not his first choice… or his second. He always chose the third place he spotted so anyone on his tail would most likely check two other places first, giving Shane the opportunity to surprise them from behind if all went as planned.

Of course, there was no plan for situations like this. A person just had to do the best they could with whatever tools the universe provided them, but Shane was an expert at improv. So when he lost sight of the guy—who, to his dismay, was much bigger than he'd hoped—Shane started to get a little nervous. And when he crept out from behind the counter and the room still seemed empty, he got even more nervous.

But that was nothing compared to the massive shot of adrenaline catapulting through his body when an obviously practiced hand yanked the suitcase handle out of his grip and an equally practiced second arm wrapped neatly, and rather snugly, around Shane's neck, cutting his air off.

It had been a brilliant move—the man had climbed onto the counter, likely knowing that was the precise place Shane would been hiding. A perfect position, with the advantage of the high ground, and one where he could spot Shane no matter which way he came out.

Shane's thoughts raced through a thousand scenarios—most of which did not end well. But he had the kind of mind that moved fast, and he prepared his stance for a counterattack, though he couldn't decide whether to try to flip the guy over his head—something the man would likely see coming a mile away—or duck and hope to catch him off guard. It was also a move that would be expected, but Shane's options were somewhat limited.

"Hey, buddy," Shane's pursuer said, his voice surprisingly jovial.

And with those two words, Shane's entire body relaxed, and he stood, turning to face his pursuer as the man's grip loosened.

Shane let out a long, exhausted and relieved sigh.

"Bug, what the hell are you doing here?"

It was the smell that first caught Ruby's attention. A very expensive, and very familiar, perfume, which she knew a person could only get once a year at the Fête du Jasmin festival in Grasse, France. She let all the air she'd been holding in out in one big whoosh.

"Are you going to get your hands off me, or what?" Ash said, having to choke the words out due to Ruby's expert grip around her neck.

"Ash? What the hell, man?" Ruby said, letting Ash go, adding just a touch more aggression than was strictly necessary.

Ash rolled her eyes. "I am not a man, and we are not in hell."

It only took a moment for Ash to straighten her coat and she was the picture of perfection again. Ruby, on the other hand, with the almost twenty hours of flights behind her, felt like a smashed bag of cow dung. She made a weak attempt at smoothing her hair back into place.

"Feels like hell to me after that excruciating flight itinerary," Ruby said, moving to a sink to splash water on her face. "And seriously, what are you doing here? I assume it's Bug you've got tailing Shane?"

She went to the automatic hand dryer, waiting for Ash to start speaking before letting it do its thing. The exasperation Ruby saw on Ash's face was even more satisfying after sitting on those damned flights and plotting her payback for hours.

When the drying stopped, Ash put a hand on her hip. "Are you done?"

"I think so," Ruby said, examining her hands, where a slight dampness still lingered.

Ash opened her mouth to speak again just when Ruby got the machine going again. It was totally juvenile and ridiculous, but Ruby couldn't help that it was damned funny too.

Still chuckling, Ruby moved her hands away from the dryer. "Sorry, couldn't help it. I'm feeling a little out of sorts after all the travel."

Ash raised an eyebrow. "That couldn't be helped," she said, with a wave of her hand that said she was quite done discussing it.

Ruby inserted the handle back into her suitcase and rolled

it along behind as they left the restroom and headed back up the deserted wing toward the gates.

"So, what happened?" Ruby asked. "And why were you tailing us instead of just meeting us like a normal person?"

"The Vault has been compromised. We were following you in case one of two things were happening. First, to keep some distance in case you and Shane caught yourselves a real tail, and second, in case anyone was watching from afar. We needed to get you somewhere secluded and lose any possible tail. Bug did his thing with his computers and gadgets and couldn't spot anything, but we wanted to be as careful as we could."

"Okay, but what do you mean The Vault has been compromised?"

"Bug discovered some glitches in the system, so he went in and checked out the code, or whatever it is he does," she said, shaking her head as if it was astounding there was something in this world she didn't understand. "In any case, he discovered someone had been in there, so now all our information is compromised—plan A, plan B and plan C are all shot."

"The whole operation is shot?" Ruby asked, panic starting to rise.

Ash shook her head. "Not the operation. We can assume the people who have Max already know most of our plan since it was already laid out by Max, and anything else we've come up with since then we've kept separate. Standard protocol. All they know is our travel itineraries and, well, now our base of operations has been compromised. So I guess that's the third reason we needed to be here when you and Shane arrived."

"So, do we have a plan D?" Ruby asked.

They had reached an area where a few more people were milling around, so Ruby started scanning for things that didn't belong. She trusted Bug and Ash would have spotted anyone who could have been spotted, but there would always be an outside chance someone was simply really, really good and didn't twig any danger vibes.

"We do now," Ash said. "I've called in some favors and secured us a new spot, which…should work."

Ruby decidedly did not like the pause in her sentence. "Please tell me it isn't some run-down warehouse, and all we have to sleep on is a bare concrete floor."

"I'm sure it's a bit better than that," Ash said, though Ruby couldn't help notice she did not seem convinced.

As they neared the domestic flight area where Shane and Ruby were supposed to meet if they got separated, Ruby tried not to be annoyed with the new plan. The whole last flight, all she'd been thinking about was a hot shower and at least a short sleep, and she wasn't sure if that was even going to happen now. But she had to think of Max. She shook her head at how insensitive she was being. The poor guy was locked up. And she knew Max would never complain about any accommodation situation if the tables were turned and he had to help one of them.

As they turned the last corner toward the domestic security area, Ruby found her gaze searching for one thing.

Shane.

Now that it was over, she hated how panicked she'd been when they split up and was surprised to realize it was more because of her worry for Shane than it had been for herself. Surely that must have been because she'd known the pursuers would likely go for him instead of her. Of course, the worry for Shane hadn't stopped after she realized someone was following her, too, but she wasn't going to think about that.

Still, her heart calmed the moment her gaze fell on him. He had his back turned as he talked to Bug, and Ruby took a moment to admire his lean, lanky frame, always relaxed, always confident. She sometimes resented that about him, the confidence. Even though she was successful, she never quite felt like she could find the assuredness he had. She never quite felt worthy in the world, which she knew was linked to the way she so often felt like she was doing something wrong—probably because she had done so much wrong in the past. Broken every rule. In theory, she could justify it, and believed in the end everything she had done had an overall positive effect on the world, but that feeling never left.

Still, even if she might never achieve that kind of swagger for herself, it looked damn good on him.

He turned, gifting Ruby and Ash with *that* smile—the one that, had it been in a cheesy commercial, would have a sparkle graphic and high-pitched ding accompanying it.

"Hey, guys," Shane said, "guess who I found hanging around."

Bug gave Shane a look. "I'm pretty sure I was the one who found you."

"Hey, Bug," Ruby said.

"We should keep moving," Ash said, never one for social niceties.

"And hello to you too," Shane said.

But Ash just kept moving, not a reply to be found inside that tight business skirt of hers.

Ash had rented a car, which Ruby guessed was also a last-minute changeup, since the four of them were squashed in there like it was a clown car. Ruby struggled to avoid accidentally touching her knee to Shane's in the tiny back seat. How in the hell could the guy possibly still smell so good after three damn flights?

Shane, of course, did not seem to be having the same idea about not touching, since he was manspreading all over the place. Either he was doing it on purpose to get inside her head, or he was oblivious to the fact that there was another person in the row with him.

Of course, Ruby knew Shane was rarely oblivious about anything.

But the other scenario didn't make much sense either. When the team split after Scotland, Shane had made sure to let Ruby know he wasn't interested in extending their relationship. He'd apparently always seen it as a sort of coworkers-with-benefits situation. The realization had struck Ruby like a sledgehammer to the face—she'd thought they'd had something that transcended the team, something lasting—but she wasn't about to beg him to be her boyfriend. That kind of humiliation was far worse than the pain of heartbreak.

Nearly an hour later, with nothing but small talk and the clickety-clack of Ash's laptop—the woman was either always busy, or always wanted everyone to think she was busy—they pulled onto a remote trail, leading toward a grove of trees. Beyond the trees was a small yard that must have been incredibly picturesque in the daytime, with a cozy cottage nestled in the center.

Ruby suddenly had thoughts of waking with her coffee to the sounds of jolly songbirds and merriment, having a morning frolic in a meadow of wildflowers, leading up to a lunch of fennel and lemongrass salad, then spending the afternoon leisurely foraging for mushrooms while wearing those trendy yellow wellies. Her evenings spent with huckleberry tea and journaling, her brain abuzz with ideas for the novel she'd always meant to write.

"This doesn't look so bad," Ruby said, though Ash didn't seem convinced.

Ruby should have known the place might not be as bad as she feared. Ash was nothing if not a glutton for luxury, and this quaint little cottage was her idea of roughing it. But after the thoughts of concrete floors Ruby had had, this was heaven.

"As long as there's running water, I'm a happy camper," she said, stepping out of the car.

The air felt fresher than any air she'd ever breathed.

Inside, the cottage was even more enchanting than it was

from the outside. Mostly a creamy white, with wood ceilings, it was brighter than Ruby imagined it would be. The furniture was a mix of rustic antiques, like the adorable kitchen chairs with hearts cut out of the backs, paired with more modern, modular furniture. Ivory cupboards and beige rugs were accented with pops of color in the drapes and pillows—and all of it put together was wildly charming.

Bug made a quick sweep of the place and came back to the kitchen where Ruby had already flopped onto the most comfortable couch she'd ever sat in. Or maybe it was just comfortable compared to an airplane seat and a tiny clown car, but she was grateful nonetheless.

"There are only two bedrooms," Bug announced, as he stepped back into the kitchen/living area.

Ruby's eyes flitted to Shane's, and he caught her gaze. Ruby did not like the way her stomach did a little somersault.

Thankfully, Ash spoke before Ruby or Shane could say anything ridiculous they couldn't take back. "Boys in one, girls in the other," she announced, making it clear there would be no arguments.

"I'll take the couch," Shane said, apparently not wanting to share a queen-size with Bug.

Which meant Ruby had no choice but to bunk with Ash.

"One of the rooms has two small beds," Bug said. "You guys can take that one if you want."

"Fine," Ash said. "I get the shower first."

Of course, Ruby thought, but didn't have the energy to argue.

Ash took her sweet time in the shower and Ruby could barely keep her eyes open, her head nodding toward her chest more than once. Eventually Ash emerged and the guys were good enough to let Ruby have the shower next.

It was one of the most glorious experiences of her life. There was just something about a hot shower after a full day, and then some, of travel, but she kept it short so Bug and Shane could get in there too. She, at least, had some sense of courtesy for other people, even if Ash didn't.

After she was clean and feeling more ready for sleep than she had in a very long time, she flopped into the other single bed in the room where Ash was already snoring like a lumberjack, which was to say, as loud as a chainsaw. But it wouldn't matter, Ruby always packed her earplugs and had no doubt sleep would find her in seconds.

An hour later, her doubt was beginning to show as she continued to stare at the ceiling. By now she knew about forty times over that there were eleven and a half tiles across the ceiling of the room, and about ten and a quarter going the other way. Almost 118 square feet of white, bare, boring tiles. Counting them should have been enough to put her in a slumber for days, but her buzzing brain had other ideas.

It was no use.

The longer she lay there, the more awake she felt, and she knew from experience there was nothing she could do to ever get her any closer to the rest she needed. So she got up, hoping she might find a book or something to help take her mind off everything that had happened and everything that would have to happen to get Max back.

But as she padded out to the living area in her bare feet, she realized she was not alone.

Chapter 12

Shane startled as he heard the back patio door slide open.

"Hey," Ruby said, as she slipped outside. "Couldn't sleep?"

She looked innocent somehow. Vulnerable, with a blanket draped over her shoulders. She was back to short hair. Apparently the bob was a wig, though this style suited her so much better. Shane shook his head. "I think I'm too far past the point of tired. You?"

"Same, I guess," she said, setting the empty glass she'd brought out onto the table and sliding it toward him. "Where'd you find the booze?"

"Back of the cupboard above the fridge. It was a little dusty, but I figured it might help me sleep." He poured her a generous shot of the bourbon.

Ruby nodded. "That's what I'm hoping too."

"It stings a little going down," Shane said, "but definitely warms you up once it hits your stomach."

"Mmm, a cozy bourbon heat in the chilly Swiss countryside," Ruby said, clinking her glass to Shane's.

Shane realized if someone had proposed that exact thing, he would have said it sounded like a good time. If only they weren't in search of a friend in a buttload of danger, it could have been a nice little vacation. Shane took another sip of what was a tad closer to the burning inferno of hell's deepest depths than the cozy sweater warmth he was hoping for, but it was getting the job done. His mind was already starting to relax.

Ruby made a face and let out a little cough as she took her first sip. “Good Lord,” she said, peering into her glass as if trying to make out what in the fresh hell was happening in there. “So, how’ve you been, Shane?” she asked.

They’d spent the past twentysomething hours alone together, but they hadn’t really been alone for a single second of it. This was the first time they’d gotten a chance to talk.

“Oh, you know, living the dream,” he said, swirling his glass, as if adding a bit of crisp, fresh air might help the burning firestorm situation.

“But how’ve you really been?” she asked, knowing his first answer had been a cop-out.

He smiled. He’d forgotten what it was like to have someone who knew him—really knew him—to talk to. He shrugged. “I’m good,” he said. “I’ve been traveling a lot, having fun, getting into trouble…you know how it is.”

Ruby tilted her head. “I’m not sure I do. I’ve spent the past three years trying to stay as far away from trouble as I can get.”

Shane’s smile faltered. “And then I waltzed back into your life.”

She looked at him for a long time. “It might not have been so bad if had been just you,” she said, taking another quick sip as if to chase the words down.

“I thought you’d never want to see me again,” he said, surprised.

“It wasn’t you, necessarily. It was the life. I just…couldn’t be around any of that anymore.”

Shane nodded. “And I feel like I’ve been chasing after that life, trying to find it again since the moment it was taken away.”

Ruby smiled a sad smile. "We're quite a pair," she said, the words thick in her throat.

"We always were," Shane said. "It's just that we used to balance each other out."

"Until we didn't," Ruby said.

"Until we didn't," Shane agreed.

Shane wished he'd never made the mistake of finally taking the bait after Ruby had pushed him away so many times. He pretended it was fine that she didn't want a commitment. That she didn't want to be "pinned down" as she always called it. But Shane had always wanted more and the harder he pushed Ruby for it, the harder she pushed back, the work or her school always more important. Always taking all her time.

After a while, he'd just given up, hoping maybe he'd find what he was looking for somewhere else. At first, he'd even flaunted it in her face, showing up with women when she was around. It was stupid—he was young and wanted to make Ruby jealous, thinking it was what would make her change her mind, but—cue the shock and awe—it had the opposite effect.

He never did find what he was looking for. Only found ways other people weren't Ruby.

They sipped in silence for a while, Shane relishing the burn of the bourbon. It felt good—like a mini punishment for all the things he'd done in the past. Or maybe he was using the heat to burn down the past. Here she was, the one woman he knew he'd never forget—the one he wanted to fix everything with for so long—sitting right in front of him after all this time.

"Ruby," he said, and she glanced up from her glass into his eyes. "I'm sorry for…everything."

She shrugged. "There's nothing to be sorry for. We didn't promise each other anything," she said, with a weak smile.

"But we knew. We both knew there was more to you and I than just a bit of fun," Shane said.

"Maybe," Ruby said. "But that's probably why everything

went down the way it did. With Scotland, maybe it was just… easier to walk away when we had the chance."

Shane sat back heavy in his seat. "After Scotland there was just…nothing anymore."

"There wasn't nothing," Ruby said. "There was finally a life. I should have seen it way before I was forced to, but getting out of that world felt like the start of my real life."

Shane half smiled, gazing off toward a towering mountain range in the distance. "Not for me. Scotland was pretty much the end[illegible]

"You[illegible]hat again," Ruby said. "If I can do it, you c[illegible]

Sha[illegible]ad. "I know that life was never for you," he said. "But it was everything I ever wanted. Sure, we weren't exactly on the up-and-up, but we were doing good in the world. It was my only chance to ever do anything important. I have to say, I'm a little bit jealous that you're still out there doing the important work."

Ruby shrugged. "It's a good job, sure. But it's not quite as satisfying as I thought it would be."

Shane raised an eyebrow in question.

"It's just…not particularly efficient. It takes approximately six thousand years to get through all the red tape. Then it's months, if not years, to recover anything. Honestly, it all feels a little useless."

"At least you're trying," Shane said.

Ruby tilted her head, conceding. "Yeah."

They sat in silence until eventually Shane spoke. "It's not that I have a shitty life. It's just… I miss everything. I miss the team, I miss the chase…" He drifted off, not brave enough to say his last words out loud as he thought them.

I miss you.

Ruby was nodding absently. "I miss all that too," she said, her voice soft and clear in the crisp air. "But I hate that we're back here. Back in the con. I feel guilty every second we're here, knowing I'm doing the wrong thing."

"That's where we're different," Shane said, "I love that we're here. Not because Max has been taken, obviously, and yeah, Scotland went bad—I get why we had to stop. But I would love nothing more than to do a thousand more jobs with the team. And with you," he said, finding her eyes.

Ruby's lips parted as if she were about to say something, but instead she lifted her glass, draining the last of her bourbon in a gulp larger than one Shane would be willing to take of the volcanic swill. She barely flinched.

Ruby could feel the burn of the liquor all the way down her throat, into her stomach, and had to fight the urge to cough the fumes still burning her nose.

She wasn't about to admit, especially to Shane, how much she missed working with her old team too. She didn't miss having to watch her back and live in a world where she was paranoid 24/7, but she missed the camaraderie. They used to have so much fun together. Except maybe Ash. But the rest of them had a hell of a lot of fun messing with Ash, which made it almost as good.

The place out in the middle of the Swiss countryside was nothing short of spectacular. It was beautiful, quiet, remote—the absolute perfect place to hide out for a bit. Or forever, Ruby couldn't help but think, wondering for a moment how much real estate in this part of the world might cost.

A breeze found its way into her blanket and a shiver rattled through her.

"You're cold," Shane said, his voice full of concern.

Ruby always used to love and hate the way Shane wanted to take care of her—she hated anyone even implying she was less than completely independent, but she couldn't say attention from someone like Shane wasn't kind of nice sometimes. Of course, in the end, she wasn't the only woman Shane showed attention to. Not even close. Not that they'd made any commitments at the time—she was adamant about that. Neither of them did anything technically wrong, even though they were both hurting each other.

"I'm fine," Ruby said, though she was getting cold, but for whatever reason—some kind of silly pride thing, she supposed—she was reluctant to admit it.

"Well, I'm getting cold," Shane said, gathering up the glasses and bottle of bourbon.

There was a time when his actions would have annoyed Ruby. She knew he was heading inside because she was cold. That, plus the gathering of the items on the table, even her glass, would have sent her into an independence spiral. Maybe she was exhausted, or maybe she had simply mellowed over the past few years, but tonight it all felt kind of chivalrous.

They headed into the cottage, Ruby opening the door since Shane's hands were full.

"Hey, do you remember the last time we ate anything?" he asked, his voice lowering to a whisper.

"I don't think you have to worry about waking the snoring twins," Ruby said, smiling.

Bug's deep snore vibrated through the place, followed almost immediately by Ash's wheezier, but no less noisy, snuffle-snore.

Shane smiled back, shaking his head. "Glad I brought my noise-canceling headphones," Shane said.

"I never thought of that," she said. "I was trying to use earplugs, but some kind of soothing sounds or something might have lulled me to sleep easier."

"I like to throw on a guided meditation sometimes," Shane said, "but my mind wouldn't slow down tonight."

"But back to your question, I think the last time we had

anything was between our second and third flights. The coffee shop at the airport."

"Right. I had a couple doughnuts," he said, "but I'm pretty sure they're long gone by now."

Ruby opened the fridge, which was woefully bare, unless you needed some hot sauce or were interested in a sad little jar of mayonnaise. Shane was already checking out the cupboards, but from the way he was moving from one to the next, he wasn't having much luck either. She started opening cabinets from the opposite side, the situation more and more dire. Eventually they met in the middle, Ruby opening the final cabinet and Shane gasping, both reaching in for a miraculous bag of potato chips, their hands grazing.

"Sorry," Ruby said, glancing Shane's way.

It was the exact moment Shane also glanced Ruby's way, their faces suddenly close. Really close. Time seemed to stop, and Ruby realized their hands were still touching around the bag of chips. Shane's eyes flitted to Ruby's lips—just for a millisecond—but it was enough to make Ruby's breath hitch.

Was he thinking about kissing her? Did she want him to kiss her? Was this the longest moment in the history of the world two people touched hands in a cupboard and stood this close together?

The moment was so strange, yet so familiar.

Shane's head moved ever so slightly, maybe half an inch, but it was enough to get Ruby's heart racing. Her thumb brushed against his, the chip bag crinkling.

Everything slowed, the air growing heavy between them. Her body seemed to forget to perform its most basic duties, like a kind of magic in the little cottage was breathing for her. For them. They were about to break the rules. The past few days had been all about breaking the rules, but this was the one that meant the most. Still, she was having a hard time reminding herself to worry. She was having a hard time getting her brain to do anything.

And then, before she realized what she was doing, her head moved to meet him and his lips were on hers, and they were kissing hungrily...desperately. There was no thought. The world didn't drift away, exactly—more like an impenetrable bubble softly enclosed them, protecting them from the world outside that moment.

Shane's hand found its way to her waist ,and he squeezed, just a little, in a way he'd done so many times. A maneuver so achingly familiar that tears suddenly sprang behind Ruby's eyes—not because she was scared or sad, but because nothing had ever felt so much like home. The feeling was so strong it startled her, a snapshot of a memory so vivid and bright it could have been yesterday, pouring into her mind. Shane bringing her coffee to bed, just the way she liked it... cream, no sugar. A streak of sun slicing over them from the gap between the curtains. His hair an adorable disaster with one un-wrangleable chunk sticking straight out the left side. The smile he reserved just for her. She was able to melt into him until the memory passed, until something more urgent swirled deep inside her.

Her hand moved from the cupboard to his waist and his moved to pull her tighter, his other hand running up the length of her arm to her still-damp hair. He held her head as he grazed her chin, his stubble scraping delightfully up to her ear, then down her neck.

The heat in Ruby's belly intensified as she grasped onto him, trying to catch her breath. The air sucked out of the room as if it were on fire, the little cottage forgetting to breathe too.

And everything fell away. There were no swirling thoughts about the operation or whether she should even be there—there were no ideas about right and wrong at all. No more snapshots of the past. Just Shane and the way his hand was in her hair, making her feel so protected, the other one sliding its way around her body, electricity sparking with every millimeter until it finally came to rest on her lower back, and he pulled her even closer.

And then one thought niggled its way through to her conscious mind—the thought that this was the only place in the world she could completely lose control.

In Shane's arms.

She sighed at the reprieve of it—like a rest from the everyday of life, its frustrations and dark moments. But she also hated this feeling of not being able to follow her own rules, to make her own choices.

In truth, it was why she'd never let him get as close to her as he wanted to.

But the thought flew away, and she fell again. Fell into the oblivion of Shane.

"Oh, shit, sorry." The jarring voice came from out of nowhere.

Ruby jumped back and nearly let out a squeak, but Shane just straightened, reaching again for the bag of chips as if nothing out of the ordinary had been going on.

"Um, just needed a glass of water," Bug said, sheepish, even though it was Ruby and Shane who should have been the guilty-looking party.

"All yours," Shane said, stepping away from the cupboard/sink area and sitting at the dining table.

He opened the chips and held the bag out to Ruby, who was having a bit more trouble gathering herself than Shane was.

"Thanks, but I think I'm just going to go to bed," she said, suddenly panicked.

How could she have let things get so far? After all the years of trying to build back the broken pieces. Years trying to forget. And the past few days had been one big reminder. She wasn't sure she could survive losing everything all over again.

She could never let it happen again. She had to keep her distance.

Chapter 13

Shane didn't know what time he finally fell asleep, but it had been late. Way too late considering the pressure they'd be under today, but it wasn't like he could just turn his brain off. Thoughts of Ruby swirled—the way her hair felt under his hand, the way she'd leaned into him, so familiar, her skin cool from the night air contrasting against the warmth of her lips.

He wondered if it had all been a dream, but his lips were slightly raw. It had been real. She had been real, and he couldn't stop the smile that crept across his face.

He'd thought of Ruby so many times over the years. She was the one he compared all the others to, so often wondering if he'd ever get to see her again, and if it would live up to all the times he'd imagined having her back in his arms.

It had, and so much more.

But now it was early. Way too damn early. And someone was up in the kitchen, not making the slightest effort to keep the noise down. How anyone even found anything in the cupboards to prepare was beyond him, but soon the scent of coffee began to call to him, and he cracked one eye open.

The noise instigator was Ash, as bright and chipper and put-together as ever. A bit maddening, since it had partially been her snoring that had kept him up—he couldn't imagine what it must have been like for Ruby right inside the room with her.

He closed his eyes and rolled over, not quite ready to let go of the feeling, trying his damnedest to memorize every second of last night's encounter. The way Ruby looked as she came outside to the way she shot back the last of her bourbon…the way the bourbon lingered in their kiss.

Then it was Bug's turn to waltz into the room. "Bless the gods," he said, rummaging around. Shane heard him pouring coffee, his body panicking that he wasn't going to get any, and so he roused himself to a seated position, rubbing his face, wishing his eyes didn't feel like they would never fully open again. He needed that coffee badly, and he was ready to fight anyone who got in his way.

"Well, good morning, Sunshine," Bug said, chuckling a little. "Looks like the couch was about as comfortable as the lumpy bed in there."

"Oh, yeah," Shane said. "It seemed real hard to sleep what with you snoring like a pack of passed-out sailors."

"It really was quite something," Ash piped in.

Shane gaped at her. "Seriously? You were worse than he was."

"Very funny," Ash said, giving him a look. "I do not snore."

Shane stared at her. "You believe that, don't you?"

"Of course," Ash said, waving her hand like it was the end of the conversation.

Which made Shane chuckle. "Have you seriously never had a partner tell you you're like a freight train rumbling through a nitroglycerine plant?"

Ash tilted her head. "No, I have not."

He and Bug chuckled a bit, but then Bug's expression turned to worry. Like he was concerned he might offend her…or maybe he was worried for her—maybe she'd never had someone get close enough for that. Which frustrated Shane a bit, considering Bug would have been that person and more if Ash would ever lower whatever soaring standards she must have in order to give the guy a chance.

The silence had grown awkward by the time Ruby padded out of the bedroom in her usual uniform of the wrinkled T-shirt and shorts she liked to sleep in. He thought of the first time he saw her all those years ago in Max's office. He remembered thinking that her features were a mix of contradictions. An extraordinary mix of things that should have never been paired together—the dark brows and light eyes, the angled nose with the soft, rounded lips. Unique. Interesting. The most beautiful thing he'd ever seen.

She still was.

Though, Shane noticed, trying to hide his smirk, the new haircut did not do well with sleep—especially the restless kind of sleep Shane assumed she had. Not for the same reason as him, of course, but because they had such a massive day ahead of them. It was a good thing Ruby had the wig to wear, he thought, because he wasn't sure how that hair would ever be tamed again.

"What's going on?" Ruby asked, sensing the tension in the room.

"Nothing," Bug said, obviously not wanting to bring up Ash's sore spot all over again. "We're all just tired, that's all."

"I guarantee not one of you is as tired as I am. Please tell me there's coffee left," Ruby said, to which Ash just rolled her eyes.

Shane grabbed the coffeepot and held it out as Ruby found a mug. She caught his eye and smiled, which made Shane forget to watch what he was doing and nearly overflowed her cup. He smiled sheepishly, feeling nervous all of a sudden.

He got to work making a new pot, figuring they'd all need at least a second cup. Ruby cleared her throat and sat. Bug was looking ridiculous trying to pretend he wasn't sneaking glimpses of Ash every five seconds. Not that Shane could talk, since he was pretty much doing the same thing to Ruby. Which then made him feel like he was a useless fool, back in high school in his nothing hometown, trying to impress the cool new girl in school.

"We're going to have to get food on the way," Ash said. "With the last-minute change to the plan, we didn't have time to get stocked up here. Hopefully I'll have a chance to get a few things if we end up staying here again tonight."

"If we stay here tonight?" Ruby asked, with a heavy emphasis on the word *if*.

"I thought we were all out of alternate plans."

Ash shrugged. "We are, but we were before we found this place too."

Out of nowhere, a clunk sounded somewhere in the vicinity of the front door, making everyone jump.

The team leaped into defense mode, all moving at once.

"What the hell was that?" Ruby asked.

"Could have been a bird hitting a window or something," Bug said.

But Shane had a feeling it wasn't a bird. The noise was a deeper *thunk* than a bird hitting glass and was too convenient coming from the front porch. He moved toward the door, pulling a gun from the back of his pants, not entirely loving the way Ruby looked at him like she was disappointed. He knew she hated guns, but in this business, you'd have to be reckless not to have one nearby.

He eased over to the door and pushed the curtains on the tiny window aside just enough to peek outside. Nothing. He grabbed the knob, turning slowly, cracking it open half an inch. There was nothing there. But as he went to close the door again, his gaze landed on a small, flat package sitting neatly on the welcome mat. He thrust the door open, quickly and efficiently checking one way and then the next, his training kicking in.

After a quick circuit around the house, Shane going one

way and Bug the other, they determined that if someone had been there, they were long gone.

"There were no footsteps in the snow," Shane said, coming back into the cottage.

Ruby and Ash had already taken the package to the table.

"Could have been a drone," Bug said.

"Wouldn't we have heard if a drone flew overhead to drop it?" Ruby asked.

"Not necessarily," Bug said. "Some of the new tech has made some drones almost noiseless."

"That's…disturbing," Ruby said.

But Bug just tilted his head. "Or rather convenient. How do you think I get most of my surveillance footage?"

"Exactly. Disturbing," Ruby said, smiling to let him know she wasn't judging.

In a situation like the one the team was in, they all knew they had to use every advantage.

"Let me get some equipment to take a look at that. It could be dangerous," Bug said. Returning to the room a few moments later, Bug scanned the package with various techy gadgets. "No dangerous chemicals detected," he said, "and there's nothing electronic inside. Should be relatively safe."

Ash picked it up and gingerly opened it, the entire team holding their breath.

She pulled out several photographs and started leafing through, letting out a long sigh as she did. "Well, so much for staying here again tonight."

"What is it?" Ruby asked, pulling the pile from Ash's hands. "Shit," she said as she flipped, then handed them to Shane.

The pictures showed the four of them in the airport, taken some time in the minute or so from the time they met up to when they got in the car. The next one showed an aerial shot of the car driving down a long, deserted road. Then the cottage. The next photo was a night shot of the backyard sometime when Shane and Ruby had been drinking out on the patio.

The final shot was the real kicker.

Somehow the drone had flown low enough to get a shot of him and Ruby through the window. A twinge of panic ran through Shane, but it wasn't quite as strong as the twinge of desire that hit Shane hard, witnessing him and Ruby fully making out like that.

"Well, I guess we know why everything feels so awkward this morning," Ash said.

"We need to check on Max," Ruby said, pacing across the kitchen floor.

"We need to get out of here," Ash said.

Shane shook his head. "They've clearly known we've been here since the moment we stepped foot in the place. If they were going to do something to us, they would have done it by now."

"Bug, could you please pull up the feed of Max?" Ruby said, trying with everything in her to keep calm.

Bug grabbed a laptop from his room and sat at the table, bringing up the page.

Max looked tired, thin and had a small gash over his right eyebrow, but he was alive. Although the feed had no sound, he appeared to be giving his captors hell the way he was wagging his finger as he gave them a piece of his mind. Ruby smiled. She'd only had that finger-wag pointed at her a couple of times, but there was nothing Max was more known for. And he always wagged with love—except maybe in the case of these jackasses who were keeping him locked up. Which made Ruby smile even more.

But her smile faded. "They know who we are," she said.

A thick silence fell over the room. Back at Ruby's apartment, Ash had assured them these people had no idea who they were. They could contact Ash, but Ruby, Shane and Bug were safe.

Ruby's stomach churned. Through all of this, the most important thing had been to stay off the radar—especially now with her job at the museum. "Bug?" she said. "How likely is it that they've figured out who we are?"

Bug looked angry, and like he didn't want to answer her. "High," he said. "There's no way people who have the kind of tech we've been seeing don't have some kind of facial recognition. They probably had us cased in three minutes."

"Shit," Shane spat out, turning away.

"Now can we get out of here?" Ash said, checking the closest window.

"Are you kidding right now?" Ruby asked. "We just find out our identities have been compromised—my whole world is blowing up—and you just want to get back at it?"

Ash blew out a long breath. "I'm sorry, okay? They never tried to find out who the people on the team were before. They never cared as long as the job got done. I didn't think anything would be different this time around."

"Everything *is* different this time around, though," Ruby said. "I have a life this time around. They've stooped to kidnapping this time around. And don't even get me started on how none of us have any trust in you this time around. Not after Scotland."

Ash looked like she'd been slapped. Ruby almost felt bad, but the truth was Ash had failed them all on that job. And now Ruby felt twice as much pressure because of it.

She had to make sure she was doing her job, plus make sure Ash was doing hers too.

She had to have the team's back, but she had to have her own now too.

She had to think of every possible scenario before it happened so they wouldn't be surprised.

Ruby glanced at the photos spread out on the table, her eyes landing on the one of her and Shane in the kitchen.

She had to keep her damned head in the game more than ever.

Shane stepped over to her, but she put her hand up. She couldn't risk him touching her when she was feeling like this. Hell, she couldn't risk him touching her at all. What had she been thinking last night? This wasn't about putting things back the way they used to be; this was about getting in, getting out, getting Max and getting on with her life.

And that was not going to happen if she got tangled up in Shane all over again.

Shane put his hands down and took a step back, hurt crossing over his features. But he recovered quickly. "This sucks—I get that. And I know I don't have as much to lose as you or Bug do, but these guys know us now. The information is out, and there's nothing we can do about it."

Ruby knew everything he said was true, but her mind still whirled, hoping, praying, to find a way she could go back to believing her life was still hers. She was supposed to be able to go back when this was all done and not have to worry about looking over her shoulder.

But there was no going back from this.

"Fine. Let's get the hell out of here," she said.

They all went to pack up—not that they'd had much of a chance to unpack. Five minutes later they were headed to the car.

"Not to be the voice of doom or anything," Bug said, "but I think we have to assume we're going to be followed no matter where we go. I can ditch our tail if we can get back into a city, but I guess my question is, do we need to?"

"What do you mean?" Ruby asked.

"Do we need to ditch the tail? Because they already know most of our plans, so...does it matter if they're watching us?"

Ruby didn't like the thought of anyone watching her in any scenario, but she could see his point.

"I don't like the idea of a potential curveball," Ash said.

"I don't think any of us do," Shane said, "but we're on a time crunch and the more time we spend dealing with this thing that might not even be a threat, the less time we have to prepare for the actual job."

"But why send the photos?" Ash asked. "We would have never known they were watching."

"Maybe they want us to know they're watching," Ruby said, the idea coiling uneasily up her spine.

"Why?" Shane wondered. But no one had an answer for him.

They got in the car and drove off, no one saying a word for a long time. Snow had started to fall in light, fluffy flakes, and Ruby concentrated on the countryside. Even the views along the highway were stunning, mountains in the not so far distance, green peeking out here and there from the snowy wonderland.

If, after all this, she had to go into hiding, she wondered what life would be like living there. But no matter how beautiful her surroundings, the thought of having to hide away from everything she'd worked so hard for was painful. She'd finally found a place in life where she was comfortable. Where she was happy.

The snow fell harder.

Ash interrupted her thoughts, deciding it was time to get to work. "Okay, we all know the drill. Shane and Ruby, you're going in as waitstaff. Bug has already taken care of getting you on the list and they'll be expecting you. Bug's going to run surveillance and security remotely. We're hoping we can get close enough with a van without raising any suspicions, but you know what to do if we can't get away with it."

Bug nodded once and mumbled something under his breath.

Ruby could only imagine what kind of awkward position

Ash was willing to put Bug into. Once she had him waiting down a sewer shaft for hours so he could get a wireless feed into an exclusive apartment building in Chicago.

Of course, Ash never put herself into any danger. She was always off parked in front of some safe house or coffee shop somewhere, ready to rattle off instructions while the rest of them put themselves on the line.

It suddenly hit Ruby that Max wasn't going to be with them on this one. He was always in the thick of it with Ruby and Shane—sometimes as hired help at an event, but more often as one of the guests, able to pull off any persona. He had an indistinct coloring about him and was able to pull off any character—from a Middle Eastern business tycoon to royalty from an obscure island off the coast of the Mediterranean...hell, he'd once even pulled off posing as a high-powered rancher from Texas.

Ruby smiled, recalling how hard it was not to break character that time, what with his thick, twangy accent and hat that made him look much smaller than he was.

But her smile slowly faded as she remembered that the stakes had never been so high.

Chapter 14

The sky was ominous. Shane had hoped the storm the weather station was calling for would hold off for a few more hours, but that had been wishful thinking. As he got out of the car a few blocks from his destination, the snow covered him in an instant.

He let out a long sigh.

This was going to make things much more complicated. At least he was going to be indoors, he thought, hoping all would go as planned and there would be no need for some of the contingency plans.

He arrived at the temp agency a few minutes before Ruby. They needed to get to the event space as soon as possible, and people on staff would arrive hours before the guests. Shane and the team had spent the rest of the drive into the city going over the plan approximately four hundred and seventeen times. To be honest, Shane had found the whole thing a little excruciating. He knew how to do this—it was the one thing he was good at, and most of his part was usually improvised anyway. He was the one who caused distractions where distractions were needed. He was the one who charmed when charming was called for. He was the one who watched the room to make sure everything went the way it was supposed to. And to do whatever it took to fix it if something didn't.

The plan was simple, though of course it wouldn't be easy.

Get in, snatch the scepter, get out. And deal with about sixty-eight layers of security while they were at it. Easy peasy.

Ruby had the harder job, even though she'd disagree. She was the one who had to keep to the shadows, be invisible. Shane didn't think he could be invisible if he tried. And honestly, he didn't know how someone who looked like Ruby could ever fly under the radar either, but she got away with it every time. That was real acting. Not making eye contact. Not leaving a single memory in her wake. Just another unimportant person that witnesses would never be able to recall enough to give a good description. Ruby always said everything about her was average, but to Shane she was the least average person on the planet. She was everything, and he kicked himself every day for ever agreeing to keep things strictly casual with her.

He hated himself even more that he let her believe anyone else could ever measure up.

And last night with the bourbon, and the cottage, and the kiss, it had all felt like coming home again, even though he'd never stepped foot in the place before. He had a suspicion it wouldn't matter where in the world he was, Ruby would always be that home for him.

But she was past all that now. She had her new job, her new fancy apartment, her new life. And Shane didn't fit into that world. Still, the kiss meant there still had to be something there, didn't it?

But he didn't have time to think about it. He owed it to Max to focus on what he needed to focus on—to do what he did best and get his friend back.

He gave the woman checking the workers in his best smile. "Bryce Hudson," he said.

The woman's eyes sparkled. "An American," she said, looking him up and down. "Something tells me you're going to be a hit."

Shane was decent at accents, but he hadn't had as much

time to prepare as he would have liked. Normally he'd get to a country ahead of time and soak in as much language as he could, but with the time constraints, he decided to go with his regular accent. Besides, it was his job to stand out, and having a different accent than everyone else made it even easier.

"I try my best to provide great service," he said, his smile never faltering.

"I bet you do," the woman said suggestively.

Shane stood and smiled a bit longer, the woman just appreciating him for a while. It didn't make him uncomfortable, the way women sometimes acted around him, but he couldn't say he enjoyed it either. It was simply one of the tools in his arsenal that made him good at this. Finally, he cleared his throat. "So, uh, what now?"

The woman blinked as if coming back to the present. "Right." She consulted her list and checked his name off, running her pen along the page. "Server, okay, perfect. Head to the back room and find yourself a uniform. The servers are pretty simple, dark pants." She leaned back and took a good long look at his crotch. "Yup, those will do," she said, nodding. "Guess this isn't your first go around," she said appreciatively.

"No, ma'am, definitely not," he said, trying to seem appreciative right back.

"Okay, so find yourself a white collared shirt and an apron and wait with the others in the big room at the end of the hall."

"Sounds great, and thanks for all your help," he said, shooting her a wink for good measure.

"Oh, you are most certainly welcome," she said, turning to watch him walk away.

He turned to her once more and chuckled a little, acting like he loved the attention she was shooting his way. Thankfully another person showed up to check in and Shane could get on with his mission.

Once he was in the new shirt and fitting in nicely with the

rest of the waitstaff, he leaned against the wall to wait. Several people filed in, one after the other, but Shane kept his eyes open for just one.

He checked his watch. It wasn't like Ruby to be running this late. Or late at all, really. Inwardly, he groaned. If she didn't make it, he was not about to go on this job without her. She was the one everything depended upon. Sure, they all had their parts to play, but without Ruby, the job couldn't go on.

Beginning to pace, Shane checked his watch once more. Soon, the woman who had checked him in came into the room.

"Five minutes, everyone. And make sure you're put-together. This is an incredibly particular clientele, and they will notice if even a hair is out of place."

A few people moved to mirrors set up around the room, smoothing hair and straightening collars, while Shane wondered when he should call it. There was no way he was going if Ruby didn't make it. He paced a couple minutes more and decided he needed to make a break for it. Would it be easiest to fake being sick, or simply try to find a way to sneak out?

More importantly, where the hell was Ruby? he wondered, his stomach starting to feel out of sorts.

If he was going to do this, it had to be now, before the woman came back and wrangled him onto the bus transporting them to their destination.

He started to move.

Suddenly, a woman stepped in front of him, stopping him in his tracks.

"Oh, sorry," the woman said, looking into his eyes in a weirdly meaningful way.

Something about her voice tried to twig something in Shane's brain, but he couldn't quite place what it was.

"No problem," Shane said, about to move around her when he realized. "Oh, hey," he said, shocked at how different she looked.

Ruby had always been the master of disguise in their little group, but she had outdone herself this time. Shane had to give the black-haired, dark-lipsticked, glasses-wearing beauty one more glance to confirm it was her.

"Hey," she said back, pushing her glasses a little farther up the bridge of her nose.

"Wow," he said quietly, giving her a nod of approval and moving back into the room.

She nodded at him, more than a little amused.

Ruby hadn't been sure if she'd fly under the radar the way she wanted to, but the moment she spotted Shane, she knew. He had no idea who she was. And if he, the person who probably knew her best in the world, didn't know right away—a thought that caught her a bit off guard—nobody else would have a clue. The people watching them would likely figure it out soon enough, but if there was even a chance she could keep the element of surprise, she was going to damn well try to take it.

She boarded the bus along with the rest of the staff hired to work the party—everyone from kitchen staff, to waitstaff, to guys who must be additional security. She spent most of the bus ride trying to memorize each person and figure out how much of a threat they could potentially be, though she was very careful not to make eye contact. She knew how to not get noticed, and avoiding eye contact was rule number one.

Ruby used several tactics to disguise herself. She left her hair just a little messy, not enough to stand out, obviously, or to garner the attention of the managers, but just enough to look less put-together. Baggier clothes were another tool she used, but not too baggy—just enough that nothing hugged her figure, to give the appearance of "nothing to see here." She'd gone a little different with her makeup than she normally would, the dark lipstick and smoky eyes more likely to draw attention, not in a sexy Hollywood siren sort of way, but more like a mainstream goth if there was such a thing.

The overall effect was a sort of non-sexy, not quite girl next door. Just an "average, everyday nice person" kind of thing.

After she'd checked in, she kept to the edges of the room and didn't make any moves to try to talk to anyone...until, that was, it looked like Shane was about to bolt.

She loved the little thrill that had surged through her, realizing Shane didn't know she was there. The way he'd been pacing made her wonder, but she hadn't known for sure until she saw the recognition dawning in his eyes and she had to work hard not to break character and laugh, or, you know, gloat. But they were on the move now and she couldn't risk eye contact with Shane again.

They traveled by bus for several miles to the base of an unnamed mountain. On the ride, they'd been told to not ask questions, not bother the guests and well, basically, not talk to anyone. Once they arrived at the base, a large group was already there waiting. Ruby pulled the collar of her jacket up higher on her neck, thankful the wig she wore was helping keep her warm. The snow that had been falling in beautiful large flakes had turned icier, with smaller flakes driving through the wind. As they waited, guards searched through everyone's bags.

What seemed like hours later, though according to her watch had only been forty minutes, Ruby was grateful to finally enter the capsule that would transport them up the mountainside. She thought she'd been prepared for the gondola ride, but she had never been on one, and had never been a fan of heights. With the increasing winds, she was in for a bit more than she bargained for. At least she wasn't the only one who looked nervous as the large capsule that about fifteen of them were trapped in swayed slightly one way and then the other, jolting a bit whenever they crossed a support pole. At least Shane wasn't on the same gondola—he'd left on the one that departed about fifteen minutes before hers.

The woman seated beside her began to turn a little green around the edges and Ruby prayed she could keep it together until they got to the top. She couldn't imagine having to finish the ride after someone had lost their lunch in the small enclosure.

Ruby had never been so relieved to exit a space in her life, sucking in big gulps of air as her feet hit solid ground again.

Taking her first glance around the grounds, Ruby wondered how rich the people who owned it were. She'd been in plenty of mansions and grand houses before, but this place was next level. Straight ahead, an enormous building made mostly of glass loomed above, several stories high. She couldn't help but think it didn't have a whole lot of privacy. Of course, when you lived at the top of a mountain where the only ways in were a secure gondola or maybe a helicopter, privacy probably wasn't much of an issue.

Ruby did not like that their potential exits were so limited, but the views from the top of the mountain were perhaps more spectacular than anything she'd ever witnessed. She'd been in mountains before, but never this high up. Three-hundred-and-sixty-degree views of snow-capped mountains with nothing but trees and nature to hold her attention. Far below a river weaved lazily through the base of the mountains as if saying, *Whatever, dude, you just stand there, I'm happy to go around—I've got all the time in the world.* Despite all the things going on, Ruby found herself smiling, trying to take it all in.

Shivering and ducking her head against the wind, she began to move toward the house, but only got a few steps before a large man stopped her.

"Where do you think you're going?" he asked.

"Um, to the house to help get the place ready for the party," Ruby said, unsure why she had caught the man's attention—something she had decidedly not wanted to do.

"No, you wait."

Ruby stepped back into the group to wait for whatever was supposed to come next. At least she wasn't the only confused one, as the waitstaff in her group all glanced at each other for guidance, which of course no one had.

Soon another vehicle pulled up, smaller than a bus, with large tracks on it instead of wheels. Ruby wondered if the thing had climbed all the way up the mountain, or if it had come by some sort of giant military helicopter or something, causing her to wonder again just who these people were. The extravagance she'd seen on other jobs was starting to pale in comparison.

"Where are we going?" someone in the group asked as the machine jostled them along to their new destination.

A trickle of worry danced through Ruby's stomach. Wherever they were headed had not been on the blueprints of the complex. She'd memorized every outbuilding on there and they'd already left each of them behind. As they moved along the bumpy trail, small buildings—security huts—came into view every hundred meters or so. She could practically feel the rest of the group around her starting to wonder what the hell they had gotten themselves into. It was something she knew because she was feeling the exact same thing.

Finally, they came to another, more typical building, a single story, though the glass theme continued with large windows on three sides. When in Rome, Ruby supposed, or more accurately, when on a remote mountaintop. Her mind whirred with contingency plans, though there had been no discussion as to what they might do if the event was held in a location they knew nothing about.

But it wasn't like they could just back away. Max's life was at stake…and since the people holding him knew who they all were now, all of theirs were too.

Chapter 15

"How you doin', Bug?" Shane asked quietly.

The comms Bug had come up with were state-of-the-art, fitting into Shane's ear like one of those new hearing aids you could hardly see when a person was wearing it. With the thing buried so far in his ear, he had no idea how the team could hear him clearly without any muffling, but he could hear the rest of them as if they were right inside his head—which, he supposed, they kind of were—so he assumed they could hear him just as well.

"Oh, you know, just hanging around," Bug answered.

Shane could hear the wind that must have been swirling around Bug, who was apparently—and quite literally—hanging off the side of the mountain as they spoke. Bug was an experienced climber, but Shane couldn't begin to fathom how he'd gotten all his climbing equipment up there, let alone all the tech he'd need to hack into the security system and keep the team safe.

Of course, true to form, Bug already had the team fully connected to each other and was well on his way to breaking into the top-of-the-line security system.

There wasn't a whole lot for Shane to do at that moment and he felt a little guilty about it. His job—watching and waiting—always seemed a little lame compared to what the others were always doing. Sure, the team used to tell him he was the only person who could do what he did, but still, he kind of felt like a useless ball of, like, lint or something. Pretty lint, maybe, lint from a set of silky, shimmery sheets, but still lint. But he was a professional, and he had a job to do, even if he wondered whether his job even mattered much.

He fed Ash as much information as he could about the exits in the place, obvious and not so obvious places where they could potentially make an escape. As he spoke quietly, making sure no one spotted him talking to himself, he'd shoot the odd smile to some of the other waitstaff. He'd instinctively always known that making as many friends as possible—on a heist as much as in real life—was a good way to magically find additional contingency plans in case things went wrong. He was the "shit! things are going south" guy. The guy they hoped never to use but who was there if they needed them.

Fortunately—or perhaps unfortunately for Shane—the crew was careful, organized and practiced, so his talents did not often come into play.

"Figuring out everything okay, new guy?" a woman asked, sidling up to him.

Shane had been so focused on making sure he hadn't missed any potential exit points, he'd barely seen her coming until she was right in front of him.

"Oh, uh, yeah, I think so, thanks," he said, hopefully dazzling her with the smile he shot her way.

She smiled back. "You seem a little distracted there," the woman said. "Something on your mind? Fight with the girlfriend, perhaps?"

Shane was used to this kind of questioning. The not-so-subtle information dig, fishing to see if he was taken. His smile went from dazzling to a bit more playful. "No girlfriend at the moment," he said.

The girl arched one eyebrow. "Boyfriend?"

He chuckled a little. "No significant other of any kind," he clarified.

"Aw, sad," she said, not sounding at all like she thought it was sad as she slid a finger up his arm. "We'll have to see if we can do something about that."

He made his eyes dance as she turned to get back to work, well practiced at keeping a person interested without making any promises. His job wasn't just to get one person willing to help if need be, but ideally, all of them.

He got back to his own work—he'd been tasked with helping to set up the tables—and he laid down another set of cutlery as he continued to scope the place.

"Three large skylights could become a factor," he said once he was confident no one was close enough to hear.

"Got it," came Ash's voice over the comms.

Ash was stationed somewhere outside too. But Shane knew better than to think she'd be even close to hanging off the edge of a cliff. More likely, she'd found an unused vehicle or outbuilding to run operations from. He chuckled to himself, wondering if she was tucked into some snowplow or tractor somewhere.

"Okay, so I'm thinking our best window to grab the target is sometime during the auction. As of now, we don't know where they're holding the auction items, so we're going to have to play this by ear a little bit," Ash continued.

A sigh came over the comms. Ruby. She did not like to play anything by ear, always wanting to plan things out and take every possible outcome into consideration. Shane, on the other hand, started to get excited, his stomach even fluttering a little. This was where he shone—in the realm of the unknown. The realm where anything was possible. He had to fight the smile that wanted to slip across his face.

Shane could also practically hear the eye roll Ash was no doubt performing.

"Anyway," Ash continued, "our best bet will likely be immediately after the item is auctioned off and is leaving the stage. There will be plenty of security around the scepter, but a lot of them will be focused on other items as well. Ruby, Shane, see what you can find out about where the stage is going to be, and any potential routes the auction items will take on and off the stage."

"Got it," Shane said, still placing silverware.

The hardest part of a job was waiting for opportunities, or more accurately, keeping your cover while waiting for opportunities. But he continued to work until all the tables were set, his eyes scanning the room nonstop, waiting for anything that might be a clue as to where this whole thing was going to go down.

It turned out, in the end, it was pretty easy to spot when part of the crew set up a podium at the front of the room. It was an obvious place for the auction to be held, the view out the windows spectacular—though Shane wasn't sure how spectacular it would be once it got dark—but it was the place Shane had been most hoping it wouldn't be held. First, because he assumed that was the very window—and cliff—Bug was probably hanging off. Having an entire room full of people staring in that direction all night was not the best scenario. And second, because there was only one way to and from that area of the room—a single door off to the side.

He needed to see what was behind that door.

Luckily, the woman who'd checked him in hours ago was standing near the staging area. He thought it might be a good idea to remind her of his existence.

"How's everything going, boss?" he asked, shooting her his trademark dazzle.

She turned, a slight expression of annoyance crossing her face—until she saw who was talking, that was.

"Oh, hey," she said, her eyes brightening. "It's, uh, good, I think," she said, though she looked a little nervous.

"Is there anything I can do to help?" Shane asked. "You look kinda stressed."

She let out a long breath. "Well, I'm always stressed during a job, but this…well, this is a really big job."

"I kind of figured," Shane said, with a crooked smile. "Can't say as I've been to too many parties on the top of a mountain."

"And that's why everything has to be perfect." She started glancing around the room again, searching for any tiny thing potentially out of place.

"I get it," Shane said. "But don't worry. I can tell by the way you run things that this night is going to be spectacular."

She focused her attention back on him, giving him another once-over like she'd done back at the check-in table. "You know, I think I'd like you to cover these tables at the front," she said, motioning to a few tables nearby—the ones closest to the stage. "It couldn't hurt for everyone to get a good look at you."

"Oh, brother," a voice said deep inside his ear through the comms unit, and he fought the urge to say something back.

"Of course, anything you need, boss," he said. "I won't let you down."

Something crashed across the room, and she rushed off, but Shane had gotten what he needed. Being stationed at the front of the room would get him close to the auction, which meant being close to the scepter.

And close to the mysterious door that it would exit through.

Ruby watched as Shane flirted with every girl in the room—and a few of the guys too. The man was nothing if not a charmer. She kind of hated that she fell for his charms just as much as everyone else—hell, probably more—but the thing was, she knew him so much better than any of these people and, to be honest, he was so much more than just charm.

But she was angry with herself about last night. She could never let anything like that happen again. When this was all over, she could hopefully get back to her life, her real life, and leave it all behind. Shane would never leave the life behind.

He always said it was the only thing he was good at, even if Ruby knew better. Shane could do anything he wanted—it was just…the only thing he ever wanted was for things to go back to the way they were. Back to the con life.

Come on, Ruby, focus, she scolded herself. She was acting like some ridiculous kid with a schoolgirl crush. She hadn't even done this when she and Shane were dating, but something felt different now. Maybe she'd just been lonely the last few years.

That had to be it, she thought, happy she'd figured it out. Now she could get on with the matter at hand.

Find a way through that damned door at the side of the room. The team had to find out what was back there before the auction started or they'd have no chance. They needed to know what exits were beyond the door and come up with some kind of plan.

"I'm in the system," Bug said over the comms.

Finally. Ruby wasn't sure if it was because he was hanging off the side of a cliff, the fact that he hadn't been on the job for years or that security had been that hard to crack, but it had taken Bug way longer than usual to get in.

Not that it mattered. They were in now and could get down to some real work.

"Anything on the door at the front of the room?" Ruby asked, tucking a piece of hair behind her ear and covering her mouth to prevent her conversation being seen by a nearby staff member.

"Give me a sec," Bug said, with lightning-fast keystrokes tapping lightly in the background.

Ruby busied herself straightening a napkin here, or moving a water glass a fraction of an inch there.

"Shit," Bug finally said. "There's nothing on the plans. The door doesn't even exist in in the system."

"What does that mean?" Ruby wondered.

"It means they have all the priceless artifacts stowed away

in a place that doesn't exist and has no security. At least no security that ties into this system."

"So, there must be a separate security system."

Bug made a musing sound. "Smart," he said. "But not good for us."

"We need to find out what's behind that door," Ash said, her voice even more grating from practically right inside Ruby's brain.

She glanced over to see if Shane had any chance of getting near the door, but he was currently surrounded by not one, but three of the female waitstaff, apparently on some kind of break. There was a *lot* of giggling going on. She suppressed the urge to look toward the heavens. She couldn't be mad—he was doing what he was supposed to be doing. It was just that sometimes she wished she didn't have to watch it.

She focused on the view behind Shane, the miles and miles of sky, the enormous old trees, the pristine snow practically begging for someone to jump into it. Ruby wondered if that could potentially start a massive avalanche, which made her think of Bug out there on the mountainside, vulnerable and likely not having the best time of his life.

The least she could do was find a damn way through that door.

And then she saw it.

A tiny, but distinct smudge on the wall of glass. A small, single smudge, as if someone had touched the glass lightly, not with their whole hand, but just a light swipe of the tip of their finger. But it was enough to give Ruby an idea.

She headed back to the kitchen area, and in a back closet, found what she needed, then headed back toward the podium area.

"Just what do you think you're doing?" Madeline, the woman in charge of the staff, asked.

"Oh, sorry, I just noticed a smudge over there," she said,

pointing to the offending mark, "and thought I should give these windows a once-over." She held up the glass cleaner and paper towel as confirmation.

"Right," Madeline said. "Good catch." She nodded toward the windows, essentially giving her permission to go ahead with the task.

Ruby silently thanked whoever had been careless enough to leave the mark, starting at the far end of the window wall away from the door. She wanted a little time to blend into the background. When a person first starts doing something new, people take notice. But once you've been doing it for a few minutes, people tend to forget you're even there.

She polished away, moving closer and closer to the door, making sure to obliterate the offending smudge along the way. As she neared the door, she began to glance behind her, getting a sense of where everyone was and what they were doing. With the room pretty much ready to go, there were only a few people left in the room. Most of the staff had been given last-minute tasks in the kitchen and at the back of the building, where guests would be arriving soon.

Ruby was not going to get a better chance.

She slipped through the door, as confidently as she could. If she was going to get caught, she wanted to be able to play it off as a mistake. The good old, "oh, sorry, thought this might be the bathroom" trick, but there was no one behind the door. In fact, there wasn't a whole lot of anything behind the door besides a long, seemingly endless hallway.

"I'm in," Ruby said quietly, her whisper echoing off the walls of the dimly lit space.

"What do you see?" Bug asked.

"Nothing really. A hallway."

"Go down it if you can," he said, but Ruby was already well on her way.

Her footsteps echoed as she walked, a sense of urgency

and unease drifting through the air. At the end of the hall was another door, just as nondescript and ordinary as the one at the other end.

"It's another door," she whispered.

"Be careful," Bug said.

Ruby took a second to still her breath and steel her nerves. She hated going into things this unprepared. But she slipped the door open anyway.

And there was…nothing there. Just a cubicle of a room with large metal doors on the other side.

"It's an elevator," Ruby said. "And it looks like it only goes down."

"Do not go into that elevator," Ash said, her "do as I say" voice coming into full effect.

But she didn't have to say it. There were a lot of things Ruby was willing to do—risks that were worth it once you calculated out the potential outcomes. But jumping into an elevator and getting essentially swallowed into the depths of the earth with, likely, a bunch of highly trained security people on the other end, was not a risk she was willing to take.

She was pretty sure she couldn't just play it off as a search for the loo.

"I'll see what I can dig up," Bug said over the comms as Ruby did the only thing she could do.

Turned around and went back the way she'd come.

She made it about halfway when a sound made the hair on her arms stand up. A whirring, much like the sound an elevator might make.

She began to move a little faster, though she was nervous about making too much noise.

Just as she neared the door back to the event hall, a tiny ding sounded.

But she smiled—she was going to make it.

But the smile faded at warp speed when the door just a few feet ahead of her began to creak open.

Ruby frantically glanced around, but her glance only confirmed what she already knew.

There was nowhere to run, and definitely nowhere to hide.

Chapter 16

"Holy hell, Shane!" Ruby whisper-yelled.

Shane marveled at the way Ruby could look as angry as she did, yet was obviously also relieved. She frantically motioned for him to go back to the event area, then stormed past him as she reentered the large room.

"What the hell are you doing?" she whispered in a rather non-gentle manner over the comms.

Shane pretended to adjust a couple plates on the nearest table. "I just wanted to make sure you were okay," he replied quietly.

"I was perfectly fine until you opened that door and gave me a heart attack!"

"Sorry," Shane said, making sure his back was to Ruby before he smirked.

It was one of those moments when you absolutely couldn't laugh. But remembering the expression on Ruby's face as she spotted him, all deer in the headlights, it took every ounce of theater training he'd had not to fall apart.

A moment later, staff began to stream in from the kitchen area, led by the supervisor.

"Everyone get ready," the woman yelled, clapping her hands. "I've just been notified that guests are starting to arrive. These people are the elite of the elite, so tonight you must serve like you've never served before. They are used to luxury and the absolute best service, and it is time to rise to the challenge!"

Shane couldn't help but be impressed by the way she delivered her speech—the pep talk giving him a little surge of adrenaline, like he was about to perform a feat like no other.

"Due to the remote location, and the weather not fully cooperating, guests will arrive slowly, so it's up to us to keep them happy. Keep the drinks and hors d'oeuvres flowing at all times. Do what you can to enchant them, and let's make this the most unforgettable night of their lives."

Okay, maybe the use of the word *enchant* was a bit over the top, Shane thought, but he admired her passion. He could certainly see why she'd been hired for the event.

Shane grabbed a tray of champagne and took his position at the edge of the room.

Ash's voice came through his earpiece. "Well, team, we were hoping we'd be able to snag the target item once it left the stage after the auction, but with what Ruby just found out, that is going to be much more difficult than we'd anticipated. Essentially, if the scepter is not intercepted before it goes back through that door, the layout of the hallway—with a single way in and a single exit out—means we won't have a chance. Bottom line, we need to do this inside the auction room, so prepare for plan E."

Shane pulled in a fortifying breath. This was not how the team usually worked. They were a behind-the-scenes kind of crew—usually getting in and out and being long gone before anyone was the wiser. Plan E meant a lot more risk.

There was a small flurry of activity as two couples entered at the back of the room. The women shed their expensive fur coats. Shane hoped they were faux fur, but with this particular crowd, he had his doubts.

The sun was just beginning to set, casting a rosy hue across the snowy landscape, shades of pink breaking through the clouds as if it were a special effect created for the occasion.

Shane wondered if people with this kind of money might be able to do that.

But none of the people arriving even noticed. Maybe they saw spectacular sights every day, or maybe since they were surrounded by it at all times, they'd become immune to beauty.

The men were dressed in tuxedos and the women in fancy evening gowns, some sparkly, some shimmery, but all impeccable, like they'd been custom-made. Shane's fingers began to itch with all the jewels walking around the room. He imagined some of them were likely the kind of item the team would go after—valuable and illicit. Ruby's head must be exploding, her mind on fire, trying to pinpoint where some of the items belonged, which was most certainly not on the necks, wrists and ears of people in this room.

He tried to relax, but mostly he tried not to be obvious about the fact that he was watching Ruby like a hawk. Plan E meant he needed to run interference if anyone got in the way of her next steps. And judging by the way their supervisor had suddenly taken notice of Ruby, whose food tray was almost empty—an absolute no-no for the event—it was time to move.

He plastered on his most charming smile and beelined for the boss lady.

"Anything last-minute that needs to be done?" Shane asked, easing in front of the woman, blocking her view of Ruby.

He knew Ruby would pounce on the moment and be invisible within seconds, but he had to hold this woman's attention for at least that long, or things would get a lot trickier.

The woman blinked, startled that someone had just pretty much bounded in front of her, an angry expression flitting across her face, though fading when she noticed who it was.

"Ah, Bryce, right?"

"That's right, boss," he said, making his eyes light up like he was delighted she remembered his name.

"I think everything's under control for now," she said, tilting her head so she could gaze at him more suggestively. "But after this is all over, I wouldn't say no to a little help…relaxing." She grazed a finger along his forearm.

Shane pretended to be shocked, then smiled wider. "That sounds intriguing," he lied, wanting nothing more than to get back to work now that he had done his job with the boss lady.

"Just keep up the good work," she said, kind of peeking behind him. "Hey, did you see where that girl went?"

"What girl?"

"The kind of mousy one with the emo sort of style. Dark lipstick never looks very good on people with pale skin," she finished off, unnecessarily.

Shane shrugged. "Sorry, I don't think I've seen her," he said.

Shane headed back toward the front of the room smirking a little, since he could say it with 100 percent confidence: the boss lady was not going to see a mousy emo girl again today.

Ruby grabbed her bag out of the locker at the back end of the kitchen and headed to the lobby area. The waitstaff were not supposed to use the washrooms in this area, but if anyone questioned her on the way in, she was going to say she was inspecting them for cleanliness.

No one would be questioning her on the way out.

She made her way to the stall at the farthest end of the room and began rummaging through her bag. She used a premoistened makeup remover on her lips to get rid of the dark, almost black lipstick. Then she applied a more muted red color that made her more mainstream than the goth situation she'd had going on, maybe made her even a little sexy. Her lightly smoky eyes would work as they were, and as soon as she took off the dark glasses and dark wig and tousled her own short, brown hair, she looked very different from when she'd walked in.

Underneath the usual gum, lip glosses, wallet, phone, etc., Ruby pulled the small tab revealing the bag's false bottom. It was only about an inch and a half of space, but it was enough for what she needed. She pulled out a shimmery, slinky slip dress in some kind of magical material that didn't wrinkle, shrugging out of the white shirt and black pants she'd been wearing as a member of the staff. She slipped the dress over her head, clicked the four-inch stiletto heels onto her convertible shoes, which she'd previously been wearing as flats, and stuffed all her gear into the small backpack. She listened for a few moments to make sure the bathroom was empty, then exited the stall, tossing the bag into the trash, carrying only a small silk pouch with her lipstick and phone inside. If she needed proof of identity, anything she'd need could be found on the phone.

Ruby liked to be as prepared as possible for any job, always researching as much as she could find on collections and targets, and then researching some more, but her work before a job was nothing compared to Bug's. For every contingency plan, Bug had to do a ton of legwork. Honestly, she wasn't sure where he found time to sleep.

For this, plan E, Bug had set Ruby up with an entirely new identity—Gabrielle Le Croix, an art dealer with a reputation for getting her clients what they wanted…even if that meant going through less than proper channels. It wasn't a real reputation, of course. But when Bug did a job, he didn't half-ass it. Gabrielle was fully set up with months' worth of social media posts, a full website, misinformation planted on the dark web—which was where her reputation preceded her—as well as identity documents and banking information.

It was just one plan out of several, for one member of the team. Each of them had several identities they'd had to memorize since they didn't know which plan Ash would eventually decide to use. And Bug had to do all that setup.

"Ready," she said quietly into her comms.

"The room is almost full," came Shane's voice in reply.

It was time to move. With her new disguise, Ruby was posing as a guest at the party—it was too risky to have both her and Shane waiting the tables at the front of the room.

As the guests filed in, Shane made sure a seat at the table closest to the stage would remain free. Ruby never could understand how he did it—she would certainly never be able to—but Shane always got the job done. If he said he could do something, which, incidentally, almost always required convincing people of things, it would happen without fail. It was one of the things she admired most about him—the ability to charm someone even if they knew you were charming them, which somehow made them respect him more. It was what he had done to her.

"The auction's set to begin in ten," Ash said in Ruby's ear.

Ruby stepped from the restroom as if she'd been there all along, and strolled into the auction room as if she was always meant to be there and didn't have a care in the world.

She did, of course, have a lot of cares in the world, but this was what their training with Max had been all about. Becoming someone else, if only for a short period of time.

In the background, Ruby's brain was going a mile a minute, taking in every face, noting details of clothes, seating arrangements...who was mingling with who. She didn't recognize any faces but knew it was inevitable that some of their names had come across her desk, either in her legitimate position at the museum, or before.

These were people who were not on the up-and-up. Or, if they were, they didn't have an issue with obtaining things through means that were not on the up-and-up. These were not good people. They were people who took advantage of others. People who made their living on tricks and schemes. They were crooks and scoundrels.

And as she walked straight to the front of the room, Ruby knew she had to be the most cunning of them all.

Chapter 17

It didn't matter how many times he'd seen Ruby enter a room, the sight of her always took his breath away. And that was when she *wasn't* dressed in a sexy formal evening gown, looking like she just walked out of the pages of *Vogue*. And okay, he hadn't read a whole lot of *Vogue* lately, but if the women in those pages looked anything like Ruby did in that moment, it was no wonder the magazine was still popular after all these years.

She'd gone back to the short hair, which shouldn't have been as sexy as it was, but the way it guided his eyes down to her bare shoulders, to the soft angles of her collarbone, nearly undid him. She so rarely wore clothes that showed off her body, but as she sauntered in—radiant, sultry, confident—the dress she wore clung to her body in a way that made Shane feel like he was seeing her for the first time all over again.

He wasn't supposed to stare. He wasn't supposed to draw attention to himself in any way. And most importantly, he wasn't supposed to draw attention to Ruby, but he was having a hard time keeping his eyes to himself. A quick glance around the room told him he wasn't the only one with greedy eyes, though, so he hoped he hadn't appeared too obvious.

He had to admit, he felt his ego blowing up a little, remembering he'd recently had his lips on those sultry ones that every man in the room—and probably plenty of women—wanted to feel under theirs.

"Okay, steady, people," Ash said over comms, as if she could read Shane's mind.

He blinked back to the task at hand—none of this was going to work if Ruby didn't get the seat she needed at the front of the room. He straightened the place setting at the last empty chair at the table at the front—the one he'd been carefully ensuring stayed empty by blocking it whenever a solo person was eyeing it up. He'd even snaked a half-empty glass of wine from one of the other guests, giving her a fresh one, of course, and set the lipstick-stained glass at the seat to make it look as if it was taken.

He whisked the wineglass away, leaving a pristine, untouched space for Ruby, turning away from the table as she approached as if he'd never been there at all. She sat without skipping a beat as if it had been her seat all along. And with the way she was oozing confidence, nobody would have dared question her.

For a while, Shane did the job he was hired—or rather, set up in a computer system by Bug—to do. He had three tables assigned to him—the staff plentiful enough to ensure the guests were well taken care of—and he was good at serving them. Smiling and flirting a little when the moment called for it, and being as invisible as possible when it didn't. He took Ruby's drink order, but besides that, kept an especially low profile at her table.

There wasn't a whole lot of chitchat at Ruby's table, but Shane did overhear her introduce herself as Gabrielle Le Croix, an alias he hadn't heard before. Bug must have gone all out, burning the midnight oil to set up the profiles for the job. Which, given the short amount of time they'd had to prepare, must have been exhausting. He thought about him out there on the side of the mountain.

"How you doin', Bug?" he asked.

"Oh, you know, just getting the job done," he said, his voice much more cheerful than Shane's would have been in the same situation, that was for sure.

"You always do, man," Shane said quietly.

"The auction should start in less than five." Ash's voice came into his ear, and he picked up his pace to deliver the last of his drinks.

Boss lady had been adamant that every person had a full drink when the auction began—they were still going to give the guests what they wanted as the auction proceeded, but they wanted as few disruptions as possible. Nothing was more annoying than bidding on a priceless item you'd been coveting for years while trying to peek around a server. Or at least that was what the boss lady would have them imagine.

Soon, movement began near the front of the room as a few people began to file through the door at the side of the staging area—the one where Ruby had taken the long stroll to the dead-end elevator. The hall of no return, as Shane had begun calling it in his mind.

He moved to the side of the room, not far from the door.

"The scepter won't be up for a while. It's one of the premiere items in the catalog, so it's likely to be auctioned near the end of the night," Ash said.

Shane settled in to wait, ready to move only when someone at one of his tables needed a drink cleared or a new one brought to them. Otherwise, he was doing his best to be invisible, though he couldn't help but notice boss lady was definitely shooting him a glance every now and then. If the heist didn't go down as planned for whatever reason, he was going to have a lot of backpedaling to get out of his implied after-evening plans with her.

"The first item up for bids is a portrait of..." the auctioneer began at the front of the room, though Shane tuned him out pretty fast.

The evening passed without a hitch other than Shane taking a few sneak peeks at Ruby, confident everyone's attention would be mostly on the auction area. Just like Ruby's was, who appeared rapt with interest as each new thing up for grabs rolled out. Truthfully, she was likely legitimately intrigued by each piece up for sale, no doubt knowing everything about each item as if it were her job to know. Which, he supposed, it was. He wondered what kind of intel she was tucking away in that big brain of hers to take back to her job at the museum.

His heart sank at the thought. After all this was done, everyone would go back to their normal lives and Shane would be left right back where he'd been. Unhappy and bored.

He shook his head at himself. He had a good life, more than good. Privileged, really, and he felt like a jackass for feeling sorry for himself, but he just didn't know how much more of all that he could take. His life had just felt so…purposeless since the team had disbanded after Scotland.

And for the first time in years, even though the situation with Max was terrifying, he finally felt like himself again.

He just wished it could stay this way forever.

The next auction item was wheeled into the room and the place fell silent.

The scepter…casting a spell over the room. People held their breath. Mouths dropped open slightly. Hearts forgot to beat.

Until the auctioneer quietly, almost reverently, cleared his throat, giving a few details about the scepter in a whispery voice.

Even Shane was impressed. The scepter was larger than he imagined, though he didn't know if it was actually larger than what he'd thought, or if it just somehow commanded all the attention in the room.

"Let's begin," the auctioneer said, and a flurry of activity began.

It was clear this was the item everyone was interested in. Of course it was. Why wouldn't the job get another step more complicated? Everything about this job had been as if they were honey and complications were flies.

The bidding was almost as fast and furious as Shane's increasing heart rate, as he waited for his signal. If they didn't hurry and make a move, they would lose their window, and with the bidding easing past sixty million, they couldn't possibly have much longer.

He glanced at Ruby, who was starting to look concerned, clearly thinking the same thing.

And then the room went black.

Without missing a beat, Shane moved toward the front of the room, the rest of the people still looking around, wondering what was going on. Shane ignored them all and headed for Ruby, who was headed for the scepter, but not as fast as the guard who'd been standing much closer to it than she had.

But the team had anticipated this.

Shane ran to the man, who, with lightning-fast reflexes, had secured the scepter into its case and was already turning toward the door he'd brought the scepter in from.

The door of no return.

But Ruby had one arm around the strap of the cylindrical case, fighting him for it with everything she had in her. The man looked incredibly strong, but distracted by Ruby, he'd left his back wide-open for attack. Shane pulled him into a sleeper hold, pulling him gently to the floor as his world went black. The guard wouldn't be out for long, but with any luck, the team would be long gone before he woke up.

Shane watched as Ruby was already on the move toward their planned exit—through the kitchen—then suddenly stopped, her eyes going wide as people began to stream from their exit point.

Rather serious people with guns.

A few women screamed and people began to get up from their tables, fleeing toward the main entrance to the hall.

"What the hell?" Shane heard Ruby say over comms, though she was already turning around, heading back toward him, surprisingly fast in her fancy heels.

The team had contingency plans prepared, of course, and Shane moved to exit strategy number two—the one near the back on the south wall. But no matter what plan they decided to change to, his job was always the same. Protect the target. In this plan, it was his job to clear a path though the panicking crowd for Ruby and the scepter. But the target—the scepter—was not his focus. It never was.

His real mission would always be to protect Ruby.

They'd only made it a few steps before he realized people with guns were streaming in from the back door as well.

Thoughts flew through Shane's head, so fast it almost made him dizzy. Who were these guys? What if the people with guns were the good guys? Some kind of raid or something? But what would that mean for the team? And worse, what would it mean for Max? There were no other exits besides the main one already fully crowed with panicked auction guests.

The whole scene took only a moment to survey and Shane realized they only had one option left.

And it was an option he decidedly did not like.

The door of no return.

Ruby knew even before Shane tilted his head to signal her, they had no choice. They had to go through the one door they absolutely could not go through. To do so was to head directly into the belly of the beast, and they didn't even know what that beast might do when they got there.

But they went for it anyway. If they could get through, and by some miracle, there wasn't anyone directly on the other side, they might be able to buy themselves a few seconds to formulate a plan. Not that the team had been able to formulate a plan in the hour or so since they found out about the surprise door, but still, desperate measures and all that.

Maybe they'd get lucky.

Not that Ruby believed in luck. She believed in having a plan, in knowing every possible outcome, in not taking uncalculated risks.

But she ran anyway, fueled by instinct and desperation, a combination she hated relying on. Shane was maybe the only thing keeping her levelheaded. If anyone could find their way out of a situation like this, it was him. He was the king of improv. The one who figured ways out of impossible situations. And as she flung open the door they weren't supposed to go through, she was heartened to see that the dim hallway was empty. With any luck it would stay that way.

Then again, there was the whole not believing in luck conundrum.

Still, the empty hall had stoked her hopes, if only a little, and as she ran, she slipped the canvas handle of the scepter case over her head and began scanning for ways out that she might have missed before. Maybe a vent, a drain in the floor…anything.

Shane was still back at the door. "It has a lock!" he yelled, and Ruby's hope rose even higher. It wouldn't keep an army of guys with guns out for long, but it might buy them another few seconds.

As Shane moved toward her, Ruby took a moment to remove the heels from her convertible shoes again—they were the universe's gift to heel-wearers—knowing the next few minutes could come down to a foot race, and if that were to happen, she needed as much help as she could get.

Shane reached her, breathing almost as hard as she was, and placed his forehead on hers, holding on to her arms, instantly calming her. "We're going to figure this out," he said.

And somehow Ruby found the courage to believe him. "Okay, let's go," she said, and they both ran toward the door where Ruby had found the elevator earlier.

It was the only choice they had, so for the moment, it was a no-brainer.

"Maybe there won't be too many of them," Shane said.

"Yeah, maybe," Ruby replied, though she knew it was wishful thinking.

Moments later, a new noise echoed in the long hallway as footsteps began pounding from the direction they were headed. Someone—or by the sound of it, several someones—must have been alerted and were headed straight toward them.

On instinct, Ruby and Shane turned around, running back toward the door that led to the auction. It was pointless, Ruby knew—there was nothing good waiting on the other side for them—but they did it anyway, completely out of options once again.

In a few more steps, the auction door burst open as the people on the other side finally busted through the lock.

Ruby and Shane halted to a dead stop, clutching each other.

The people on either side of them stopped as well, the space becoming eerily quiet.

For a moment no one moved. Ruby didn't dare to even breathe.

As they stood like statues, even the air stilled in anticipation of what was to come. Ruby and Shane were out of options, simply waiting for the people on either side to close in. It's strange what goes through a person's mind in situations like that. Scenarios should have been playing through Ruby's mind…options, contingencies, desperate choices. But in that moment, when every one of those scenarios had already been exhausted, everything calmed. For just a second, she was so incredibly present. More present and aware than perhaps she'd ever been—the massive glass wall before her providing the most spectacular and surreal view she might ever see in her lifetime.

A large clearing with massive, snow-dusted trees and mountain peaks in the background, the clouds parting just enough to showcase the moon hanging huge above, casting its light onto the snow and creating millions of tiny sparkles, like she was standing in front of a sea of jewels. Ruby blinked—once, twice, an intense calm settling deep into her bones.

And then, the world exploded.

Well, the glass wall in front of her anyway.

Ruby ducked as Shane leaped on top of her, shielding her with his body as glass rained down.

The word *run!* invaded her head as Ruby glanced up and saw a sight that made a tiny ray of hope burst into a big, shining sun ball of it.

Ash—her arms outstretched to either side, guns in each hand, shooting in either direction.

Ruby had zero time to think, only able to react as she ran out into the open air of the night, Shane alongside her.

Ash paused her firing just long enough to let them pass, then what seemed like a thousand shots rang out, though Ruby wasn't sure if they were only from Ash's gun, or if they were from the other people too. So she just ran harder, her only thought to get away.

Unfortunately, that getaway was heading straight toward the cliff's edge of a damn mountain.

But she kept running, Shane a bit ahead of her, though he was not leaving her behind. The world grew darker, the light from the building receding as they neared the edge.

Just before she was about to go over, Ruby risked one glance back toward the building. It was lit up like a beacon in the dark and her stomach seized as she caught one last, horrific sight.

Ash. Standing in the hall she and Shane had just vacated.

Ash. Pummeled by bullets from either side, her body convulsing with shot after shot.

Ruby choked on a scream as she jumped over the edge.

Chapter 18

The ground slipped away from Shane's feet. Where once it was solid underneath him, now there was only air. Thoughts that slip through one's mind when confronted with an impossible situation can be a strange thing, such as wondering if he looked like one of those cartoon characters who hang in the air for a moment until they realize they're about to fall. Because that was sort of what it felt like. The ground beneath his feet, then what seemed like a legitimate moment of hang time before he began to plummet into the darkness.

Shane didn't even know when to expect the landing. It felt both like a long time and no time at all before he felt the impact, the landing at odds with itself, too, feeling both unbelievably hard, yet somehow strangely soft. When he blinked his eyes open, he was buried almost completely in snow.

Digging his way out, he couldn't see Ruby anywhere. But then a groan, both inside his ear and somewhere off to his right reached him. He ran toward the spot, where Ruby was beginning to climb her way out. He reached for her and pulled her the rest of the way, realizing she must be freezing in her tiny dress.

"Hey, guys," a voice said, in echo, like Ruby's groan had been.

Shane turned where only a few yards away stood Bug, grinning like the cat that ate the canary. "How's it going?"

Shane couldn't help but grin back. "Oh, you know, just dropping in for a chat."

Bug chuckled. "Wanna get out of here?" he asked, motioning to the three snowmobiles he had waiting.

During the hours Shane and Ruby had spent setting up inside, and before he'd hacked into security, Bug had been running snowmobiles up the mountain with Ash. First, bringing two sleds up, then taking one back down together to retrieve the third.

His equipment was already packed up and he was ready to go.

"Hell yes," Shane said, moving toward the nearest sled.

"Wait," Bug said, a note of worry slipping into his voice. "Where's Ash?"

Shane glanced back up the mountainside, only realizing then that she hadn't jumped behind them. He glanced at Ruby, but the expression on her face did not make him feel better.

"Guys," Bug said again, his voice sounding panicked and angry all of a sudden.

But then a sound came over the comms. Someone clearing their throat. "I'm right behind you."

Ash.

Relief flooded over Bug's face. "We're not going without you," he said.

"You get that scepter the hell out of here now. That's an order," she said, though something didn't sound quite right with her voice.

"I said I'm right behind you. Go, go, go!"

There was a pause while the three of them stood on that mountain in the dead of night. It felt like one of those moments where if you didn't make the right choice, life would never be the same. Although, Shane thought, maybe life was never going to be the same either way.

He glanced at Ruby, who had tears in her eyes, and he knew. It was too late for Ash.

Shane swallowed the giant lump trying to choke off his breath.

Ruby wasn't facing Bug, so there might still be a chance.

"Well, you heard the woman," he said, his voice overcompensating, sounding more cheerful than he'd meant for it to. "Time to go."

They didn't have time for much besides stepping into heavy winter boots and shrugging into the large parkas Bug had waiting for them. Ruby looked a bit ridiculous in her evening gown and parka, but she must have been grateful to have a little protection from the cold.

Shane climbed onto the closest sled and Ruby climbed on behind him so they could leave the last sled for Ash.

"Come on, man," Shane said, starting up the engine. "You have to lead us. We don't know the way down."

Bug stood for a moment, but then noises above them—yelling...more gunshots—seemed to shock him into a decision. "Yeah, okay, we're going, boss," he said.

"Good," said Ash. "I'll be right there," and Shane knew it would be the last time he would hear her voice.

Bug revved his machine and took off down the hill, slowly at first, and then picking up speed as the mountain began to flatten out a little.

If the situation hadn't been so terrible, Shane would have had a lot of fun on that sled. The untouched snow, the crisp air, the gorgeous woman hanging on tightly to his sides. The beauty of that place on that night almost took his breath away, but he also couldn't stop thinking about Ash, and how the hell they were going to get Bug to safety.

If the people at the top of the mountain had sleds of their own, the tracks they left as they went would lead the bad guys, and their guns, straight to them.

Once at the bottom of the mountain, the team drove the

snowmobiles the final few miles through the valley, all the way to their car, which was waiting on the edge of the city.

"Where the hell is she? She should have caught up to us by now," Bug said, his eyes straining through the darkness toward the direction they'd come.

Shane got off his snowmobile and removed his helmet. "Bug, I don't think she's coming."

The look that flashed in Bug's eyes was pure anger, a hatred Shane didn't think Bug had in him. He moved toward Shane like he was about to hit him.

"Bug!" Ruby yelled, sort of jumping in front of Shane.

Bug could have pushed Ruby to the side without much effort but seeing her made something change behind his eyes. He was still angry, but now there was a fear there too. And then his face crumpled completely. "What do you mean you don't think she's coming?" His voice was pitched higher than normal, as he fought the rage and desperation inside him.

Then Bug turned and faced out toward the mountains again. "We have to go back," he said, a few tears breaking free.

"Bug," Ruby said, moving around to stand in front of him. "She's gone. I'm so sorry, but she's gone. I saw it. There's no way she could have survived."

Bug glanced between Ruby and Shane. "And you assholes let me leave?"

His fist balled up again and he started to pace.

"I'm sorry, Bug," Ruby said again. "There was nothing any of us could do—if there was, we would have done it. She… she sacrificed herself to save us. To save Max," she finished, her voice trailing to a whisper.

Bug broke down then, and they both guided him into the back seat of the car. Ruby climbed in beside him, turning to Shane. "We have to get out of here."

She was right. The snowmobile tracks led directly to the car. The plan had been to ditch the machines there and once in the car, their tracks would blend in with the thousands of others on the street. The team knew they were still being tracked by the people who had Max, but that wasn't their concern at the moment. The real concern was the group from the auction, wanting their precious item back.

They had to find a safe place to go.

But Ash had been the only one who knew what the plan was.

"Just get off the street," Ruby said. "Find a hotel or something. I have cash in my suitcase."

Thank goodness they had their luggage, Ruby thought. She was definitely done wearing slinky evening gowns for a while. The giant snow boots could go too—they were fine for plowing across the side of a mountain, but were a bit much for regular city activity. She rummaged in her case for some pants, socks and shoes, all while keeping one arm around Bug.

Shane drove for a long time. Thankfully, the city was relatively large and should be easy to get lost in, at least for a little while to give them a chance to regroup. In movies and on TV, people are always headed to seedy little motels to hide, but that wasn't the best way to get lost in a sea of people. A person wanted to go to a regular old motel where any family would stay if they wanted to remain unnoticed. The people working in low-end places were always on edge, sizing people up as they approached—always vigilant for their own safety. But the people working in some random Holiday Inn in the suburbs rarely had to think about anything like that, which made them less suspicious, and more likely to forget they even had an interaction with you.

Still, to be on the safe side, Ruby made Shane go in and get a room so they could lie low and figure out their next move, while she and Bug stayed in the car. Using his key card at a back entrance, Ruby and Bug snuck in without anyone the wiser, and the people at the front desk thought Shane was just like any other solo businessman in town for the night.

For a while, Ruby and Shane left Bug alone with his grief. Ruby couldn't imagine what it must be like to lose someone you cared so much about without ever having told them your real feelings. She glanced at Shane. Her feelings were a lot more than she'd ever told him about, too, but she was going to have to live with the fact that it was going to stay that way.

She closed her eyes, centering herself. They had to get the scepter to the people who had Max and get Max back. They owed at least that much to Ash.

She approached Bug cautiously. He'd been staring at the same spot on the wall for the past twenty minutes. Ruby wasn't sure if he'd even blinked.

"Bug?" she said, her voice soothing. "I know you don't want to think about this right now, but do you know anything about what the next steps were supposed to be? Do you know how we're supposed to get Max back?"

Bug turned his head and his glossed-over eyes took a moment to focus on her. "Next steps?"

"Yeah, like was there a meeting place where we were supposed to swap the scepter for Max?"

He blinked. "Oh, I don't know," he said, turning his head back to the wall, looking like he was thinking hard. "She never told me," he finished, his voice cracking a little.

Ruby had hoped he might elaborate, but Bug fell silent again.

She went over to Shane on the other side of the room. It wasn't a large room, so Bug would be able to hear them talking, but Ruby didn't think he was paying attention to them. There was too much going on in his mind.

"What do we do?" Shane asked. "Why the hell didn't she tell any of us what the exchange detail were?"

Ruby shrugged. "Was there ever a job where you knew

any of those details? I sure as hell never knew anything like that. The exchanges were always done after the fact, after you and I had already done our jobs and were on our way home."

Shane ran his hands through his hair. "How did we not see that this could happen?"

Ruby was surprised she'd never thought of it either. Ash had always just been so…reliable. She never imagined Ash, of all people, getting hurt during a job. She certainly hadn't imagined her ever storming in with guns blazing either, though. It was so unlike her. Which sparked a whole new pang of guilt inside Ruby. She didn't think Ash would ever be the one to sacrifice herself, but she was willing to do it for Max. God… Max. How were they ever going to tell him?

Well, she realized, they sure as heck weren't going to tell him anything if they didn't get him back.

"Bug?" Ruby said, moving back across the room. "What about The Vault? Do you think the info would be in there? Can you get access to Ash's Vault?"

He shook his head. "I designed it so no one could access it, not even me. All of your Vaults are like that. Unless…" He trailed off, his gaze going back to the wall.

"Unless what, Bug?"

Bug shook his head a little, blinking again. "I might be able to if I can get to her secured network at her place."

"Her place? Like her house?"

Bug nodded absently, only half paying attention to the conversation.

"I think we should wait here. We know these guys are watching us. They must know we have the scepter. If we can't get to them, they'll come to us, won't they?"

"Maybe," Ruby said, a new idea forming. "We need to check on Max. We had to be careful about it before, right? Because we were worried they would find us too easily, so why don't we just do that?"

"Yes!" Shane said, already pulling his laptop out of his bag.

Bug didn't seem to be paying attention at all.

Shane typed in the web address, the hotel Wi-Fi taking forever to load the live feed.

And then finally, there he was on the screen. Max looked a whole lot less feisty than the last time they'd checked in on him, but he didn't look any worse for the wear. Other than the fact that he looked exhausted, Ruby thought. Then again, she imagined she didn't seem too chipper at the moment either.

"He looks miserable," she said.

"I think we all look miserable right now," Shane said. "At least he's still alive." Realizing what he'd said, Shane glanced to Bug. "I'm sorry, man, I didn't mean to be insensitive."

Bug glanced up and sort of half smiled. "I'm glad he's still alive too. I mean, if they didn't mess with the feed, that is."

"Mess with the feed?" Ruby asked.

Bug tilted his head. "In theory, they could have filmed him before and could be running the feed in a loop."

Ruby's eyes grew wide, which Bug noticed, coming a bit more back to himself instead of lost in his thoughts and grief.

"But there's no reason they would want to. We still have what they want—for them, nothing has changed."

Ruby's stomach knotted, hating that these people were getting what they wanted while their entire team was being ripped apart.

"Is there a way to check to make sure?" Shane asked.

"Probably," Bug said, struggling to ease himself to a standing position.

He moved toward the computer and sat down hard in the chair, like his body had grown twelve times heavier in the past few hours. But then he just sat there, staring.

Ruby was beginning to wonder if he was searching the feed itself for clues, until he finally spoke.

"I know where this is."

Ruby searched the room on the screen. Max was sitting on a sofa that could be any old regular sofa that might be in anyone's house. The place was decorated minimally—a few books on the coffee table, a lamp in the corner, a couple prints of insignias on the walls. Nothing that would make the place particularly stand out.

"Where is it?" she asked.

"It's Ash's place."

So many thoughts whirled through Ruby's mind. She wondered if Ash had information on the team filed away at her house, including their identities. Was she going to have to upend her life and move, go into hiding and start all over again? Was this always going to be the meeting place, or were these people trying to mess with their heads?

There was only one thing she knew for sure—they were headed back home.

Chapter 19

Shane, Ruby and Bug had one big problem.

The scepter.

"It's not like we can just carry a massive, stolen scepter through airport security with no one batting an eye," Shane pointed out.

"What about disguising it in some kind of case? Like maybe a guitar case or something."

Bug was shaking his head. "Airport security is designed to pick up on things like that. Even if we had the time to construct something that might have a chance at working, it's still taking a huge risk."

"Is there any way to get fake documentation to get it through?" Bug asked.

This time it was Ruby's turn to shake her head. "It's almost impossible to get anything to appear authentic without help from a world-class forger, and something like that would take time. Plus, there's a good chance the scepter is already in antiquities databases. The people who work customs at airports are trained to spot these things."

"Whatever we do, time is definitely not something we have to spare," Shane said.

"Ugh, this is so frustrating," Ruby said. "I never even considered we'd have to find a way to get this thing back home. I thought we'd make the trade for Max somewhere over here."

She began to pace. Shane didn't know what was going on

inside that magnificent mind of hers, but he could tell she was worried, and if she was worried, they all needed to be worried. Bug was a computer and tech genius, but strategy had never been his thing. Ruby, on the other hand, could give Ash a run for her money any day, and Shane sometimes wondered if Scotland would have turned out very differently had Ruby been in charge.

But then, she stopped pacing, which worried Shane even more.

He went to her, putting his hands on her arms, just below her shoulders. It had taken everything he'd had in him not to react to her, not to focus only on her when they'd been in character, but now they were back to being themselves, and Shane was tired of pretending.

She stiffened, but didn't move away.

"Talk to me, what are you thinking?" he asked.

"I don't know what I'm thinking," she said. "A million things, and none of them feel like the right choice. Every possible scenario ends up with someone getting hurt."

"Just…stop thinking about the scepter for a second." He tried to pull her into a hug, but she pushed him away.

"This can't happen again," she said.

Bug shifted his position on the edge of the bed. Shane had almost forgotten he was there. Christ, here he was trying to get closer to Ruby right after the poor guy had just lost the love of his life. Not to mention that love was also a good friend of his too.

God, he was a selfish asshole. It was just that having this time with Ruby again had made him realize one thing. Nothing mattered without her.

He gently pulled Ruby out into the hall. "Can we please talk about this?" he asked.

She closed her eyes and tilted her head upward. "There's nothing to talk about, Shane."

"Ruby, last night—"

"Please," she whispered. "We can't go there."

"Why the hell not? What's stopping us?"

Ruby shook her head, like she was struggling with what to say. "I just… We have other things to figure out," she said.

Shane's shoulders fell. She didn't even want to talk about them—about the two of them being together again.

A woman came out of a room down the hall and shot them a strange expression. Shane supposed they did look a little out of sorts, after being chased down a mountain and all.

Shane smiled at the woman, who gave them a wide berth as she passed.

"I won't be able to think about anything else until this is taken care of," Ruby said, quieter.

"It will be fine. I'll carry it through the airport and—"

Ruby cut him off. "Don't be stupid. You know that isn't an option."

"If we can just hide it somehow, put it in a case like you said…"

She was shaking her head more now. "No." Ruby finally looked up at him then. "It wouldn't work. No crew in the world would take that chance. The likelihood of getting caught is like, 95 percent, and the consequences of getting caught means game over. Whoever is holding that thing will be put away for years."

"Maybe it's worth it for Max," he said.

"If we get caught, it's over for Max." Ruby still shook her head, like the whole situation was just impossible.

Which, he supposed, it was.

"Can you take care of the flights home? Just get us on a plane first thing in the morning. I'll be back in a couple hours."

"What do you mean you'll be back in a couple hours? It's the middle of the night."

"It's not even midnight," she said, as if that made it any better.

"Exactly," Shane said.

"I'm fine," she said. "It'll be fine."

She grabbed the scepter on her way out.

"What are you doing with that?" he asked.

"I'm taking care of our problem," she said, and walked away.

Shane wanted nothing more than to follow, but he knew if he did, it would just delay whatever it was she was going to do. He knew he would never stop her. Once Ruby put her mind to something, there was no holding her back.

Shane had a feeling whatever it was she was about to do, it was the only chance they had.

He also had a feeling it was a very bad decision.

Ruby purchased a burner phone to check in on a couple of old friends in the area.

An hour later, she was seated across a diner booth from Jessica Weber, a colleague who worked for a renowned national museum in Zurich. They'd never met in person, but Jessica had been instrumental in a few of Ruby's overseas transactions with her job.

Jessica was taller than Ruby had imagined, although it was a bit challenging to tell height from a small profile picture on the internet. She'd been incredibly helpful to Ruby over the years and Ruby hoped she could trust Jessica to do what needed to be done as quietly as possible.

"I'm so sorry to have to meet at such an inconvenient hour," Ruby said.

Jessica waved the comment away. "It's fine. So much of my job is working with museums and galleries all over the world—I'm used to working all hours of the day," she said, her smile warm and friendly.

"Thanks so much for meeting me."

"Of course, it's great to finally meet you in person. And I must say, you certainly have my interest piqued."

Ruby took a deep breath, gathering courage for what she was about to propose. If anything went wrong here—if Ruby had miscalculated, and Jessica wasn't the ally Ruby hoped she would be—the whole thing could be over, and Max might be gone forever.

She let out the breath slowly, stalling. "I have a favor to ask."

"Of course," Jessica said, as if it were no big deal.

Except the favor *was* going to be a very big deal, potentially landing the two of them in hot water. There wasn't much question Ruby would be in hot water after all this was over, but she hoped she wouldn't take Jessica down with her.

"I need to get an artifact back to the States."

Jessica shrugged. "Sure, easy. I can fill out the paperwork and ship it out in the morning," she said, though curiosity crossed her face, like she wasn't sure why they might be meeting at a diner in the middle of the night for something so insignificant.

Ruby cleared her throat. "So, the thing is, it's not just any artifact. I've…uh…" Ruby wasn't sure how to word the next part. "I've recovered a stolen artifact, and, well, there could potentially be some controversy over how it was obtained."

Jessica began to nod. "Well, since you've invited me down here at this hour, I'm going to go ahead and assume there might be some…fudging that needs to be done with the documents?" She raised an eyebrow, though Ruby couldn't tell if it was one of those intrigued "ooh, this is interesting" eyebrow raises, or more of a scolding, looking down on her kind of a situation.

Ruby was suddenly starting to worry about the decision to contact Jessica. She barely knew the woman and had called her based on nothing but instinct. And maybe a little desperation.

"Maybe this wasn't such a good idea," Ruby said.

Jessica put a hand up to stop her. "I know we don't know each other well, but I'm honored you trust me. I'm going to need a whole lot more information before I agree to do this, but I'm willing to hear you out."

Ruby relaxed her shoulders a bit. "Thank you," she said. "And just know I wouldn't be here if it weren't a potentially life-or-death situation."

Jessica leaned forward a bit. "Are you in some sort of danger?"

Ruby shook her head. "I don't think so—at least not yet. But someone who is very important to me is, and this is the only way to get him back."

Jessica nodded as if it all made perfect sense. Which it absolutely didn't, but she'd obviously seen a thing or two in her day.

Ruby started in on the story about the auction. She didn't tell Jessica every detail behind what the team had to do to get the scepter, or why, but Jessica was a smart woman. She understood if Ruby didn't give her certain details, it was out of protection for her.

"Can I see what it is?" Jessica asked, and Ruby handed over the case without question.

Jessica opened the end of the case and pulled the scepter partially out, her eyes going wide. "This is quite the find," she said.

Ruby wasn't sure if Jessica knew the full history of the scepter, or if she could simply see the value from the jewels and gold, but she closed the case back up, giving a quick glance behind her.

"You can see why I wanted to find someone I trusted and who knows how to handle this particular type of item," Ruby said.

Jessica nodded. "I'll do it," she said.

"Really?" Ruby asked. "It's a big ask."

"It is," Jessica said, "and I also know you're the one putting your neck on the line for this. My part it simply filling out a few forms based on information you've given me and having an artifact sent overseas. In my job, this is what happens every day."

"There are risks, though," Ruby said.

Jessica nodded. "There are. And I'm willing to stick my neck out a little for someone who has helped me so much over the past few years. But I'm also going to mitigate my risk. I'll put down on the paperwork what you've told me. I don't know how the artifact came into your hands, and so I will simply leave that part out. If I'm questioned about it later, I'll explain just that—that I don't know."

"They could say you didn't do your due diligence," Ruby said, not sure why she was playing the devil's advocate.

"They could, and I'll simply say that wasn't the important part of our meeting. I believe an artifact like this needs to be back on the record books, and the true owners deserve to be found. It's my position that retrieving these types of items back from…less than legitimate sources is far more important than specifically how they were retrieved in the first place. My integrity wouldn't allow me to let the piece get lost to history yet again."

Ruby's whole body relaxed. "I knew you were the right person to call. That's exactly how I feel too."

Chapter 20

Shane was uncharacteristically anxious as he went through airport security, even though he was doing nothing wrong. Other than, you know, using a false passport—but he'd done that a hundred times over the years and not once had he been this nervous.

Maybe he was just on edge in general.

Things had been…tense with Ruby ever since she left to go on her secret errand in the middle of the night, and she still hadn't let him know what she'd done with the scepter. She'd come back and fallen into a deep sleep. Thankfully, Bug had also gotten a few hours of sleep, albeit restless, but sleep had eluded Shane. There was just too much to think about, though if he was being honest with himself, most of those thoughts centered around Ruby.

Even in that moment, it felt like they were miles apart, though they couldn't be sitting much closer together than they were—side by side in the economy section of an airplane.

"We won't have the, um, thing back right away," Ruby said, surprising Shane. She'd hardly talked to him all morning. "And we can't get Max back without it."

Shane nodded. "They must know we wouldn't have been able to bring it through when we came back."

"That's what I keep thinking about. Why would they want to do the trade back home? It doesn't make any sense."

"Unless the people who want it live there," Shane said. "Maybe that's the whole reason behind all this. It might have been much easier just to buy it at the auction if they wanted it that badly. These people don't strike me as being hard up for cash."

Ruby was the one nodding now. Shane could tell her thoughts were flowing fast. "What if they… Shit," she finished, looking a little wild.

"What if they what?" Shane asked. "Wait, what did you do to get it sent back?"

"Nothing, it's fine. Don't worry about it," she said, though Shane did not think it was fine at all.

If there wasn't anything to worry about, Ruby would just tell them how she was getting the scepter back. The fact that she wasn't was making Shane more uneasy by the second.

"We'll still have to go to Ash's place," Ruby said, more to herself than Shane, but Shane was going to take every opportunity to keep her talking.

Maybe he could figure out what was going on before it all blew up in their faces.

"Of course, we have to," he said. "It's the last place we know they had Max."

"Yeah," Ruby agreed, "but he won't be there anymore. We were too far away, they've had too long to move him."

"Probably, but I'm still going to hope."

"Even if he was still there, we don't have the scep—" She cleared her throat. "We don't have the thing to trade."

Shane leaned back into his seat and sighed. "You're thinking this was all set up from the beginning, aren't you?"

"It had crossed my mind," Ruby said.

"Ash would never do that to us." Shane leaned his head out into the aisle to make sure Bug wasn't listening to their conversation.

Ruby shrugged. "It wouldn't really have been *us*, though, would it? Just me."

Shane shook his head. "Unless..."

"What?" Ruby asked.

"Unless she wanted to get the team back together. She knew she'd never be able to convince you, but if you lost all your other opportunities, then maybe."

"I guess she didn't know me as well as she hoped she did, then," Ruby said. "I would never go back to that life. Never."

"Was it really so bad?" Shane asked.

"Yes."

They sat in silence for a long time. Shane was hurt Ruby thought of their old life—the only part of his life worth anything—as something she regretted. As something bad.

And yeah, Shane got that they were doing things that weren't on the right side of the law, but in the end, they were on the side of what was right.

"Look," Ruby finally said, her voice softer. "I'm not saying it was all bad. Obviously, there was a lot of good that came out of those days. But I'm sorry, I could never go back."

"I understand," Shane said, "I do. But so much of it was incredible—the excitement, the adventure...you."

He swore Ruby's neck turned a little red.

Her voice was still quiet. "All of that stuff was good...great, even. But my anxiety about getting caught just grew and grew until it consumed me. I could never go back again. These last few days have only confirmed it."

"I'm sorry," Shane said, though he wasn't sure what, exactly, he was sorry for.

It just felt like he was responsible for some part of it.

She shook her head a little, as if to say, *Don't be sorry*, but the conversation drifted off. There was so much to say, but Shane couldn't seem to find a way to say any of it.

Because of the time difference, it was still early afternoon when they landed, though Shane couldn't remember the last time he'd been so tired. It was a huge inconvenience, especially considering how much he traveled, but he'd never been able to sleep on a plane. He was happy Ruby didn't suffer from the same condition, but her tiny snores only flooded his thoughts with memories of lying side by side with her through the rest of the flight.

After landing, the three of them went straight from the airport to Ash's condo.

Shane was surprised when they pulled up to the building. It was just a normal apartment-style building in an average part of town. He'd always imagined Ash living the high life in some luxury place in the trendiest part of town, and this was just…so plain.

No fancy shops on the bottom floor, no doorman to greet them, just a regular old buzzer and lock on the door. It was the perfect place to hide in plain sight—he just never thought Ash would settle for something so ordinary. The building was on a fairly busy street, so the trio moved around to the back.

Bug checked for security cameras before Shane made quick work of the lock on the back door.

"There's probably more to this place than meets the eye," Bug said. "I wish I'd paid more attention the last time I was here."

"Why were you here?" Shane couldn't help but ask.

It was a question he'd been wondering since the moment they'd seen the feed and Bug recognized the place.

"Ash reached out to me about a year ago. Had me do a little freelance work for her."

Shane raised an eyebrow. "Was she still in the business?"

Bug shrugged. "I didn't ask a lot of questions. Just got in, did the work and got out."

Shane knew better than to push. Bug was a professional. He

wasn't about to spill Ash's secrets, even if she wasn't around anymore to be upset.

Bug led the way upstairs. More surprises. The condo wasn't even on the top floor. Then again, it wouldn't have been keeping with the hiding-in-plain-sight thing if it had been. Every person in the building would know who lived on the top floor, and Ash certainly wouldn't have wanted to be in that spotlight. Shane began to wonder if this was just a shell apartment Ash got mail sent to or something. He just couldn't picture her there. She was more of an "own her own private island hideaway" sort of person.

Shane put his lockpicking skills to work once again when they reached her door. "Heads up, everyone, we know they've been here. Could still be here."

He turned the knob and pushed the door.

As expected, the place was deserted.

Once inside, they split up, Bug heading off doing his techy thing, and Ruby headed straight for the art hanging on the walls. Shane had never seen her do that before, but considering their former occupation, maybe Ash had some particularly interesting pieces.

Shane went for a den area off the main living area. If Ash had worked out of this place, this was where she would have had her office. There was a laptop on the desk, but Shane thought that was best left for Bug. He began to sift through the few papers next to the computer.

It didn't take long before he found something he knew was from the kidnappers. The reason he knew this was because it had his name on it. It had Ruby and Bug's name on it too. But it didn't have Ash's.

Which meant they knew she was gone. It wasn't surprising, but it made Shane angry. Max's captors were watching them and he hated it. Worse, it felt like they were messing with them.

"Guys!" he yelled.

Ruby and Bug came to the doorway.

"I found something," he said, and turned the page around for them to see.

Saturday, 2 p.m.—
Market Square Beside the Church

"Well, that seems pretty clear," Ruby said, immediately thinking back to the last time she'd been in the market square.

Her mind was already running through scenarios about what could happen given how crowded the area would be that time in the afternoon on the market's busiest day. It was a smart place for the exchange with so many variables in play. Her brain wouldn't stop running through the possibilities until she'd exhausted each and every one at least three times.

"I'll scope the place out before we meet tomorrow," Bug said. "Make sure there are no surprises."

Ruby nodded. "Okay, good. Thank you," she said, though she knew there was no way to plan for every potential surprise that could be thrown their way.

"I'll get the scepter back. Let's meet up at Bug's place before we go," Ruby said.

"I can come with you," Shane said.

Ruby's heart gave a little tug, but she shook her head. "I need to do this on my own."

"Ruby," he said, frustrated. "You don't always have to do everything on your own."

She smiled a sad smile. "I know," she said, even though she wasn't sure if she believed it. "But I have to do this one on my own. Trying to sneak you in with me would make it a thousand times harder."

He tilted his head in confusion, but thankfully didn't question her.

Ruby went home, showered and changed into her best work

suit—a gray striped pantsuit that always made her feel like she belonged in the world-renowned museum. She was unstoppable in that suit.

At least she hoped she'd be.

She arrived at work after the place closed. With any luck, most of the employees would have gone home and the ones who hadn't would just think she was working late. They'd all know her face, though hopefully they wouldn't know she was supposed to be on vacation.

She paused at the top of the steps before she made her way in. This was the moment when everything was about to change. After she walked through those doors, there would be no going back.

But she knew she was going to do it anyway. She owed that much, at least, to Max.

She took a deep breath and used her key card to unlock the door and let herself in.

Her heels clicked more loudly than seemed possible in the quiet of the building. On Fridays, everyone was so ready for the weekend they usually sprinted out of there after work. Tomorrow the place would be bustling with museumgoers again, but for now, the place was a ghost town.

She made her way to the basement—the most secure area of the building, where the most valuable items that weren't on current display were stored.

"Hey, Dave," she said as she approached the man on duty at the secure locker.

Ruby knew he'd be there. Dave was always there after hours—the place manned by trained security 24/7.

"Ruby! I haven't seen you in ages. You burning the midnight oil today?" Dave smiled. He was an easy guy to like, and she suddenly wondered if she would see him again. "What can I do for you?" he asked.

"There should have been a high-priority package sent from

Zurich in my name," she said. "I was hoping to do some preliminary screening of it before I left for the weekend."

Dave started typing into the computer. "Yup, looks like it just got here this afternoon," he said.

He rolled his office chair back and went down one of the shelf-lined halls to retrieve the scepter.

Ruby held her breath until he slid the package under the cage window. "Key card and punch code, please. You know the drill," he said, winking.

"I sure do," Ruby said, hating that his day was going to become a lot more hellish later on, and that it would be her fault. "See you in a bit."

"I'll be here," he said, turning his focus back to his book and giving her a little salute.

Ruby went to her office and pulled her gym bag out of her small closet, emptying its contents onto the closet floor, closing the door behind her. Footsteps made their way down the hallway toward her office, and she scrambled to shove the scepter and bag under her desk.

"Ruby! What are you doing here?" Barb, her boss asked, poking her head around the door.

"Hey!" Ruby said, a bit too enthusiastically. *Dial it down*, she scolded herself. *You're supposed to be a professional.* "Yeah, just got back a bit early and thought I'd come in and see if there were any emergencies or quick to-dos to tackle, so Monday wouldn't be such a nightmare." She made a goofy face that was supposed to convey that Mondays after vacation were almost not worth going on vacation for.

"You do have quite a bit piled up there." Barb motioned to the pile of papers, mail and a few packages, then shooting her a goofy face back, which warmed Ruby's heart. "That one looks fun," she said, pointing to a large box on the pile.

Ruby nodded. "I think I'll leave it until Monday," Ruby said. "It'll give me something to look forward to."

"Smart," Barb said, turning to leave. "Have a good week-end." She raised her hand in a wave as she walked away.

It struck Ruby that over the past three years, Barb had become more than just her boss. She had become a friend. Ruby was going to miss the after-work drinks on paydays, the Monday-morning catch-ups about the weekend, the two-hour chats in the middle of the day about whatever scandal was going on in the world of priceless artifacts.

Ruby was going to miss this whole life, really.

She carefully packed her gym bag with a very specific item not meant for the gym and walked out of the museum for the last time.

Chapter 21

Shane spent the next morning staked out on the roof of a building across the street from the meeting point at the market square. After the sleepless flight, his body had finally given out; he'd drifted off early, which meant he woke up early too. The restlessness kicked in quickly, since he knew what they had to do later that day.

"Be prepared for anything" had always been the team's motto, which Shane used to hate—he was the one whom they depended on in case they needed to improvise, after all. But after Scotland, he'd come around to the idea.

And so, instead of pacing around his rental place, he went to check things out. Scope the area for potential hazards and find areas they could potentially use for contingencies in case things didn't go according to plan.

When he arrived, the place had been quiet—a single car rolling through the square in the entire first hour of his stake-out. But soon, city workers came to cordon off the street and vendors started to set up their wares. Folks were unpacking boxes of homemade jellies and jams alongside artists with dozens of canvases, and booths filled with graphic T-shirts popped up beside farm-fresh produce. The street was a bustle of activity and Shane began to get overwhelmed with all the variables at play.

He slowed his breathing. There was no way their small team

would be able to account for every possibility, so it was no use trying to determine how it would all go down. Ruby was better at that sort of thinking, and Shane had to focus on what he did best. Trust his instincts. They had never failed him before.

Other than Scotland.

He still didn't know how he hadn't seen it coming. The girl, the daughter who'd come home from college, had been such a surprise. Ash had been so sure no one would be home. Still, he should have felt a presence…should have heard something sooner. By the time he heard the gun being cocked, it was too late. She was already shooting. He would never forget the look in her eyes—the fear.

Focus, Shane.

He wasn't going to do anyone on the team any good if he couldn't stop thinking about how he wished everything had gone differently that horrible day three years ago.

Shane made his way to ground level and tried to blend in with the rest of the people at the market. The busiest time—midmorning—had already come and gone as he'd watched from above, and now the crowd thinned for the lunch hour, but it would pick up again soon enough, just in time to make things more complicated for the exchange.

He waited until a bench freed up, then sat to wait. To watch.

Forty minutes later, Bug sat down heavily beside him. There was no point in trying to hide that they were working together anymore. The people who had Max had been onto them since the beginning.

The thought sparked…something in Shane's brain, though he wasn't sure what bothered him exactly, or what it might mean. There was just…a weirdness about it all.

He shook the thought from his head. He was just being paranoid.

"How are you doing, man?" Shane asked.

"Not great," Bug said.

Bug had always been a man of few words, and Shane got the feeling he was going to be a man of even fewer words for a while. Ash had meant so much to Bug, and Shane couldn't imagine what it must be like for him. He wasn't sure what was worse—stumbling into the love of your life and taking it for granted like Shane had with Ruby, or pining after someone for years but being too scared to do anything about it.

"I'm so sorry," Shane said again.

"I know," Bug replied, the words pained but heartfelt, like he did understand Shane wanted to help him but didn't know how.

A short while later, Shane spotted Ruby coming up the block, the now familiar scepter case slung over her shoulder. He watched as she approached, glancing in every direction, but appearing completely natural as she did it. To the outside world, she could have been carrying anything in the case—a rolled up canvas, or perhaps some blueprints for an architect she was interning for. No one would have guessed she was sauntering along with a priceless artifact. She appeared relaxed, calm, not suspicious in the slightest, and Shane was the only one who noticed she was on high alert.

"Hey," she said, smiling as she approached, hugging both Shane and Bug as they stood to greet her as if they were any old friends meeting for lunch or a drink.

"Good to see you," Shane said, loudly enough for the people in the vicinity to hear.

It was a perfect spot for the trio to meet. Anywhere else, one or all of them may have stood out, but in a trendy neighborhood where everyone was trying their hardest to put on a persona of some sort, a biker dude, a guy who could easily blend in with a Hollywood crowd, and a small woman dressed plainly with sunglasses and a ball cap didn't stand out as much as a person might think.

They chatted as if they hadn't seen each other in years—

maybe old high school friends having a mini-reunion—until two o'clock neared and Ruby said quietly, "Heads up, guys, we're getting close to the time."

They continued to make small talk, each one of them facing a different direction, watching closely past each other as the tension rose by the second.

Shane tried not to check his watch constantly, but it was a struggle. It was like time had slowed with the anticipation, like he could feel each individual millisecond tick by.

"I've got someone coming this way up the alley," Ruby said quietly.

Shane glanced to his right, where, sure enough, a shadowy figure was making their way toward the group. "I see him," he said.

Bug visibly stiffened, his training not working as well as it should be. It was always harder to stay in character when your emotions were humming so close to the surface.

"Hey, guys," the stranger said as if he approached, clapping Bug's shoulder as if they were all old friends.

Shane had to hand it to the guy, blending right into the ruse they had going, confirming they'd been watching them for a while.

Ruby gripped tighter to the strap of the case.

"Ready to head out?" the man asked.

Shane cleared his throat, plastering on a smile. "Where are we headed?"

"It's just through the alley," the man said, not missing a beat.

Shane, Ruby and Bug glanced at each other, questioning. None of them loved that they were about to be led down a secluded alleyway, but what choice did they have?

"Great!" Shane finally said, his acting slipping a little with his overenthusiasm, as the three of them followed the stranger into the unknown.

* * *

Ruby didn't want to call attention to the case on her back, but she couldn't stop checking the strap every twenty seconds or so to make sure it was still there. The scepter was relatively heavy, and she would have noticed if it suddenly wasn't there, but she was having a little trouble controlling her impulses. There was so much at stake. They'd already lost one member of the team, and Ruby wasn't sure if she'd be able to handle it if they lost Max too.

Thankfully, she had Shane in front of her and Bug at her back, both protecting the case just as intently as she was.

Near the end of the alley, the guy made a surprise move toward a door at the back of the church.

"Really? The church?" Shane said, as the man ushered them through.

The guy shrugged, surprisingly congenial about the whole exchange. "As good a place as any," he said, grinning.

Ruby hated entering dark spaces. The precious seconds it took for eyes to adjust felt like a lifetime in a dangerous situation. The best advantage was always knowing what was going to happen, and making sure the people on the other side of the equation didn't.

Ruby hated being on the wrong side of the equation.

The man led them up a steep set of stairs and into the large congregation area. It was strangely eerie walking through an empty church, different from other gathering spaces with its pews, hymnbooks and pulpit up at the front. But perhaps most strange was the way the stained glass windows reaching to the high ceiling bathed them in multicolored light, making the moment seem even more surreal.

He led them out of the main area toward another doorway, opening it to reveal a small room—perhaps the place where the minister waited until it was time to start the service.

And in the middle of that small room was Max, tied to a chair and gagged, but alive, though his head was tilted downward as if he was trying to sleep.

Ruby's heart leaped and she tried to rush to him. "Max!"

"Not so fast," the man who'd led them there said, putting his arm out to stop Ruby from charging in.

"The case?" he said, raising an eyebrow, almost as if he thought it was mildly amusing that she'd forgotten.

Ruby pulled the strap over her head and practically shoved the thing in his hands.

As if coming out of a dream, Max raised his head slowly as Ruby rushed to him, Shane and Bug following close behind.

At first Max looked confused, like he hadn't expected anyone to come for him, let alone his former students and coconspirators. But he blinked out of his confusion and his eyes went wide, almost as if he was scared—like he didn't want them there.

And then there were footsteps, coming from just outside the same doorway the three of them had just come through. Heels—high heels—clicking on the tile floor.

And there was something familiar about the cadence of the walk that made Ruby's stomach seize.

Shane was working on Max's restraints, and Bug worked to untie the cloth wrapped around his mouth. As the fabric loosened its grip, three desperate words escaped from their mentor's mouth. "It's a trap—"

Still crouching, Ruby had just enough time to twist and face the doorway as a person she thought she'd never see again came into crystal clear view, framed in the center of the ornate doorway as if she'd designed her reveal to be as dramatic as possible.

Ash.

And the look on her face, so satisfied—a smirk of knowing she'd outsmarted them all alongside a sparkle of pity behind her eyes, no doubt thinking they were a bunch of gullible doorknobs. The man, who had already opened the case and was in the process of pulling out the scepter, handed Ash the case.

Thoughts whirled through Ruby's head. She'd felt all along something had been off, but she'd never imagined her old teammate, a person she'd been so close with, would do this to her. And yeah, maybe she and Ash hadn't always seen eye to eye, and she could accept that maybe she'd be less than loyal to her, but to Shane and Max? And especially Bug?

A strangled, shocked sound escaped from behind her as Bug began to understand what had happened. Ruby couldn't bear to look at his face. He deserved privacy in that dagger-to-the-heart moment.

Ruby wanted to lunge at her. She'd never been prone to physical violence, but something about the smug expression on Ash's face sent her into a rage like she'd never felt before.

But all she could do was whisper, "Why?"

Ash tilted her smug head to somehow look even smugger and began to pace in front of the two guys she had holding guns on them.

Ruby knew Shane was already trying to work out how he was going to take the two of them down so they could get to Ash, but since it was exceedingly risky to go after guys with guns already pointed at them, she also knew he wasn't going to come up with anything.

Ash no doubt knew it, too, just sauntering around like she'd won the damned lottery. If, you know, the lottery had been rigged and she was the mastermind of it all who liked to toot her own horn.

"Well," Ash said, drawing the word out as if to make sure everyone was listening, "turns out the scepter belongs to me."

Ruby squinted her eyes. "It was stolen from a family in Switzerland in World War I."

Ash nodded. "Exactly. My family."

Ruby knew there had been something familiar about the prints of insignias in Ash's apartment. The crest on the scepter was so similar… Of course, all family crests looked a bit the same, but still, Ruby was a professional. She knew something about them was off. She just hadn't put the pieces together.

How could I have missed that?

"If the scepter belonged to your family all along, why didn't you just go through the proper channels?" Shane asked.

"The scepter was already on the black market," Ash said, as if they were missing a few brain cells. "It was about to be sold again to some new unknown person. I'd finally just found it. I couldn't risk it going underground, to possibly never see it again."

Ash pulled the scepter farther out, the jewels glinting in the light of the room. Her gaze seemed almost hungry, as if she was about to swallow the damned thing.

"So, you used us to do your dirty work," Ruby said.

"Well, at first I thought I only needed Shane and Bug," she said, shooting Bug a wink.

The poor guy looked like he was trying to fight tears. He still hadn't said a word since the moment Ash had strolled in, still alive. Ruby admired his restraint. Or maybe it was simply shock.

"But then there was the question of getting it home," Ash continued. "I knew it would be impossible to smuggle it into the country. And that's when I realized Ruby had the perfect way to do it for me."

Acid rose in Ruby's throat.

"Of course, asking you to give up your entire career wasn't going to work, so that's when I came up with the idea of getting Max involved too."

Ruby breathed hard through her nostrils, trying not to yank the scepter right out of Ash's hands and whack her over the head with it. Unfortunately, there was the small issue of the two dudes with guns who looked like they were hoping for a reason, any reason, to use them.

"Ruby?" Shane asked, still confused, but Ruby knew the pieces would fall into place soon enough. "What did you do?"

But Ash waved his words away. "Don't worry your pretty little head about it, Shane. In a few minutes, none of this is going to matter anyway."

She walked toward the door, turning back one final time with a sigh. "I'm going to miss you guys and all your antics." She smiled and walked out, her heels clicking along the tile floor.

The two guys backed out of the room behind her, and a series of locks clicked with finality on the other side.

Ruby tried the door, even though she knew it was pointless, and as expected, it was locked tight.

"Oh, my protégés," Max said, in awe that the three of them were there, but with an edge of guilt that they were now in the same situation as he was.

"Are you okay, Max?" Shane asked, looking him over to make sure he didn't have any injuries.

Max waved his concern away. "I'm fine, I'm fine. I'm just sorry to have gotten all of you into this mess."

"Max, this is not your fault," Ruby said, only then noticing Bug pacing behind Max, like he was getting ready to punch something. "Bug?" she asked, her voice tentative and quiet.

And then Bug balled his fists and let out a loud, growling scream, as if trying to rid himself of the rage building inside. Ruby had never seen him lose his cool before, and frankly, it was a bit frightening, though she knew he would never do anything to hurt any of them.

He took a breath, blowing it slowly out his mouth. "How could she?" he asked no one in particular, the hurt thick in his voice.

Ruby's heart cracked in two, watching her friend try to process that this woman, their partner and friend, the person he'd thought he loved for so long, had become something he could have never understood. Someone who let her people believe she was dead, all the while setting them up for a massive fall.

She'd played them all.

But most of all, she'd played Bug. Ruby couldn't help but wonder just how far Ash had gone to get inside Bug's head, to make him trust her and, as it turned out, do her dirty work for her.

"Oh, Bug," Max said, sounding like his heart was breaking too.

Still shaking his head in disbelief, Bug straightened, and suddenly he looked a whole lot better than he had since the moment he learned of Ash's "death." Ruby supposed finding out the woman you loved was not, in fact, dead would do that to a person. Especially when said person had suddenly become your enemy and a new fire was lit. A fire of anger and vengeance.

Ruby wasn't sure if she wanted to see what Bug would do fueled on vengeance, but she supposed it was better than watching her friend's heart break over and over the way hearts do with grief.

"Do you know?" Bug asked, turning his attention to Max. "Do you know why she did this?"

Max shook his head. "She couldn't figure out any other way, I suppose," he said.

"But why us?" Shane asked. "How could she double-cross the people who've had her back all these years?"

Max cleared his throat. "From the way she talked to those men, and to me after I'd been captured, she didn't seem to feel we'd had her back at all. She talked about how we had abandoned her after Scotland. How we all blamed her for everything."

"Because it was her fault," Ruby couldn't help but spit out.

A pained expression crossed Bug's face. "Sorry, Bug," Ruby said.

She couldn't imagine the array of emotions storming inside him.

"No," he said, his voice gruff. "I used to think it was unfair so much of the blame for Scotland fell onto Ash, but I'm starting to see more clearly." He shook his head, as if he couldn't believe he'd ever been so fooled. "We need to get that scepter back. We need to find her and make sure she never does this to anyone else," he finished.

"Don't worry about the scepter right now," Ruby said. "We have more important things to worry about, like how the hell we're supposed to get out of here."

As they talked, Shane moved across the room to check the windows. "Locked," he said, though even if they weren't, Ruby wasn't sure what the plan would have been. Judging from the number of stairs they'd climbed to get into the church, the drop would not be something they'd want to risk. Broken bones were decidedly not at the top of her wish list.

"Max, you've been here the longest," Ruby said. "Have you figured a way out yet?"

She was hopeful he had a plan but just couldn't execute it since he was being watched, not to mention tied to a chair.

"I thought about the windows…if there was a balcony or a drain pipe to shimmy down or something, but as you can imagine, I haven't had much opportunity to check."

Ruby nodded, and Shane was already climbing onto a chair to look outside, no doubt hoping for a miracle. "There's nothing like that out here," he said, "and the drop is worse than I thought."

Ruby let out a long, slow breath. "There has to be another way."

As she was saying it, Bug began to sniff the air. "Does anyone else smell that?" he asked, at about the same moment Ruby noticed the smoke beginning to slither its way under the door.

Chapter 22

Shane was still reeling at the idea that all this had been a setup. He and Ash had never been bosom buddies or anything, but he'd always considered her a friend. And he'd never been double-crossed by a friend before. His instincts were usually better.

But people changed, he supposed.

These were the types of moments when Shane was at his best. When things were starting to look dire, with no solution in sight.

Clearly, they couldn't go through the main door. Not only was it locked, but they'd be running toward Ash, who Shane could only assume was getting her feet wet in this new, and alarming, hobby of arson.

The windows were clearly out—especially for someone Max's age. He was in pretty good shape, but the fact that he'd been toted around and kept captive for the past several days would not help.

Bug was at a second doorway on the other side of the room, but he shook his head. "Locked tight from the outside."

It made sense, of course. They had been holding Max captive here, after all, but still, even if Ash needed that scepter so badly, did she want the rest of the team to die? He and Ruby were one thing, he supposed, but Max...who'd given her the opportunity for this life in the first place, and Bug? Shane had always thought they'd been close…the guy must be devastated. Not that he looked it in the moment, suddenly far more focused on finding a way out than lamenting his current status of betrayal.

Shane pulled out his phone. Maybe if they could get the fire department there fast enough, the windows would become an option. After trying his call three times, it became clear that Ash and her new crew had set up a cell phone jammer, rendering all their phones useless.

"Calls won't go through," Shane said. "They must have them blocked. Bug, is there any way to reverse a jammer?"

Bug shook his head. "Not without finding the physical jammer, and I highly doubt it's in here."

The rest of the team exhausted the options they'd been pursuing. Ruby ripped a large curtain right off the wall and was shoving it under the door to slow the smoke, but it was only a matter of time before the fire made its way into the room.

They gathered near the back of the room as far away from the danger as possible, but Max let out a weak cough and reminded everyone they did not have a hell of a lot of time.

Shane glanced desperately around the room, hoping for a miracle idea.

"The ducts?" Ruby asked, pointing to a large return air vent in the ceiling.

Bug shook his head. "You only see that in movies. In real life the vents usually aren't strong enough to hold a person's weight, not to mention we wouldn't get very far. We'd go about twenty feet at most before running into a damper or tight corner or some other kind of obstruction."

But Bug's words got Shane's mind moving in a new direction, the thoughts circling through his mind in fast, jerky sequences.

"In movies you always see people crawling around in the

ducts for a long time, right? But what if we only needed to go a short distance?"

"Sure, but there might not be another fresh air return in this area of the building," Bug said.

"Okay, but you also said it might not hold a person's weight, which means in theory it's a very lightweight material," Shane said.

Bug nodded, starting to catch on.

Shane was already moving toward the vent, pulling the chair Max had been tied to underneath it. He pulled out his utility knife, which had about a million gadgets one might need in almost any sort of pinch, including when you needed a screwdriver. He began to remove the vent cover as quickly as he could, trying to ignore the smoke filtering in faster by the second.

He dropped the grate to the floor and Bug came over to give him a boost up into the opening. It was a bit of a feat trying to wriggle his way up there, and he could only hope the last person who had to make the trek would figure out something to get them closer to the duct than Max's chair, but this could work. The duct was definitely large enough for Shane to crawl through, but, as expected, made a rather alarming groaning sound as he inched forward, his full weight putting the flimsy metal under way more strain than it was designed for. But it held, at least for the moment.

Inside the duct, it was slightly smoky, but most of it seemed to be coming from the same direction as he was, which meant hopefully he'd be heading away from the fire.

Shane began to move more quickly, hoping if he moved fast, he wouldn't put too much strain on any one joint or weak spot long enough for it to give out. He crawled until he thought he was far enough away from the room. Once he got to the next joint in the ductwork, he started to push on it. It let out some groans of protest but didn't want to give.

"Of course," Shane grumbled to himself as he inched his way farther until his feet were close to the joint.

He started to kick, as the stubborn material continued to hold. But then, the groaning turned into an even more alarming noise—a horrid metal-on-metal screech that would have normally signaled disaster, but in that moment, was music to Shane's ears.

"Shane?" Max's voice reached him.

It was as if Max was yelling from somewhere far away, not from just twenty feet or so.

"One minute," Shane yelled, his foot finally breaking through the stubborn metal—then promptly getting caught between the two pieces now ripped apart at the seams. As he lay on his stomach, he used his other foot to free the first foot, and continued kicking, until a substantial hole had formed. He shimmied back so he could use his hands to continue working the duct apart. Soon he could see the room below was dark and small, but it wasn't filled with smoke. As Shane's eyes adjusted, he could just make out the outline of a door, light coming in underneath.

He continued to push on the metal until it resembled a can, peeled open to reveal the contents.

The room below was a storage or janitor's closet. Shane tried to think ahead, realizing if he jumped down into the room, he might not have a way back out if he was locked in there too.

But what else could he do? He decided he had to take the chance.

"I found a closet of some sort," he yelled back through the duct. "I'm going in."

No doubt the team would realize as quickly as he did that if there wasn't a way out of this room, they were out of options.

Shane wriggled his legs and body through, lowering until

his hands were hanging above his body. He let go, dropping the few final feet to the ground.

The place was dark, and it took a moment for Shane to get his bearings, but he quickly found the door and grabbed for the knob.

Locked.

His stomach gave a little jolt before he realized that even though it was locked, most doors locked from the inside. He felt for the locking mechanism and turned it with a small click, the door swinging brilliantly open.

There was definitely some smoke in the hallway, but if they hurried, they might have a chance.

Shane worked up his loudest yelling voice, worried now that he was out of the duct, his voice might not carry back to the others. "We're good to go!" he yelled.

His words were met with silence.

"Guys! We have a way out. Get your asses over here!"

He waited a moment, listening for something…anything. Shane flicked on the light in the closet, and after blinking for a moment, searched for something he could stand on that would be high enough to get him back up into the duct, but all he could see was a five-gallon pail that might get his fingertips to make their way back to the hole, but he wasn't sure how he'd be able to pull himself back up.

"Ruby! Max! Bug!" he yelled one more time, still scrambling to find more things to get himself higher.

"Dude," a voice said.

It was so quiet, so calm compared to the yelling he'd been doing that it was almost startling.

"Enough with the yelling, we're here," Ruby said, popping her head over the opening and shooting Shane her best grin, promptly causing Shane's stomach to give a little jolt for an entirely different reason.

"Well, get down here then," Shane said, grinning back.

Ruby shimmied over the hole until her legs could get through, then lowered the rest of her body down. It was an excellent opportunity for Shane to help her, grabbing her legs as she descended. Once he had her, she let go and he lowered her gently to the floor—her descent much more graceful than his foray into the closet had been.

Max was next, maneuvering over the opening in the duct with a bit more difficulty than Ruby'd had. Although Shane couldn't help but think it wasn't so much "a bit more" difficulty as it was "a whole helluva lot" of difficulty.

He glanced at Ruby, whose face held as much concern as Shane was feeling, as smoke began to billow through the duct.

Mercifully, Max's legs finally appeared through the hole and he started to lower himself down, though he must have been weak from his time in captivity, and lost his grip before falling the last few feet.

But Shane had quick reflexes and managed to sort of half grab him, and half get his own body under Max's to cushion the fall. The result was a mess of limbs and muffled cries, but zero injuries besides maybe a bruise or two. Probably mostly on Shane.

Which was a gloriously small price to pay than what the alternative could have been in the situation, Shane decided.

Bug struggled his way through the hole—his shoulders much bulkier than anyone else's, and his cough much more pronounced, since he'd spent more time in the smoke than the others.

But they were all there, and they were free.

At least free of the locked room. The rest of the church was still a question mark.

Shane led the way down the hall away from the fire. He had no idea where they were headed, but it wasn't like they were going to go back the way they'd come. A building like this—one meant for the public—would have several exits for the exact purpose of fire safety.

At the end of the hall, a set of double doors led them to a stairwell. Shane led the team down, and as he turned on the landing, a sign came into view with perhaps the most beautiful word in the English language.

Exit.

He pushed through the door and immediately a high-pitched wail sounded, the exit having been rigged with an alarm. But the air was crisp and cool, and tasted delicious, like the essence of life itself.

He made it about three steps before he realized several guns were pointed directly at his head.

He sighed. "Really? This again?"

Like Shane, Ruby was getting sick of people pointing guns at her. These weren't the same people, of course, but the feeling was pretty similar no matter who was doing the pointing.

The good news was, they found out their lives were not in nearly as much danger as they had been in the church.

The bad thing was, this time they were being taken into custody for questioning.

She supposed it should have been more surprising, but Ruby had thought so much about this moment, about getting caught, it almost seemed like an inevitable conclusion to her story.

Her thoughts jolted ahead the way they always did, picturing the monotony of her life from that moment on. She wondered who she'd have to make friends with in prison for protection. But most of all, she felt a deep sense of loss when they put Shane in the back of a police cruiser, watching until he'd been driven around the corner and out of sight.

She wondered if it would be the last time she saw him.

And then she was the one being led into a police cruiser

and driven to the station, assuming Bug and Max were close behind.

They kept Ruby waiting for what seemed like hours, though time worked differently when you're locked inside a room with nothing besides your uncooperative thoughts to keep you company.

Eventually, a man and woman sauntered into the room like there was nothing out of the ordinary—just chillin' with my coffee, nothing to see here.

The worst part was, they didn't even offer her a cup.

Maybe she didn't deserve coffee anymore, Ruby thought. If they knew even half the laws she'd broken…well, they had every right to lock her up and throw away the key.

The duo sat, the man dropping a thick file onto the table.

The woman took a long swig of her coffee before she spoke. "This is Anover," she said, pointing to her partner. "And I'm Mills. Care to fill us in on your part in all this?"

"My part in what?" Ruby asked. She wasn't trying to be difficult; she was simply trying to gauge how much they knew.

The corner of Mills's lip curled up a bit. "Oh, you know, the breaking and entering of a church, the little matter of the arson of said church…the heist of a certain priceless piece of history?"

The detective's eyebrow rose at the end of her sentence and Ruby realized they knew everything and there was no point in lying.

Of course, she opened her mouth and lied her face off anyway.

"I planned the whole thing," she said. "I was working with another woman to get the scepter and then was too blind to see she was double-crossing me the whole time."

"Really?" Mills said.

Ruby nodded. "Really."

For the next fifteen minutes, Ruby went into detail about

Ash and the heist, careful to keep Shane and Bug out of it. She mentioned Max's role, but said he was innocent of any wrongdoing—he had just been a pawn.

The detectives listened quietly. The man, Anover, took notes while Mills stared at Ruby, almost unblinking.

Finally, Mills cleared her throat. "I gotta say, that is the most popular story I've heard all day." She turned to her partner. "Seems to be a bit of a theme, don't you think?"

He nodded.

"Sorry?" Ruby asked.

"Well, it's just that the whole lot of you seem bound and determined to take all of the blame and make damn sure everyone else looks as innocent as a baby bunny in the springtime."

Ruby swallowed.

Mills narrowed her eyes. "Your story wasn't quite as good as your boyfriend's, though."

Ruby narrowed her eyes right back. "I don't have a boyfriend."

"You could have fooled me, the way both of you talk all swoony about each other."

"I do not talk swoony," Ruby said, working her jaw.

"I wouldn't have pegged it either, but here we are."

Ruby huffed, crossing her arms. "Just…don't listen to what he says. He can't be trusted."

Mills chuckled a little. "First you try to convince me Shane Meyers is as trustworthy as a kindergarten teacher, and now you're telling me he can't be trusted." She turned to her partner again. "You know, I'm inclined to believe the one who's not changing his story so much."

"I'm not changing my story. I'm just saying my story is the truth."

"Ah, the truth," the detective said. "You know what they say about the truth. There's your truth, my truth and then what actually happened."

“What I just told you is what actually happened,” Ruby said.

Mills tipped her head back and forth, as if thinking. “I don’t doubt everything you’ve told me is the truth. It’s just that I don’t believe for a second that it’s the whole truth.”

Chapter 23

Shane had given his all with the story he told the authorities, selling it as if he was hoping to get an Oscar. He explained what went down, of course, but he might have gone a bit off script with the ending. Specifically, the part where Ruby sent the scepter back to her museum. In his version of the story, he'd held a gun on her and forced her to ship it using her credentials. It hadn't been her idea at all. He was the one who was working with Ash.

Ruby was going to lay into him if he ever saw her again, but that was a small price to pay to make sure she could keep the life she'd worked so hard for. He was more than willing to trade his freedom for hers.

He just didn't know what was taking so long for them to haul him away.

Shane hated to wait. When given too much time to think, his brain tended to be like an unattended toddler in a kitchen—messy and dangerous.

Eventually, the two detectives—Mills and Anover—returned.

"You're free to go," Mills said, holding the door open so Shane could simply walk out.

"Wait, what?" Shane said, panic starting to rise in his chest.

"I mean, you can sit here longer if you want," Mills said, "but it's not like we're the Ritz here. We aren't going to bring you room service."

"But what changed? I told you, I'm guilty."

"Yeah, yeah, yeah," Mills said. "You're all guilty. I get it." She turned to Anover. "Weird bunch of friends, if you ask me," she finished under her breath.

Shane tried to formulate a coherent thought. "But—"

Mills held up a hand to stop him, clearly impatient. "We caught Ashlyn Greaves and have been questioning her for the past hour."

"What? How?" Shane asked.

Mills sighed as if she didn't have the time or the patience to deal with his questions but was resigning herself to the idea that he wasn't going to leave until he heard the full story. She sat heavy in one of the chairs across from Shane, and Anover followed suit as if he was her shadow.

"At approximately four fifteen this afternoon, Ashlyn Greaves was apprehended by authorities as she was boarding a Greyhound destined for Florida."

Shane blinked. The thought of Ash on a public bus, let alone one to Florida, which would have taken, like, thirty hours, did not compute. Although it wasn't like she could get the scepter on a plane. But why not a car?

Maybe she figured the bus would be the last place anyone would search.

"Florida?" he finally asked when his brain started to focus again.

Mills nodded. "She purchased a property under an assumed name down there. A place to lie low until she could coordinate the sale of the scepter."

"She was going to *sell* the scepter?" Shane asked, dumbfounded. "I thought she wanted it so bad because it was a precious family heirloom."

"Oddly enough," Mills said. "It did once belong to her family—generations back, of course. But Ms. Greaves had no interest in sharing her find with her family. She'd been estranged from them for over a decade. The scepter had been a story told from generation to generation, but no one ever thought it could be retrieved."

"Except Ash, apparently," Shane chimed in.

Mills nodded. "When she did somehow find it, she had no intention of ever sharing the spoils with anyone."

Shane stared at Mills, unable to comprehend what must have been going through Ash's head. A thought struck him. "If it was under an assumed name, how did you know about this place in Florida?"

Mills half smiled. "Your friend… Mr. Elliot," she said, "had an enormous amount of intel on Ms. Greaves—it seems he had a bit of an infatuation with her—and, well, after the way she double-crossed all of you, he was willing to give the info up."

"Bug?" Shane was shocked he'd revealed anything to the authorities, including that he was able to find out almost anything about anyone. He must have been seriously pissed at Ash—not that Shane could blame him. He was more than a bit miffed at her himself. "He's not going to be in trouble, is he?"

Mills shook her head. "His retrieval of the information on Ms. Greaves certainly did not follow the proper legal channels, but after agreeing to use his…skills on a few cases for us, we've agreed to let that slide."

Oh, man, Shane thought. Bug was going to hate that, but he supposed it would all be behind him soon enough. Plus, it must have felt damn good to turn her in after the devastation she'd rained down on him.

"And you were able to get Ash to talk?" Shane asked.

Mills shrugged. "We don't think she'll be too hard to crack, but for now, we're accepting Mr. Elliot's and Max Redfield's accounts of the story, which actually match, and are the only ones that make sense. Yours and Ms. Alexander's are a little too far-fetched," she said, almost rolling her eyes.

Shane only had one question left. "So, Ruby's free to go too?"

"We have a few more questions for Ms. Alexander," Mills said, her voice serious.

"But she didn't do anything—"

Again, Mills cut him off by holding up her hand. "What Ms. Alexander did, she did of her own accord. We won't be pressing criminal charges against her, but she will have to answer to her workplace over the things she's done."

Shane slumped further into his seat.

"But mostly," Mills continued, getting up from her seat, followed by the ever-silent Anover, "what we'd like to figure out is how Ashlyn Greaves was caught trying to smuggle a so-called priceless artifact that was, in fact, a counterfeit."

Ruby could have had six thousand guesses as to who the next person who strolled into her interrogation room would be, but she wouldn't have been successful.

"Barb?" she asked, gawking at her boss from the museum.

"Hey, Ruby," Barb said, like she didn't have a care in the world. In fact, she sounded practically jovial.

"How… Why…" Ruby said, struggling to form a thought, let alone a sentence. "What?" she asked, her forehead crinkling.

Barb chuckled a little. "Good to see you too," she said, sitting across the table from Ruby.

"What are you doing here?" Ruby asked.

She knew she'd be let go from the museum, but she didn't think Barb would have to come all the way down here to tell her. Frankly, she thought the authorities would be the one telling Barb that Ruby wouldn't be at work Monday morning.

"Heard you were having a little trouble with these fine folks down here at the station," she explained.

Not that it was much of an explanation.

"And I thought I'd come down to see what I could do."

"How did you even know I was here?" Ruby asked.

A smirk twitched at the corner of Barb's mouth before they were interrupted with Max poking his head into the doorway. Ruby's whole body relaxed in relief. At least Max was being set free. That was something, at least.

"I heard you were in here," he said. "Thought I'd come by and say thanks."

Max was so sweet, Ruby thought and opened her mouth to say as much, but promptly shut it when Barb's chair scraped back and she headed for Max. As Barb embraced him in a big hug, Ruby realized Max hadn't been talking to her at all. For the second time in a matter of seconds, she was struck silent.

Silent, and so very, very confused.

When they finished greeting each other, both Max and Barb came to sit in front of Ruby. Ruby's brain always wanted to work every question out as soon as possible, but in that moment, it had given up. There was no way she could explain any of this.

"I hear we have you to thank for saving our Max, here," Barb said, squeezing Max's hand that had been resting on the table.

Our Max?

Barb's eyes sparkled with secrets and mischief as she turned to Max. "This is even more fun than I thought it would be," she said, bouncing a little in her seat.

Max smiled. "You better tell the poor girl what's going on before her head explodes from trying to figure it out."

"Right," Barb said, though she sounded like she wanted to draw it out even longer. "Well, I guess I should start by saying I know a lot more about your past than you think I do."

Ruby's stomach clenched with that same old feeling. The one where she was terrified someone she knew had found out who she really was.

A flood of shame washed over her.

"I didn't mean to deceive you," Ruby said. "I just wanted

so badly to do something with my life that was good, for once. I…I guess I wanted a future."

"Ruby," Barb said, her voice kind, "you haven't done anything wrong. I mean, I know you and Max and the team didn't always do things within the strict confines of the law, but trust me when I say you did it for the right reasons. For the overall good of the people you were helping."

Ruby shook her head, her gaze focused on her lap, unable to look Barb in the eye. "It wasn't right…"

Barb shrugged. "Maybe it wasn't, or maybe it was," she said. "But in the end, your intention was to help people and fix what had gone so, so wrong. And that's a noble cause." She cleared her throat. "It took me a long time to realize that, too, but I think I'm finally there."

Ruby's eyes snapped up.

Barb smiled. "As you've no doubt guessed, Max and I are old friends. Well, Max was my mentor, really."

Ruby looked from Max, who appeared to be enjoying himself to no end, then to Barb, and back to Max again. "You were one of his students."

"One of my best," Max confirmed.

"And you got out," Ruby said.

Barb tilted her head. "Sort of," she said. "Though Max and I have never stopped collaborating."

Ruby's eyebrows pinched together.

"I've been working on a project for several years now, trying to find the right people to help me…expedite some of the work we do at the museum, along with other partner museums around the world."

"I'm not sure I understand," Ruby said. "Why are you telling me this?"

"Because I'm hoping you'll agree to work with me on the project."

"Um," Ruby said, gazing around. "I'm not sure if you noticed, but I'm about to be arrested and likely put away for a very long time."

"You are not about to be arrested," Barb said. "In fact, the people who have spent the better part of the day questioning you are partners in the project. Folks in law enforcement who are going to help us speed the process of finding stolen antiquities and getting them back where they belong."

"It's just like what we used to do, Ruby," Max chimed in. "Except this time, it will all be aboveboard."

Something sparked in Ruby, though she wasn't sure she could trust it.

"We've been given the go-ahead to assemble our task force—funded in part by the museum. Though, thanks to Max and his various teams, several rather grateful families whose stolen items have been returned over the past decades are more than happy to show their appreciation with monetary investments as well."

Ruby shook her head. "I'm sorry. The people who have been given back their heirlooms are funding some kind of task force?"

"Precisely," Max said. "They want to see justice for even more families, and frankly, so do we. And we're hoping you'll agree to help us. The work will still be dangerous—as you may have noticed, I have several…precautions at my house—but something tells me that sort of thing isn't going to stop any of my former students."

"And you'd be able to keep your credentials with the museum intact," Barb said. "If, at any time, you decide the task force isn't for you anymore, you'll have your job back at the museum."

Ruby was speechless. She rarely let herself admit it, but she missed so much about her old life. Once a person lived with that kind of adventure—the travel, the adrenaline, the satisfaction of having families immediately reunited with their priceless heirlooms—it was hard to let it go.

"You'd be helping people the way we used to," Max said, "except you'd never have to feel like you were doing something wrong."

Ruby hadn't even realized she was nodding until Barb said, "So, does that mean you'll join us?"

"What?" Ruby asked, as if snapping out of a daydream. She looked at Barb, her boss and friend, then to Max, someone she cared for so much, but who was from an entirely different world.

The whole scene in front of her was jarring, but Ruby decided she could live with her two worlds colliding.

"Yeah," she said. "I'm in. Absolutely, I'm in."

"Great! I think that pretty much takes care of business," Barb said, getting up and holding her hand out for Ruby.

It was a weirdly formal gesture for someone she'd grown so close to, but Ruby had to admit, when she shook Barb's hand, it felt like the start of a new chapter.

Barb turned to go, but paused at the door. "Oh, there was one more thing," she said. "The little matter of a priceless scepter I found abandoned under your desk at work?" She raised an eyebrow.

Ruby smiled, a bit sheepish. "Oh, that." She cleared her throat. "I may have gotten an old friend of mine to whip up a counterfeit. Something about the whole job just felt…off. I never did know what felt wrong, but I thought maybe I'd try to pull one over on the bad guys—with the real one safe at work for backup in case they figured it out."

"At the risk of your job," Barb said.

Ruby nodded. "I wouldn't be able to live with myself if we didn't get Max back…or if the scepter got into the wrong hands."

"I'd love to know how you did it," Barb said.

Ruby shrugged. "I have an artist friend who specializes in reproductions," she said. "Before I had the real scepter sent back to the museum, I had my contact, Jessica, do a full 3D scan of the scepter. It's amazing what my friend Jerome can do with a few good photo renderings and computer-generated specs."

It had been a risky move. If the people who had Max even suspected the scepter wasn't the real deal, they could have killed Max, plus the rest of the team. Ruby had mitigated the risk, knowing they'd have to be an expert to tell the difference between the real deal and the fake scepter. Still, she felt bad for putting Max in that position.

But Max was beaming. "You can never be too prepared."

"Great job," Barb said as she turned to leave again. "See you Monday morning, Ruby."

And Ruby wasn't sure she'd ever heard five better words in her life.

Chapter 24

Ruby couldn't wait to fall into bed and sleep half the weekend away, but there was one thing she needed to do first.

Get the travel filth, the fire soot and the police station grime off her.

She threw her keys onto the console table near her door and began to strip her clothes off, dropping each item on the floor on her way down the hall to her bathroom.

She made the shower hot—hot tub–style hot—and scrubbed the last few days away.

She could hardly believe all the things that had happened, but most of all she couldn't believe she still had her job at the museum. Well, a different job within the museum, she supposed—one that would give her everything she wanted.

Almost.

There was still one big question mark, but she couldn't think about him. If she did, she'd never get the sleep she needed.

She wrapped a towel around herself before making her way back down the hall. Halfway to the kitchen she realized something was off and stopped, heart racing. There didn't appear to be an immediate threat, but impossibly, her clothes were no longer scattered on the floor. A sound of a glass clinking came from the kitchen where the clothes she'd discarded sat neatly folded on the counter.

A voice floated from the shadows. "Still doing the same old rituals, I see."

This time she met his smirk. "And just how did you get in?" she asked, accepting the wine he'd poured for her, but before she could drink, he raised his glass. "What are we toasting?" Ruby asked, her voice sultry, playing along.

"I'm hoping we're toasting to working together again," Shane said.

Ruby raised an eyebrow. "Ah, they talked to you, did they?"

Shane grinned. "When they told me you'd have to answer for the scepter being counterfeit, I thought I was going to lose it. My mind started trying to come up with something, anything, I could say to get you out of trouble with the museum. Some way you could keep your job. Thankfully, they put me out of my misery pretty quickly and told me about the task force." He chuckled. "Or maybe they just couldn't bear listening to my absolute bullshit one more time."

"You always did try to be my protector," Ruby said.

A strange, restless feeling shimmered through Ruby, who was torn between annoyance that he thought she couldn't take care of herself and a weird thrill that he wanted to be her rescuer. It was uncomfortable, like her insides itched. Suddenly she knew what it was.

Vulnerability.

An idea that scared her way more than any jump off a dark mountain could.

"I guess I was hoping that someday, just once, you'd let me," Shane said.

Ruby was scared. No longer worried about losing the life she'd built for herself, but of losing a life from before.

"Shane, I—"

He shook his head. "You don't have to say anything. This doesn't have to be anything. We can just have right now."

"That's not what I want," Ruby replied.

The hurt that moved over his face nearly broke her heart.

"No, I mean…" She sighed, then looked him in the eye.

"I mean I don't want it to be just right now. I want it to be… something else. Something longer."

"But you always said you never wanted serious," Shane said, his eyes questioning. Hopeful?

Ruby's head swam with every moment she'd ever been here. Every time she'd been close to saying what she felt, then chickened out, made up excuses. Even now, everything in her screamed to take it back, to keep things light, stay on the surface. Real feelings could too easily go wrong. Could break a person.

But then…hadn't she already felt broken? Felt like she was missing a piece of herself?

"Shane," she said, tears prickling. "I never really wanted that. Not with you. I just…" She glanced away. "I wanted things to be easy. You wanted things to be easy. What we did for work, it was so dangerous, always felt so impermanent. Anything could have changed at any moment. Everything did change in a single moment. It didn't make sense for either of us to get tied up in a relationship."

"Except you were the one thing that always made the world make sense," Shane said, his voice quiet. Serious.

She looked up at him, the tears threatening to spill over. "I think I finally know that now."

"So, you're on board with working together again? The way we used to?"

Ruby put her wine down and took a step closer to Shane. "I'm on board with a lot more than that."

She felt breathless with the admission. Before the words had tumbled out, she wasn't even sure if she'd be able to say them, but in the end, it was easy. Probably because she'd never been so sure of anything in her life.

"For real this time?" Shane asked.

"For real this time."

Shane set his glass beside Ruby's and closed the remainder of the space between them as his gentle hands lifted her face and he kissed her deeply. There was no desperation in it this time, only certainty.

Every cell in Ruby's body sparked, every flutter of emotion racing straight to the surface of her skin, prickling each nerve ending with sensation. Delightful little prickles of heat, electricity, light.

Her hands found the back of his neck, curling up into his hair, and she only had one thought. That this felt right. Nothing in that moment could have made her feel like anything she was doing could be wrong.

Shane kissed down her neck and Ruby sighed with relief and desire, the tingling dancing even brighter between her thighs.

She pulled his head back to hers, kissing harder—almost frantic.

He kissed her back just as hard. Heat swelled inside Ruby—the kind of heat she hadn't felt in a very long time. She needed a moment for air, the sensations almost too much to handle, and she took a step back, keeping her gaze locked on his. She smiled and reached for the place where she'd tucked her towel into itself.

Shane followed her lead, starting to unbutton his shirt as she let the towel fall to the floor.

Shane flung his shirt to the ground and moved his hands to his belt, then stopped. He didn't smile. He didn't say a word. He just looked.

Emboldened, Ruby reached for her wine and took a long sip as Shane fumbled with his clothes, every sparked sensation burning brighter as his eyes roamed over her.

Nothing in Ruby's life had ever felt this right. This necessary.

Shane came out of his trance and rid himself of his clothes by the time Ruby had carefully made her way backward to the couch, wine still in hand. She sipped as Shane moved toward her. Muscled shoulders leading to a lean chest and torso. His legs holding their own, too, though she didn't quite get past the erection that most certainly did not disappoint. Shane took the final steps toward her, keeping the slightest gap between them, looking into her eyes, silently asking if she was sure.

And my god, was she sure. There was a familiarity to the moment, like coming home, but it was all new, too, the desire somehow more intense than it had ever been.

Shane took the wineglass from her and set it on the side table, while every cell in Ruby's body screamed that if she didn't close the distance in the next few seconds, they might never forgive her.

She arched, her chest grazing his, his lips finding her throat. As she leaned back, waves of heat flooded her, frantic, alive—senses spiraling out of control. Shane's lips explored, tasting his way past her collarbone, slowly working their way to the sensitive nerves of her nipple, instantly igniting a fuse straight down her center. He took his time, swirling…savoring, as the invisible fuse burned brighter and hotter, inching closer to sparks, fire, explosions.

Shane lifted her then, setting her gently on the top edge of the couch as he traced the invisible thread farther down, past her chest, toward her belly button. Mercifully, he did not stop there, searching for the fuse's final destination, and she spread her legs, letting her head fall back, as if opening herself to the universe, but more importantly, to the man below.

He grabbed her hips and closed his mouth over her, his expert tongue stroking, caressing…then sucking with a gentle pressure until she could barely hold herself up any longer, the blaze building to combustible levels, until she couldn't hold it inside any longer and cried out with an explosion unrivaled by any she'd experienced before.

After some luxurious moments allowing herself to revel in

the satisfaction, Shane holding her tight, always her protector, Ruby gathered enough composure to slide down the back of the couch, and Shane laid her gently across it. They began again slowly, a kiss here, a soft touch there.

Ruby's body had always responded to Shane's. His lips, his arms, the muscles down his torso. Her body had not forgotten. Only screamed at her that it had been too long since she'd been here with Shane. Since she'd come home.

They'd found their way back to each other and Ruby wondered how she could have allowed the part of her that fought this to win. To be without for so many years.

And Shane treated her like she was his home too. Treasured, valued…loved.

Their slow kisses and soft touches soon turned more urgent, Shane setting a faster pace as Ruby helped him find the way to his own, much-deserved explosion.

Afterward, they lay quiet for a long while, Shane stroking her shoulder as she rested on his chest, and Ruby found that her thoughts had calmed. She'd forgotten being with Shane used to do that. Made her feel less…out of control.

"I can't believe everything that's happened," Shane said eventually. "I feel like we get to have our old life back."

A familiar twinge shot through Ruby at the thought of going back to that life, to that world. The old combination of excitement mixed with a heavy dose of dread…but then she remembered she could push those feelings of dread away.

"Not our old life," she said. "The old life never quite felt right. Like we couldn't quite fit all the right pieces together."

Shane made a musing sound. "So maybe it's like we get to have all the best pieces of our old life back."

Ruby nodded. "Plus some new, very interesting pieces," she said, draping her arm across his chest.

A sense of contentment washed over her then, an unfamiliar feeling that she couldn't quite place.

"Some very interesting new pieces," Shane agreed.

"And this time they all fit together," Ruby said, suddenly realizing exactly what the sensation was.

A falling into place of the pieces. A completion.

A life she knew could never be flawless—nothing was, not even the most precious piece of art—but this life, with this man in her arms, was about as close as she could imagine to perfect.

* * * * *

SPECIAL EXCERPT FROM

Set aflame...
by danger—and him!

Hotshot firefighter Michaela Momber is used to saving people from peril. But when a saboteur puts Michaela's team in their sights, *she's* the one under fire. Ambivalent bar owner Charlie Tillerman could be a prime suspect. But Michaela knows another side of the gruff Charlie: he's the father of the baby she thought she could never have! Together, can they elude a killer to save their unborn child…*and* one another?

Read on for a sneak preview of
Hotshot's Dangerous Liaison*,*
the next book in Lisa Childs's
miniseries Hotshot Heroes.

Prologue

Sixteen months ago...

Smoke burned his nose and dried out his throat, drawing a racking cough from him that jerked him awake. He lifted his head from the leather blotter on his desk, coughed again and blinked. But the smoke burned his eyes, making them tear up and blur his vision.

What the hell is going on...?

Still half-asleep, Charlie Tillerman dragged himself up from his desk and staggered over to the door. When he wrapped his hand around the knob, the metal was warm but not too warm. Wasn't there some rule about that?

He drew in a breath, coughed as it burned his lungs and pulled open the door. The hall was all hazy, like his office. He stumbled down the hall toward the game room area of his bar, where the pool tables, dartboards and arcade games were—or where they should have been, since he couldn't see them through the smoke. But he could feel the heat coming at him in waves as the flames rose higher as he neared the front dining room area of the bar. The fire crackled, almost as if it was laughing while it consumed his livelihood, his family legacy: the Filling Station Bar and Grille. His fondest memories from childhood were from this place, from helping his grandfather out at the bar on the corner of Main Street and Lakeside Drive in Northern Lakes, Michigan.

Grandpa had died around the same time that Charlie's life had fallen apart in the big city, so he had two reasons to come home to Northern Lakes. And after inheriting the bar, he had a reason to stay.

The Filling Station once had a gas station on the property. He could smell gasoline now. It burned his nose like the smoke burned his eyes. But the pumps had been removed long ago, along with most of the soil from around where they'd been. So how could the scent be so strong?

He coughed and sputtered, his lungs and throat burning from the smoke and fumes. When had the fire started? What time was it, even? He'd left his damn cell phone in his office. But his primary concern was making sure everyone got out and none of his customers or employees were trapped inside like the local Boy Scouts—one being his nephew—who had been trapped in the middle of a wildfire in the forest a few months ago.

He blinked and wiped his eyes, trying to peer through the smoke and flames to see if anyone else was still inside the building. Because people were what was important, not possessions. If only his ex-wife had realized that…

Or if he'd realized sooner that possessions were all she cared about.

No, that hadn't been all; she cared about appearances and power just as much as her material things. When he'd lost the election for a seat in the state senate, he'd lost her. But now he was about to lose even more. He couldn't breathe, the smoke searing his lungs, and he found his legs giving way beneath him. He dropped to the floor, onto the peanuts that had been strewn across the scratched hardwood boards.

Was he dying?

Because, just before consciousness slipped away from him,

the last thing he saw was the face of an angel framed with short, pale blonde hair. She had the most beautiful blue eyes he had ever seen.

And then he closed his eyes for maybe the last time.

Chapter 1

Sixteen months later...

Charlie Tillerman was a dead man—or he would be if the other hotshots were right…

If *he* was the saboteur.

Michaela Momber listened to her fellow hotshots' voices rumbling around the airplane cabin as they speculated over the identity of the saboteur who'd been messing with them for way too long. The incidents had been happening for over a year now. Stupid things at first that they hadn't even realized were intentional—like equipment that had been checked suddenly breaking. But because of the nature of their jobs, those things had been dangerous. Especially when the firehouse stove had exploded, sending Ethan Sommerly to the hospital with burns. Fortunately, his beard had saved him from any significant wounds, but once his beard was gone, all hell had broken loose. He wasn't just a hotshot firefighter, he was heir to some famous family.

That situation could have been worse, like when their vehicles had been tampered with, brake lines cuts. But now the attacks had become physical, with the saboteur striking Rory VanDam over the head so hard that he was in a coma for two weeks. *Saboteur* really wasn't a strong enough word for this person.

Rory had recovered from his traumatic head injury, which happened after the hotshot holiday party six months ago. He'd also recovered from a gunshot wound he suffered when a corrupt FBI agent had gone after him. Again.

Rory was flying the plane now, so his wasn't one of the voices Michaela heard from where she sat in the back of the plane. She'd boarded first, eager to take a seat and get some much-needed rest after the two weeks they'd spent battling a wildfire. But even though she tried to sleep, the majority of her twenty-member team kept talking. It wasn't just their voices keeping her awake but also what they were talking about—or rather, whom.

"Charlie had access to my drinks," Luke Garrison remarked. "He could have been the one who drugged me. Maybe he was working with Marty Gingrich."

Marty Gingrich, a former state trooper, was the one who'd tried to kill Luke and his wife, though. Not Charlie.

But had Charlie helped? The thought had Michaela's stomach churning with dread, but she shook her head, rejecting the idea.

"It's more likely that Trooper Wells is helping Gingrich than Charlie," Michaela said, then stiffened with shock over the fact that she'd instinctively come to the bartender's defense.

"True," Hank said. "I could definitely see Wynona Wells being involved in this."

Henrietta "Hank" Rowlins was Michaela's best friend, so her quick agreement was no surprise. But did she suspect that Michaela had a reason for defending Charlie? Michaela felt a jab of guilt that she hadn't told her anything, but she'd hoped there would be nothing to tell. That it had just been a one-time thing on a night when she felt just too damn alone.

But it had been more than once.

"I don't trust Wells either," Patrick "Trick" McRooney said.

He might have just agreed with Hank because he was engaged to her. "But Charlie definitely has easier access to us."

Damn. Did Trick suspect?

He was the brother-in-law of the hotshot superintendent, Braden Zimmer. Braden had brought in his wife's brother to investigate the saboteur, figuring that he would be more objective than the superintendent could be about his team. But then Trick had fallen for Hank and lost all his objectivity.

Michaela hoped she hadn't done the same thing. Lost her objectivity.

Not falling for anyone. That was never going to happen, she would never risk her heart again. She couldn't trust anyone, most especially herself and her own damn judgment.

"Charlie's got more access at the bar," Ethan Sommerly said. "But at the firehouse?"

Carl Kozak, one of the older hotshots, snorted. "Thanks to Stanley, everyone has access to the firehouse. Sorry, Cody."

Cody Mallehan was Stanley's older foster brother and the reason Stanley was in Northern Lakes. He had moved the teenager here after Stanley aged out of the foster care system. Cody sighed. "We're working on it."

"We're also working hard on finding out who the saboteur is and on keeping the team safe," Braden added, as if trying to reassure them. With the dark circles beneath his eyes, he looked as exhausted as Michaela felt, he probably wasn't sleeping any more than she was.

"It's bad enough fighting a wildfire," Donovan Cunningham murmured. "But to have to worry about getting hurt at home, too..."

Apparently, Michaela wasn't the only one on edge right now. The stress had to be what was making her so sick. At least the wildfire they were returning from was in Ontario, so the plane ride would be short, which was good since Michaela's stomach went up and down with every bit of turbulence.

"That's why we have to investigate every possible suspect," Trick said. "Even Charlie."

"What's his motive?" Michaela found herself asking.

"You know," Cody said. "You were the one who was there when his bar burned down. You saved him."

Michaela smiled. "And he would want revenge on us for that?" He certainly hadn't seemed to want revenge on her, anyway, since he'd refused to let her pay for anything in his bar since the fire. And then they…

"He might want revenge because the arsonist who burned down his bar was really after us. He and the Filling Station were nearly collateral damage," Donovan said. He was an older hotshot, too, like Carl. Guys who'd been working as elite firefighters for a long time.

"The Filling Station is more than his bar," Braden said. "It's his home, and his family legacy."

So that did give him motive.

Even the superintendent who was usually loath to suspect anyone seemed to think Charlie had a motive. But…

If Charlie Tillerman was the saboteur, Michaela Momber had been sleeping with the enemy.

Had she done it again? Had she made a horrible mistake, trusting someone she shouldn't have? Not that she really trusted him. Not that she could really trust anyone…

Her stomach churned again, and she closed her eyes and arched her neck against the headrest of the airplane seat. She didn't usually get motion sickness, but lately everything had been making her queasy. For months now, she'd been feeling so damn nauseous and bloated. So bloated that she couldn't even button her pants anymore.

If she didn't know better, she might have thought she was pregnant. But that wasn't possible. She couldn't get pregnant. But it was good that she hadn't gotten pregnant with her ex.

She shouldn't have trusted him to be a faithful husband, so she certainly wouldn't have trusted him to be a responsible father.

No. She wasn't pregnant. But with as sick as she'd been feeling, she probably had an ulcer. And no matter if he was the saboteur or not, Charlie Tillerman was partially responsible for that too.

After her divorce, Michaela had no intention of ever getting involved with anyone again. Not that she and Charlie were *involved.*

But they were…

She wasn't sure what they were. But if anyone found out about them, they might think she was working with him, that she was complicit in the sabotage, too, just like so many people thought Trooper Wynona Wells might be complicit in all the horrible things her training sergeant Marty Gingrich had done to the hotshot team. Michaela really wished that it was her and not Charlie.

But she also had to be realistic and cautious, or she might wind up getting hurt, like Rory. She didn't want anyone else getting hurt, either, though. She desperately wanted the saboteur—whoever it was—caught and brought to justice.

Especially if that person was Charlie.

And if that person was Charlie, she wanted to be the one to catch him first. With the access she had to him, she might be the only person who could catch him.

The flames sputtered and cowered, shrinking away from the water blasting from the end of the hose Charlie Tillerman held tightly between his gloved hands. After the arson fire had destroyed his bar and nearly claimed his life over a year ago, Charlie had no interest in ever going near another one. But here he was, suited up in fire-retardant jacket and pants, battling a blaze.

Sweat rolled down his back and off his face. Despite it being June, the weather hadn't warmed up much yet this year, and this late at night, it was extra cool. But the fire burned hot, especially with as close as Charlie was standing to it, just inside the open garage door.

The flames flared up, trying to reach the wood rafters of the garage, but another blast of water sent them crashing back down…below the raised hood of the vehicle inside the garage. The hood and motor were black, and the windshield and headlights had shattered in the heat. It was too late to save the car, but the battle was now to save the structure, to stop the fire from spreading any farther.

From destroying anything more.

Like his livelihood and his home had been destroyed over a year ago. He'd rebuilt the Filling Station Bar and Grille within months of the fire, working alongside the contractors and the townspeople who'd volunteered to help. While the town in the Huron Forest, with its many inland lakes, was a seasonal tourist destination, it was the locals who had been his loyal patrons.

And it was those loyal patrons—even the hotshot firefighters whom some people held responsible for the fires in the first place—who'd helped him rebuild. The arsonist who'd torched his bar and started the forest fire that had trapped the Boy Scouts six months prior to the bar burning down had been holding a grudge against the hotshot team for not hiring him. But even though he had been apprehended and brought to justice, other tragic or near-tragic things kept happening in this town. And while the hotshots seemed to be at the heart of the threats, too many other people had been put in danger as well from the violence.

The most tragic of these incidents had been a murder. But people had also been nearly run down walking across the street or, while in their vehicles, had been run off the road. There had also been shootings and explosions and fires.

Like the one he was battling now, the hose from the rig between his gloved hands, blasting water onto the flames. If only he'd had the rig and this equipment the night his bar had burned down…

If only he'd had some control over the situation and hadn't felt so damn helpless and vulnerable…

But he'd learned long ago there was no controlling anything, sometimes not even himself. At least when it came to a certain female customer.

The flames died fast, extinguished by the water, which now dripped from the blackened shell of the vehicle. While the car was a total loss, they'd managed to limit the damage to the garage it was inside. This fire was probably just an accident, like the homeowner had claimed it was. He'd left the classic car running while he was working on it, and something must have sparked and started the engine on fire.

This wasn't like all those other things that had been happening in Northern Lakes. And this fire had nothing to do with the hotshots, since they weren't even in town. They were off somewhere battling another wildfire. There had been a lot of them lately, which had left the Northern Lakes Fire Department so short-staffed that they had put out an emergency call for volunteers.

Even though he'd had no intention of going near another fire, Charlie hadn't been able to ignore the call. Not after so many of his neighbors and the townspeople had helped him rebuild his business and his life. So he'd gone through training and had been out on—fortunately—just a few calls since he'd finished that training a month ago.

Maybe things were quiet because the hotshots had been gone so much. That quiet, from fires, also extended to other parts of Charlie's life. Professionally, the bar was quieter without the hotshots' business, and personally…

No. He could not risk having a personal life. He just… couldn't. After his divorce, he had decided relationships were too damn unpredictable, kind of like fires. There was just no way of knowing which way it would go, so the chances of getting burned were just too great to risk. And Charlie wasn't nearly a good enough judge of character to trust anyone with his heart again.

To trust *anyone* again. Even the angel who'd rescued him that night in his burning bar. He was actually the least likely to trust *her* because she was one of *them*. A Huron hotshot.

No. He definitely couldn't trust her. He had only seen her a few times since the night of the hotshot holiday party, which had been a private event at the Filling Station, six months ago.

Not that he wanted to see her again. It was easier if he didn't. Then he wasn't so damn tempted. But damn, he missed her too.

"Hey, you awake?" Eric asked as he stared into the back of the rig, where Charlie was sitting alone.

He didn't even remember climbing inside the truck at the burned-out garage, much less riding back to the firehouse. But that was definitely where the rig was now, parked in one of the bays of the three-story concrete block building. That building, on the main street of Northern Lakes, was just down the road from his bar, which was too damn close, given some of what had been happening at the firehouse over the past year or so. The shootings, the explosions…

He shuddered at the memory of those things that had rattled the windows and the walls of the Filling Station, which wasn't just his business but also his home since he lived in the apartment above it.

Charlie shook his head, trying to clear thoughts of those

dangers and of *her* from his mind. But that hadn't been easy to do even before they…

He definitely couldn't let himself think about *that*. So he drew in a deep breath and nodded. "Yeah, I'm awake," he assured his fellow volunteer, who was also his brother-in-law.

Eric Veltema was a big guy with blond hair that turned reddish in his mustache and beard. He had a booming laugh and a big personality, just like Charlie's sister. Valerie was the one who should have followed their father into politics, not Charlie.

Charlie had always preferred tending the bar, like their grandfather had most of his life. Charlie looked like Grandpa Tillerman, too, with dark eyes and black hair, and now that he was getting close to forty, the stubble on his jaw was starting to come in gray.

"You're the night owl," Eric said, "staying up late and closing the bar. I didn't think you ever slept."

Charlie chuckled at the misconception. "I sleep. Unlike you, I don't have kids." A pang of regret struck him, along with a sense of loss for what might have been, what could have been. His ex-wife hadn't wanted any children, though, and after what had nearly happened to his nephew, Charlie had changed his mind too. The world was entirely too dangerous to bring children into, especially in Northern Lakes.

Eric chuckled too. "Is that the reason you're staying a bachelor now? Because you want to sleep?"

"That's one of them," Charlie admitted.

But he had other reasons, and his brother-in-law was well aware of them. He and Eric had been friends since they were kids. They'd gone to school together and grown up together. Eric had been like family even before he'd married Charlie's sister, who'd always thought her younger brother's friend was annoying. Despite falling in love with him, she claimed she still found him annoying.

"Seriously, though," Charlie continued, "is Nicholas sleeping through the night yet?"

Eric's grin slid away, and he sighed. "Most nights now, but he still has the occasional nightmare about the fire."

"He's not the only one," Charlie muttered.

He'd felt so damn helpless then, when those Boy Scouts had been trapped in the burning forest and they'd had to rely on the hotshots to rescue them and put out the fire. He hoped to never feel that helpless again, but just a few months later, he'd been trapped in his own burning bar.

"That's why you have to win this election, man," Eric said. "With you as mayor, you'd have some clout to get this fire station away from the hotshot crew. Let them use someplace else as their headquarters, someplace where they don't put anyone else in danger with all their enemies and secret identities and crap."

Charlie's stomach churned with the thought of putting himself through another campaign. While he was a town council member, he hadn't had to campaign for that position because everybody had just written him into the open seat his grandfather had left behind when he died, like he'd left Charlie the bar.

But mayor was a position some other people wanted, like a local Realtor and the CEO of the lumber company that owned whatever forest wasn't state land. These two guys, Jason Cruise and Bentley Ford, had influence and money, like the people Charlie had run against before. And they would probably be just as cutthroat as his old opponents had been for that senate seat.

He took off his hat and pushed his hand through his hair. He was tempted to pull out some of the dark strands, that would probably be less painful than going into politics again. But his brother-in-law, sister and quite a few other locals had been putting the pressure on him to run. Even the incumbent mayor was offering to step down now and have Charlie assume his duties as an interim mayor, figuring that if he had the job before the election, he would have the advantage over his opponents. The deputy mayor had passed away from old age a few months earlier, so the mayor could appoint one of the town council members to take over for him.

Because Charlie wanted to protect his hometown—not just from the danger the hotshots posed but also from the danger that ambitious real estate developers posed—he was going to have to take some action. And at the moment, he could think of only one.

He uttered a weary sigh and admitted, "I know something has to be done about them."

Every time there was a shooting or someone was nearly run down or there was an explosion or a fire, everyone in the vicinity was in danger, not just the hotshots.

"And I think you're the best man for the job, Charlie," Eric persisted, like he had been doing for the past few months. "Tillerman is the name that people in this town instinctively trust."

The election was six months away yet, but the current mayor had already publicly announced that he wasn't going to run again. Then he'd privately offered to step aside now if Charlie would agree to be interim mayor until the election. Being the "incumbent" would give him the advantage over any rival, all but guaranteeing him the win, especially if he did what the townspeople were lobbying for the mayor to do.

"You're just saying that because you want me to get rid of the hotshots," Charlie said.

"I'm not the only one who wants that," Eric reminded him. "And it's what *you* want too."

But he didn't really want to get rid of all of them. At least, not one blue-eyed blonde beauty who made his pulse race just thinking about her.

When he finally stepped out of the back of the rig, his gaze met that blue one of hers. She was standing a little way behind Eric at the foot of the stairs that led up to the second and third stories of the building.

So the hotshots were back in town.

And from the angry expression on Michaela Momber's beautiful face, she had clearly overheard everything he and Eric had been talking about. Was she outraged for professional reasons, though, or for personal reasons?

The saboteur was feeling bold. They'd gone so long without being discovered that they felt invincible. It didn't matter who came after them or tried to find them—that person was going to fail, just like everyone else kept failing.

Braden Zimmer. The hotshot superintendent hadn't been able to figure it out. Nor had his assistant superintendents, Wyatt Andrews and Dawson Hess. Even his smart new wife, the arson investigator, hadn't been able to figure it out.

And then Braden had brought in his brother-in-law to help find the saboteur. But Trick McRooney had failed, just like Braden had.

They had no clue.

But if, by some chance, someone started getting close to figuring it out…

Started putting it all together…

Then that person was going to have to die. The saboteur hadn't actually considered murder before—not that someone couldn't have died during one of the *accidents*. Hell, a few nearly *had* died. And because of that, because of all the things that had happened and how many people had been hurt, the saboteur would definitely face jail time if they were discovered.

And if that happened, they would lose everything that they had, everything that they were. But none of that mattered as much as the saboteur's quest for justice.

For revenge…

Chapter 2

Charlie should have been used to Michaela walking away from him. That was what she'd been doing for the past several months. No. Longer than that. She'd walked away the night she'd rescued him from the fire at his bar.

Once she'd gotten him to safety, to an ambulance waiting outside, she'd walked away from him. She'd walked back into the fire. That was a little how Charlie felt as he rushed out after her—that he was walking back into a fire.

That was how he felt every time he got close to her, like he was going to get burned by the heat between them. The passion that ignited whenever they were alone or even just looked at each other. But they'd done more than just look. Eventually, after months of him flirting with her, of trying to get her to give him a chance…

She'd given him more than that. She'd given him more pleasure than he'd ever known.

Clearly nothing like that was going to happen tonight. He was more likely to get burned by her temper because she looked really mad about what she overheard them saying. But instead of unleashing her anger, she just walked away. And he realized that beneath her anger was the vulnerability he'd found beneath her toughness.

She wasn't as tough emotionally as she was physically. And as angry as she was about what she'd heard, she probably felt equally betrayed. That sense of betrayal was something Charlie understood all too well from the things that had come out during his campaign.

The secrets he hadn't known about his ex, the secrets she'd purposely kept from him. Like her affairs and the money she'd taken from his campaign contributions.

At the time, he hadn't appreciated how much gratitude he owed his opponent for digging up that dirt. He'd just been angry at him for humiliating him and at her for her betrayal. He'd been angriest at himself, though, for being so damn blind.

But underneath his anger there had been pain. He hoped that wasn't the case with Michaela, he didn't want her hurting because of him, thinking that he'd betrayed her.

Needing to make sure that she was okay and to explain what she'd heard, he tried to break free of his brother-in-law's grasp. When he started after her, Eric grabbed his arm before he could get past him.

"Charlie, what's the deal with you and the lady hotshot?" Eric asked. "The way she looked at you…" He shivered, then chuckled.

Michaela had a reputation around Northern Lakes for being tough—icy, even. But while she was tough, there was nothing cold about her.

"You must realize that she'd be pissed about what she overheard us saying," Charlie pointed out.

"So." Eric shrugged. "The hotshots are going to know soon enough when you're the mayor of Northern Lakes and they're looking for a new place for their headquarters. They wore out their welcome here."

"I don't have time for this now." Charlie tugged his arm free of his brother-in-law's big hand, and he rushed toward that side door.

The last thing Charlie wanted to talk about at the moment was running for mayor. Right now he just wanted to run for

Michaela, to catch up to her so that he could explain what she'd heard.

And that wasn't just because of…what they'd both agreed was a bad idea. This attraction between them, this strange and secret arrangement they had…

He stepped outside, letting the door slam shut behind him. Once it closed, it was as if someone had extinguished all the light. It was alarmingly dark without the glow of the fluorescent lights from the garage chasing away the night. Clouds must have obscured the moon, but there should have been more light.

While the streetlamps didn't quite reach the side of the building, there were light poles in the parking lot next to the firehouse that illuminated the entire area. Usually…

What had happened to them?

And more importantly, what had happened to her?

"Michaela!" Charlie called out to her now, concern gripping him, making his muscles tense. "Michaela!"

"Shh…"

The whisper from the dark raised goose bumps along his skin, despite the heaviness of the firefighter gear he was still wearing. He would recognize that husky female voice anywhere. He heard it so often in his dreams, and then he would wake up to find himself reaching for her.

But she was never there.

She never stayed, as if what they'd done was some embarrassing secret she was determined to keep. And he wasn't sure why—except that, for some reason, he hadn't been any more eager to share than she had. After his last political campaign had exposed more about his personal life than even he had known, like his wife's affairs and overspending, he was doubly determined to keep his private life private. Which was another reason he was reluctant to accept even the interim mayor position, let alone run in another election.

Lowering his voice to match her whisper, he asked, "Where are you?" And why couldn't he see her? She was still wearing her yellow hotshot-firefighter gear when he'd seen her inside just moments ago. But it was so dark that he couldn't even see her uniform.

"Shh..." she hissed again from the darkness, but she sounded closer now, and there was a strange sense of urgency or caution in her voice.

She wasn't just trying to shut him up because she didn't want to hear his explanation. There was something else happening.

"What's going on?" he asked.

Then he heard what must have drawn her attention already: the sound of shoes or boots scraping across asphalt. They weren't alone. Someone else was out in the dark parking lot with them.

He opened his mouth to call out to them, but Michaela must have been close enough to see him now, because she whispered again, "Shh..."

What was going on?

Did she consider whoever else out there in the darkness a threat? And was that threat to their relationship she seemed so determined to keep secret? Or, given all the dangerous things that happened to and around the hotshots, was that threat to their lives?

Moments ago, when Michaela had stepped out into the darkness, she had already been reeling from what she'd just seen and heard in the firehouse. Charlie Tillerman, in the back of one of the rigs, in firefighter gear. Not yellow gear, like the hotshots wore, but black, like his thick, glossy hair and his dark eyes and apparently his soul.

He did want to get rid of the hotshots, and he and that other man had already been plotting how to do it. Her team was right to be suspicious of Charlie Tillerman. And she, once again, had been wrong about a person. On the plane ride into Northern Lakes, she'd decided to find out the truth about him, to find any evidence of him being the saboteur. She'd even intended to go over to his place tonight and look around. But maybe that had just been an excuse to see him again.

She hadn't even had to go to the Filling Station to find out the truth about him. But in that moment, she'd realized how badly she wanted him to not harbor any resentment toward the hotshots, to not want to hurt them.

But she was afraid that he had. At least, he'd hurt one of them…

So, feeling sick again, she'd rushed outside for some air, only to step into total darkness. Despite the darkness, she could feel someone else's presence. But she couldn't see who was out there. And she desperately wanted to see them.

Were they this close? The saboteur? It had to be the saboteur because she could hear the hiss of air, like tires deflating. A lot of trucks, like hers, were parked in the lot because many of the hotshots had been too tired to go home and were sleeping upstairs in the bunkroom right now. She hadn't wanted to make the drive home, either, since the firehouse in St. Paul—where she and Hank worked and lived when not out with the hotshots—was more than an hour away.

She'd intended instead to go to the Filling Station, despite the fact that the bar would have closed a couple of hours ago. Then she'd heard his voice rumbling out of the back of that rig, and after she'd heard him admit to wanting the hotshots gone, she just wanted to get away from him.

But he wasn't the one out here letting air out of tires. And if he wasn't…

Did that mean he wasn't the saboteur?

Charlie was here now, though. When he had opened the door seconds ago and light spilled into the parking lot, she glanced around the area, trying to find whoever else was out there.

But the door closed too quickly again, extinguishing that brief flicker of light and the flicker of hope Michaela had to see who was still hiding in the darkness. They must have shut off the lights somehow, or Michaela would have seen them already.

Had they seen her when she'd opened that door? And Charlie? Were the two of them in danger now, like Rory had been the night that the sound of all the engines running had lured him out into the hall?

She had no weapon, and she doubted Charlie had one too. So what had she intended to do if she actually caught the saboteur in the act?

But she wanted to see who it was so damn badly that she hadn't considered how she would actually apprehend the person. She just wanted to know who'd been messing with them for so long, putting them in danger and also doing some petty, stupid stuff like this. Letting air out of tires.

For a second, when she'd heard Charlie talking, she thought it was him. And while she'd been angry, she'd also been…hurt. But now, knowing that it wasn't him but someone else—some *anonymous* someone else, who quite possibly was a member of her team…

Fury bubbled up inside her, and she wished she had a weapon. Or at least a flashlight. Her phone had died on the return trip from Ontario, and she hadn't had the chance to charge it yet. Or she would have used that to not just see the person but take a picture of them in the act of sabotage.

Maybe Charlie had his phone on him. When he'd opened the door, she'd started back toward the building. Toward him, drawn to him, as she'd been for too damn long. She'd tried to resist the attraction, but he was just so good looking and so charming. But those were the very reasons she should have resisted him, because she knew those traits were her weakness and made it as hard for her to see clearly as it was for her to see in the dark parking lot right now.

But as she moved closer to him, she could see him a bit in the faint light seeping out from under the door of the firehouse. She needed to find out if he had his phone on him, but she didn't want the sound of their voices to draw the saboteur's attention or to send the person running before they could see who it was.

So she moved even closer to him and whispered near his ear, "I need your cell."

His body moved in a slight shiver. And he nodded and pulled out his phone. "Call the police."

The police wouldn't get there in time to stop whoever was out in the dark with them. And neither would anyone inside the building because she had no doubt that if the door opened again, the person would run off.

Why hadn't they done that already, though? When she'd walked out or when Charlie had?

What was the saboteur waiting for?

Did the person want to get caught?

Another sound emanated from the shadows, something that made Michaela gasp even before the flash of the flame. She'd heard the tell-tale flick of a lighter.

Then a bottle rolled toward them, right before footsteps pounded across the asphalt, running away from what they'd tossed: an explosive.

"Get down!" she yelled as that bottle, the rag inside burning brightly now, rolled right near them. They were close to the building but not close enough to open the door and get inside before the glass exploded in a fireball from the accelerant inside the bottle.

Fragments of glass flew, and the blast, as close as it was, knocked Michaela back into Charlie, whose arms closed, almost reflexively, around her. But he fell back, too, into the steel door behind them.

And then, a moment later everything went black again when she lost consciousness.

Braden Zimmer was in his office on the second floor of the firehouse. He'd just intended to take care of a few things on his desk before heading home. Sam, his wife, wasn't home right now. She'd just wrapped up an arson investigation out west and was staying in Washington for a couple of days to spend time with two men who were both nicknamed Mack: her dad and her oldest brother. The younger Mack had mysteriously shown up in Northern Lakes four months ago, just in the nick of time to save the life of another hotshot, one he'd known from their military service.

Mack Junior was back, but nobody really knew from where or what he'd been doing while he was there. Sam was determined to find out, but even as good as an investigator as she was, Braden wasn't sure she would get much information out of her oldest brother.

That wasn't all she was going to ask Mack, though. She wanted his help. Because even as good as an investigator as she was, she hadn't been able to figure out who the saboteur was either.

Mack had already helped out once, when he'd shown up in town all those months ago. If he hadn't, Braden would have wound up burying another member of his team. Rory VanDam or whatever his real name was. Like Ethan Sommerly, Rory insisted on keeping the name he'd assumed five years ago when he and Ethan, who was really Jonathan Canterbury, had survived a plane crash.

A member of your team isn't who you think they are...

Braden had received that anonymous—and ominous—note more than a year ago, but he was no closer to finding out who'd sent it or who they were referring to. At least two people on his team weren't who he'd thought they were.

They were even better. Really good guys, and Braden would have lost one if Mack hadn't shot the FBI agent trying to kill Rory VanDam. Mack knew who Rory really was from serving in the military together.

While neither Rory nor Ethan Sommerly was who they'd said they were, neither of them was the saboteur. They'd both been victims of the saboteur instead, as well as victims of the enemies from their own pasts. With the danger they'd been in, they were lucky to be alive.

The saboteur hadn't killed anyone yet, but Braden was worried that it was only a matter of time before one of the "accidents" that the saboteur kept staging caused fatal injuries for another hotshot.

And then Braden felt it.

The slight shudder of the building, as if something had struck it. He jumped up from his chair and rushed around his desk to pull open the door to the hall. He barely made it to the top of the stairs when he heard the yelling.

"Help! We need help!"

Braden didn't recognize the voice, but there were some new volunteers in the local fire department. The new crew had a rig out when he and his team had returned from Ontario earlier that evening. Maybe they'd struck the building trying to drive it back into the garage.

"Call an ambulance!" another voice shouted.

That voice, Braden recognized: Charlie, the bartender and owner of the Filling Station. He was one of the new volunteers, much to Braden's surprise. He hadn't shared that news with any of the other hotshots yet because they were already suspicious of Charlie. And he didn't want any of them trying to investigate on their own and getting hurt. It was bad enough that he'd put his brother-in-law Trick in danger by having him help investigate and protect the others.

But Braden would have to check out Charlie now. He'd known him and the Tillerman family for years, but he knew, after what Marty had done, that anyone was capable of being dangerous. And Braden couldn't deny that Charlie volunteering at the firehouse gave him easy access to it.

Of course, Carl had pointed out that, thanks to Stanley—the nineteen-year-old who helped out around the firehouse—frequently forgetting to lock the doors, pretty much anyone had access to the building. Maybe someone else—or some-*thing* else—had caused that disturbance he'd just felt.

"What happened?" Braden asked, running down the stairs to the garage area. Once he hit the bottom step, he gasped, and he could see why there was such urgency in Charlie's voice because of what he held in his arms: Michaela's limp body. Her head lolled back, blood dripping from her temple, staining her pale blonde hair red. "Oh my God!" His hand shook as he pulled out his cell.

The other man, who'd yelled first for help, was on his phone, speaking to a 911 dispatcher from the call center.

But Braden called Owen. The paramedic was closer than the hospital since he was probably just a street over at his girlfriend's apartment. "What happened?" he asked Charlie again.

"Something blew up—a bottle. There's glass and something...gasoline...and fire," he said, his deep voice vibrating with concern and confusion.

It was clear that there had been another explosion of some kind and Michaela had been injured in it. Braden relayed those details to Owen, who assured him that he was already on his way. One of the paramedic rigs was parked in the garage, though, so Braden pulled open the doors to it. "There's a stretcher in here we can lay her on, and we can get something for her wound…"

And hopefully, Owen would be there as fast as he'd promised.

As Charlie carried Michaela toward the open doors of the rig, Braden stepped forward to help, but the bar owner's arms tightened around her as if he didn't want to let her go. "She's breathing. I think," he said, his voice gruff. "And she has a pulse but…"

He was scared.

And so was Braden.

Charlie was also hurt, blood running down the side of his face like it did from hers. Maybe that was why he seemed so confused. He could have a concussion.

"Help's on the way," the other man—the new volunteer—said, and he shuddered as he stared at Michaela too. Then he looked at Charlie and gasped. "You're hurt, too, man!"

Ignoring him, Charlie jumped up into the back of the rig, and finally, he released Michaela's limp body onto the stretcher. The side door opened again, and Owen rushed inside and across the garage toward them.

"The asphalt's on fire," the paramedic said. "What the hell happened?"

"Some kind of explosive again," Braden said. "Michaela's still unconscious."

But then she moved slightly, shifting against the gurney as she started to regain consciousness. And her jacket fell open. Unlike the rest of the team, she hadn't changed out of all her gear yet. She wore the yellow pants, but they were unsnapped and straining over the slight swell of her belly.

And Braden, whose wife was expecting a baby within the next few weeks, realized that the female hotshot was pregnant too. She'd never said anything to him. Hell, he hadn't even known she was seeing anyone.

But from the way Charlie was sticking so close to her side, even as Owen started treating her, Braden had another suspicion about the bar owner: that maybe he was the father of Michaela's unborn child.

But none of that mattered as much as making sure that Michaela and her baby survived the saboteur's latest attack. Or Braden's fear might be realized, he might be losing another hotshot.

Don't miss
Hotshot's Dangerous Liaison
by Lisa Childs,
available July 2024 wherever
Harlequin® Romantic Suspense
books and ebooks are sold.

www.Harlequin.com